D0712653

A Night in The Manchester Store and Other Stories

A Night in The Manchester Store and Other Stories

Stanley Cohen

Five Star • Waterville, Maine

Copyright © 2002 by Stanley Cohen

Additional copyright information on pages 299–300.

All rights reserved.

This collection is a work of fiction. Names, characters, places, and incidents are either the product of the author's imagination, or, if real, used fictitiously.

Five Star First Edition Mystery Series.

Published in 2002 in conjunction with
Tekno Books and Ed Gorman.

Set in 11 pt. Plantin by Rick Gundberg.

Printed in the United States on permanent paper.

Library of Congress Cataloging-in-Publication Data

Cohen, Stanley, 1928–
   A night in the Manchester store and other stories /
Stanley Cohen.
     p. cm. — (Five Star first edition mystery series)
   ISBN 0-7862-3935-2 (hc : alk. paper)
   1. Detective and mystery stories, American. I. Title.
II. Series.
PS3553.O43 N54 2002
  813′.54—dc21   2001059219

To the memory of Jake and Stella,
my beloved parents . . .

Table of Contents

I was invited to join the Adams Round Table a short time before I retired from the corporate world, where the major focus of my work was the carpet industry. When I was told that the title for the Round Table's next anthology was A Body Is Found, *I decided that I wanted a story which would involve both murder and floor coverings.*

Hello! My Name Is
Irving Wasserman

Morty Kaplan was definitely excited about something as he arrived home from his office on a perfect summer day. When he entered the co-op building on East 67th at Third, even Tony the doorman noticed it while pulling the door open for him.

"You just swallow the canary, or what?" Tony quipped.

"Mostly what, Tony. I gave up on canaries years ago. Nothing but feathers and bones."

"Yeah? What about that feather on your necktie?"

Morty grinned. "You're quick, kid. I'll give you that. See you later."

Morty took the elevator to the seventeenth floor, unlocked the door, and went inside. He threw his jacket across a chair and walked into the kitchen where Evelyn was at the sink, rinsing lettuce for the salad.

"And how's the world's most lovable endodontist?" she asked, not looking up from her work. "You root a few hot canals, today?"

Morty walked over to her and gave her fanny a little caress, his usual way of letting her know he was home. Then he gave her a pleasing little kiss behind her ear, an action that was

9

maybe a little less routine, but not out of character. "I just might have a pleasant little surprise for you, today."

She whirled around to face him, a bright expectant smile on her face. "What?" She was into pleasant little surprises.

"You know the rug you've been wishing we could find for the den?"

"What about it?"

"You know, something authentically Navajo, or even quasi-Hopi, something that looks like it had been made by real, honest-to-goodness American Indians?"

"Oh, cut the crap and get to the point, Morty."

"I may, and listen closely, I'm saying, I may, I may have found you the rug you want."

Evelyn was all smiles. "Where? I've been shopping for months and I'm convinced there's not one in this city that's even close. At any price."

"Well, I may have found one. In fact, when you see this rug, you're not going to believe what you're looking at."

"Is it going to cost a fortune? You're always saying that you're not willing to spend a fortune for it . . . Wait a minute. Where would you be seeing any rugs today?"

Morty's eyes gleamed. "I saw one. And we could have it for nothing."

"What are you talking about?"

"Are you ready for this? As I was walking home from the office just now, I saw this rug that somebody had thrown out on top of a pile of stuff left for pickup, and I took a look at the corner of it, and it really does look like just what we want."

"All you saw was a corner of it?"

"It was tightly rolled up and taped with heavy tape."

"Well, if somebody threw it out, it's probably a mess."

"Not necessarily. Not in that neighborhood. East Sixty-second between Second and Third? That block is all million-dollar town houses. Latching onto a discarded anything in that block can be very promising. Very promising. Nothing about throwaways in that block would surprise me."

"Well, why didn't you just pick it up and bring it then?"

Morty smiled at her and then shifted into a poor excuse for a body builder's stance. He was slight in build, with a paunch, a receding hairline, glasses, and delicate hands. "I know you think I can lift the world," he said, "but that thing was heavy. I could tell just from pushing at it. And it was bulky and lumpy. Whoever threw it out must have gotten rid of a lot of other junk, heavy junk, by rolling it up inside before they taped it up. Admittedly, after we get it up here and get a look at it, we may decide we don't want it, but considering how long we've been shopping for this thing, I certainly think it's worth a look."

"It'll probably be gone before you can get back. This is New York, you know."

Morty smiled. "I thought of that when I looked at it. So, I sort of rearranged the pile a little. I put some other stuff on top of it."

"Get our neighbor down the hall to help you. The big Swede. Lars. He'd be more than glad to, and he could probably carry you and the rug. And go now. Before somebody else gets it."

"Why don't you give him a call?" Morty said. "He likes you."

★ ★ ★ ★ ★

The rolled-up rug was definitely heavy. Very heavy. But Lars, their big Swedish neighbor from down the hall was up to the task. And they were something to look at as they moved along, carrying it. Lars, a giant of a man, had the bulk of the load on his shoulder. Morty walked with his considerably less powerful shoulder under the front end of the thing, where he

11

provided little more than balance. If that.

When they reached the building, Tony the doorman pulled the door open for them. "A new rug, huh? What? D'you find that somewhere?"

"Does it surprise you?" Morty asked.

"Surprise me? Nothing surprises me in this city." Then he grinned at Morty. "What? You couldn't carry it yourself? You had to get Mr. Swenson to help you?"

"You want to try carrying it, Tony? Go ahead. Take it upstairs for us. Lars and I will watch the door for you."

Tony grinned. "I gotta stay here."

It took some negotiating for Morty and Lars to get their burden into the elevator, but they managed. When they reached the door to the apartment, Evelyn opened the door for them. She took one look at the rolled-up rug and had trouble containing her excitement. Since it was a handwoven Indian rug, its design was the same on both sides.

"Blacks and grays and whites," she said in a controlled manner. "Morty? Do you happen to know what this might be?"

He smiled and nodded. "I think so," he said with certainty, sensing that she didn't want to discuss too much in front of Lars. He and Lars continued struggling with the rug, placing it finally in the den, in position to be unrolled.

"Well," she said, looking at Lars and then at Morty, "I've got to get the fish out of the oven or it'll be spoiled. So I guess we'll have to leave this till after we eat. Lars, would you like to stay and have a bite with us?"

"Oh, thanks, no," he answered, "but you call me if you need any more help. Any time. Okay?" And he meant it. A gentle giant. And a friend among friends.

"Another time," Evelyn said warmly, trying not to let her sense of relief be too obvious. She wanted to get him the hell out of there so she could look at the rug.

After she'd seen him to the door and closed it, she turned to Morty. "Are you thinking what I'm thinking?"

"I sure am." He loved when she got really excited about something.

"That rug looks like an authentic 'Two Gray Hills.' And an early one, at that. If it's in any kind of good condition, do you have any idea what it's worth? That size rug?"

"A lot of money, I'm sure."

"I saw a tiny throw rug that was supposedly a 'Two Gray Hills' at that Indian Museum on upper Broadway, and it cost nearly a thousand dollars. I don't think you can even order them in room size any more. Morty, this rug could be a real collector's item."

"Believe me. I've been thinking about it."

"Let's go look at it," she said.

"I thought you wanted to eat first."

"The fish's not going anywhere. I've got to look at that rug."

They went into the den to examine their prize, or confirm that it was in fact a prize. Morty very meticulously cut the duct tape wrapped around the rug in four places, and they began unrolling it.

Evelyn liked what she saw as they unrolled it slowly along the floor. The colors! The design! Based on all her research and endless shopping, it was just what she'd pictured in her mind's eye. And it wasn't stained, or even soiled. It was in beautiful condition. Almost like new. Why would anyone throw it away? A piece of art, no less . . . Only in New York. And especially an area like that block of East Sixty-second. Someone was redecorating? Out it went . . . But why was the rolled-up rug so bulky and misshapen? What bunch of junk was inside it?

When they reached the end of the rug, she found out. And she fainted dead away. Inside the rug was the body of a middle-aged man, dressed in a fine dark suit with an expensive silk tie. And affixed to the lapel of his jacket was one of those familiar sticky labels which read:

Hello! My Name Is
Irving Wasserman

Morty revived her with a cold, wet towel.

She sat bolt upright and looked around. "Where is he? Or was I dreaming?"

"I dragged him into the bedroom."

"Not our bedroom!"

"The *other* bedroom."

She reached for the towel that was soaking wet at one end and patted her face with the dry end. Then she began to examine the rug with a decorator's eye. She got to her feet and walked around it. "I like this rug. I LIKE this rug. I'll bet the Museum of the American Indian would like to have this baby. And it's in perfect condition. Perfect."

"Well, almost perfect."

"What about it is not perfect?"

"It's missing one of the corner fringes. See, down there at the other end? At the corner?"

"I'd hardly have noticed it. Even I'm not that fussy."

"Well, don't get too excited about it. What makes you so sure the police'll let us keep it?"

Evelyn looked at him with alarm. "Have you called the police?"

"No, but I'm getting ready to, right now."

"No!"

"What do you mean, no?"

"I mean, no, don't call the police. I want this rug. If you call the police, you know as well as I do that they'll take it. It's evidence. Morty, I want this rug. Do you know how long I've been looking for exactly this rug? Exactly this rug?"

Morty threw up his hands and looked skyward, his usual gesture when faced with one of Evelyn's absolutely immovable sudden positions. Maybe *this* time he could get some help from above. "Evelyn, listen to me."

"Forget it," she snapped. "I want this rug."

"Will you listen a minute?"

"No. I don't want to hear it."

"Okay, you don't want to hear it. But what are we going to do with Irving in there?"

"I don't know. We'll have to think of something."

"Evelyn, if we call the police now and tell them exactly what happened, and with Lars Swenson as our witness, everything'll be fine. And after the smoke clears, and the excitement is over, I'm sure they'll let us have the rug."

"You're sure? How sure? Can you call them and ask them? No. And I want this rug. Morty, I want this rug. I don't want it leaving this room."

"Then what do we do with Irving? Shall we put him in the bathtub and start buying ice?"

"We'll have to think of something. All we need is some way to get him out of here. I don't have any guilty conscience, Morty. We didn't kill him. We're not responsible for his being dead."

"Well, whoever was sure knew what he . . . or she, but presumably he, was doing." He smiled a little smile of respect. "A real professional, whoever did that. A really neat job."

"What are you talking about?"

"I've read about cases like this one," he said, reflectively. "They take a small caliber gun like a twenty-two short that shoots with a fairly low muzzle velocity and they stick it under the chin, pointed sort of up and toward the back of the head, and they fire. It's instant and painless. And neat. Because with the low muzzle velocity, the bullet doesn't come out. It just enters the cranial cavity and ricochets around, making scrambled eggs out of the brain. But from the outside, neat. The victim looks normal. Just a tiny clean hole where the bullet enters."

"How do you know so much about muzzle velocity? You've never touched a gun in your life."

"I've read about it. I think it was an article in the *Times* magazine about professional hit men and their techniques . . . Evelyn, what do you propose doing with Mr. Wasserman?"

"I'll think of something."

★ ★ ★ ★ ★

Morty took the garbage out to the disposal chute, which was located in a utility closet off the corridor. The closet was completely at the other end of the corridor from their door. And there were eleven other co-op apartments on the floor. What were the odds, say, in the middle of the night . . . ? And if somebody did see them? What then?

He opened the port to the chute and dropped in the bag, and as he listened to its descent, he studied the opening. It was a close fit for the small garbage bag. For a man the size of Irving? Who was also a mite paunchy? He thought about Irving getting stuck between floors. But that presumed getting Irving into the chute at all, which wasn't possible. Forget it. The garbage chute was definitely not a viable solution.

When he reentered the apartment, he found Evelyn tugging at a window. "Evelyn. You don't just throw bodies out of windows."

She turned to face him. "Then we'll have to think of something else. Right?"

16

"Listen to me. We've got to call the police, and quick. Lars is our alibi for having him here, and the longer we wait, the more questionable our story's going to be. Lars won't lie about *anything*. Am I right?"

"We're *not* calling the police."

"Well, if we wanted to call one, we wouldn't have to go far. There's one on duty right across the street from this building at all times . . . God, I'm sure glad it's Friday, at least. I don't expect to get much sleep while Irving is with us."

"We'll have to come up with a plan for getting him out of here. That's all. Because we're keeping the rug."

"Evelyn, listen to me. Number one, we live next door to our temple. Next door. But that's nothing. Forget that. As long as we don't try to carry him out while services are letting out, we're okay there. Now for number two. Number two, we live across the street from the Russian Embassy. The Russian Embassy! And directly across from our front door is a guard shack which just happens to be occupied twenty-four hours a day by two of New York's Finest, because the Embassy is there. That's number two. And it's not bad enough that they're *there,* they even come across to *this* building to use that bathroom down in the basement. And if that wasn't enough, now for number three. Number three, we have our own doormen on duty, also twenty-four hours a day."

"Morty, we didn't kill this man. Someone else killed him. Someone murdered this poor man and left him out there on the street. We brought him in here by mistake, and all we have to do is figure out some way to get him back outside without anybody noticing. And without calling the police. Because we're keeping the rug."

"Evelyn, you're repeating yourself." Then he stopped, and started wondering if he would ever be able to make himself believable when he began explaining what he was doing with the corpse of Irving Wasserman. Surely some of the prisoners in Attica, or wherever, would need root canal work.

And with that notion, and unable to think rationally because of the feverish state of his mind, he went into the living room and dropped himself into his big chair and flipped on the tube. The Mets were two behind going into the sixth. Couldn't they have been winning big this one time?

During the bottom of the ninth, with the Mets still two behind, but with two on and nobody out, Evelyn came and stood between Morty and the television. "I have a plan," she said. "It's not a wonderful, grandiose plan, but it's a plan, and I think it'll work. And I frankly can't think of any other way to do it."

Behind her, on the tube, there was a lot of excitement and a lot of cheering, but he wasn't quite sure what had happened. He'd set the volume low. And it was always her practice, when he was watching and she wanted to talk to him, to stand between him and the screen to be sure she had his attention. So, under the circumstances, about the best response he could manage was a rather annoyed, "Tell me about it."

★ ★ ★ ★ ★

Saturday. Morty entered the surgical supply store and looked around. He made a point of going to a store other than the one he used for his own office needs because, as he ruminated about the situation, when you've got a house guest like Irving, it tends to make you a little self-conscious. He certainly didn't want to have to discuss with people who knew him what a dentist needed with a wheelchair.

The night before had been bad, but perhaps not quite as bad as he'd anticipated. The Mets had managed to tie the score in the ninth and then win it in the fourteenth, and staying with this had helped him fall asleep, for a couple of hours, anyway, before he woke up, starkly awake, thinking about Irving in the next room.

He paid for the chair in cash, of course, reflecting on the fact as he did that he was thinking like a criminal, leaving no written records or receipts. Then he asked the clerk if the rather large carton could be wrapped.

"Wrapped? You want this wrapped?"

"It's . . . it's going to be a gift." And as he said it, he flushed with guilt, realizing that although he might have paid with cash, he was certainly leaving an indelible impression on the clerk's mind.

"You want it gift-wrapped? A wheelchair?"

"It doesn't have to be exactly gift-wrapped. Just wrapped. In plain paper is okay. With a rope around it so I can handle it." Things were going from bad to worse. That clerk would never forget him. But he wanted to get the carton past Tony, and into his building without its contents being obvious. Problems. Nothing but problems. At least the store wasn't close to home. It was a ten-dollar cab ride there. And it would be another ten-dollar cab ride back. But worth it.

He helped the clerk, and another clerk, finally get the carton covered with plain brown paper and a few dozen yards of tape, then a rope for carrying. Before walking out, he rather sheepishly asked, "Uh, if this is not exactly right, it can be returned, can't it?"

The two clerks looked at him in disbelief. After a moment, one of them said, "In the carton. And keep the cash receipt." And the other said with a grin, "Don't let it get messed up."

Morty lugged the carton to the street and hailed a cab.

Tony pulled the door open for him when he arrived, and he dragged the carton inside.

"You need a hand with that?"

"Thanks, Tony, but I can handle it okay."

"Hey, we won last night. In the fourteenth."

"I stayed up and watched it. Till the end."

"It's about time Strawberry did something, huh?"

"Yeah."

He carried it into the elevator and pressed seventeen. Another hurdle passed. Tony did as he was supposed to do for a change. Just open the door and not ask a lot of questions. When he reached the seventeenth floor, he started to lift the carton and the rope came loose. He pushed the carton along the carpeted hallway to their door, unlocked it, and then shoved the carton inside.

★ ★ ★ ★ ★

"You're awfully quiet, tonight, Morty. You, too, Evelyn. Everything okay?" Arnie Perlman, a dentist and close friend, and one of Morty's best sources of referrals, kept looking, first at Morty, then at Evelyn."

"We're fine, Arnie. I stayed up a little late is all. I got hooked on the Mets game."

"The Straw-man really hit that thing," Arnie said. "When he connects, he can give it a ride."

"You watched it, too."

"What else?" Arnie said.

And in a separate conversation between the women, Phyllis asked Evelyn, "What'd you do, today?"

"I spent most of the day shopping. I felt like getting out today."

"Speaking of shopping, did you ever find that rug you were looking for? You know, for your den?"

Evelyn flushed and looked at Morty, who'd heard the question. Then she looked back at Phyllis.

"Did I say something wrong?" Phyllis asked. Then she smiled. "Oh, God, don't tell me I brought up a sore subject or something."

20

"No, of course not," Evelyn answered. She glanced at Morty again, and then, "As a matter of fact, we may have spotted one that we're going to consider."

"Really? Where'd you find it? I figured you'd probably have to go to New Mexico or somewhere."

"Oh, at a little shop over on . . ." Evelyn looked at Morty. "Morty, where was that little shop we found?"

"I don't remember, exactly. Somewhere down in the Village. I have it written down at home."

They finished dinner and walked outside.

"Why don't you guys come back to our place for a nightcap?" Arnie asked.

Morty and Evelyn quickly begged off. And Morty looked nervously at his watch. They didn't have a lot of time left to get back home, according to their plan. Service in the restaurant had been slower than usual. The doormen at their building changed shifts at eleven, and they had to be back before Tony left. They hoped the old man, Manolo, who worked nights, wouldn't show up early and see them come in alone. If that happened, they'd have to postpone their plan another night, and that could be disastrous. Would Irving keep that long? Morty pictured himself going into the Food Emporium and trying to look casual when he checked out with thirty or forty five-pound bags of ice.

But they'd elected not to cancel their date with the Perlmans. It might provoke some questions. Besides, they could use the evening out. And Irving certainly wasn't going anywhere.

They made it back in time. Tony greeted them, and the old man was nowhere in sight. There was a bit of activity, however, around the guard shack across the street. The cops changed shifts at eleven, as well. They watched for a moment as the blue and white police van drove away, and then went inside. They entered the elevator and both exhaled.

★ ★ ★ ★ ★

Waiting time. One, one-thirty, two. They sat and stared numbly at the tube.

"I think we should start getting him into the chair and ready to go," Evelyn said.

Morty nodded. "I think you're right."

"You know what I was thinking," Evelyn said. "I was thinking that he really needs to be wearing a turtleneck so that the hole won't show. You know. Just in case."

"You're probably right."

"I think a white one, to be dressy enough to go with that dark suit he's wearing."

"My new white turtleneck. Right?"

"I'll buy you another one. Besides, you'll get to keep his tie. You said you liked his tie . . . And maybe we should stick a Band-Aid over the hole."

Morty, with his most resigned sigh, breathed, "Okay, why don't we go do it? Come on."

"We? You'll have to do it. I'm not touching him. Oh, and another thing. Why don't you put some of my makeup on him so he doesn't look so pasty-faced? A little rouge, maybe."

"What do I know about applying makeup? Can't you do that one thing?"

"I told you, I'm not touching him. You'll do it fine. Just a little rouge so he has some color . . ." She smiled. "My husband, the undertaker."

Not at all amused, Morty got slowly out of his big chair and moved toward the bedroom.

★ ★ ★ ★ ★

Four-thirty A.M. That moment of darkest night and deepest sleep. That moment when, even in New York, the pace of life slows to a crawl. A crawl, maybe. But in New

York, one can never count on the pace of life grinding to a complete halt. Not at any hour. There is always a reasonable likelihood of activity on the streets of Manhattan.

Irving was in the chair, ready to go. And getting him there had been no easy task for Morty. He'd struggled with the clothes while Irving was still on the floor. First the jacket, then the shirt and tie, the Band-Aid, and then Morty's new white turtleneck. And a struggle it had been. Especially the turtleneck. Finally, the jacket, once again. The sticky tag was still on the lapel. Morty was beginning to get into the macabre humor of the whole business as he smoothed out the tag, making sure it was on there securely.

Hello! My Name Is
Irving Wasserman

After he'd finished dressing Irving, he'd dealt with the makeup. Like a real pro, he'd covered the crisp white turtleneck with a towel. The more he fussed with the stuff, the worse things seemed to get. But by this time, he was really amused by what they were doing. Almost giddy. To the point of giggling as he put on too much rouge, then tried to wipe some off, then tried a little powder, then more wiping and rubbing and smearing. He thought about using a little mascara, or adding a touch of lipstick, and this made him whisper aloud, "I am from Transylvania." The final effect was one of Irving looking not just healthy, but ruddy, in fact, even more than ruddy. Flushed. And that was perfect.

Then came the job of getting Irving into the chair. And Morty was almost not up to it. With his physique, he was not used to lifting people. Having his hands in their mouths, yes, but not lifting them. In the process of straining and struggling, he was face-to-face, no, cheek-to-cheek with Irving and as he puffed and sweated, the lyric strains of "Dancing Cheek to Cheek" tripped lightly through his head. Once Irving was into the chair, Morty went into the bathroom and wiped the makeup off his cheek, deciding finally that nothing less than a shower would do. And with time to burn, he'd taken a nice long one.

They rolled Irving to the door, and Evelyn opened it and peered out. No one in sight. As it should be. She could think of no one on their floor that she'd expect to be up and around at that hour. They moved soundlessly to the elevator, pressed the button, and waited. It arrived, they pushed Irving into it, and pressed LOBBY. As the car began its less than reckless descent, Morty held Irving's collar with one hand to keep him from pitching forward.

The car stopped at the ninth floor, and they looked at each other, panic-stricken. The door opened and a rather nice-looking young man, perhaps in his late twenties, entered the car. He looked at Irving curiously and then at the two of them. Then he looked away, not wanting to appear intrusive or judgmental. Morty sized him up as probably leaving some young woman's apartment. At four-thirty in the A.M.? Morty felt a twinge of jealousy.

When the young man glanced again at Irving, Morty, feeling obliged to comment, said, "Demon rum."

And the young man, feeling obliged to respond, said, "It can do it."

"We're taking him back to his place," Morty said. "It's not the first time."

"But it's going to be the last," Evelyn said, suddenly. "He's disgusting," she added. "He does this every time he comes over, and the next time, I'm not giving him anything to drink. I'm sick and tired of his passing out like this."

The young man nodded and looked relieved when the car

stopped. The door moved slowly open and the young man hurried across the lobby.

They rolled Irving out of the car, and as they had hoped, Manolo, the old night man, was dozing on a sofa in the lobby. Manolo woke up when he heard the young man press the inside release and exit to the street. Manolo glanced around and saw them coming toward the door, pushing Irving.

As Manolo started to get to his feet, Morty said quickly, "It's okay, Manolo, we can let ourselves out. Thanks."

Manolo nodded, smiled, and made a thank you gesture with a nod and a wave of his hand. Then he dropped back on the couch and got comfortable again.

When they reached the sidewalk, certainly the tensest moment in the plan, Morty said, "Get back with the car as quick as you can."

And Evelyn promptly responded, "Would you expect me to drive around for a while, first?"

"Just be as quick as you can. Okay?"

Evelyn headed across Third and east on Sixty-seventh to the all-night garage a block away where they kept their car. Morty pushed the chair into what he hoped was the least illuminated spot in front of the building. He looked across the street at the little police shack, but could not tell if the cops inside were watching him. Realizing Evelyn would not be able to bring the car right to the door of their building because of a couple of POLICE LINE sawhorses, he moved a short distance toward the corner of Third Avenue, gripping Irving's collar tightly, and trying to appear as relaxed and casual as possible.

Suddenly a cop emerged from the shack and started across the street toward the building. Morty watched in horror, his heart pounding so furiously he could hear it. Was the cop coming toward him? The cop glanced in his direction and

25

went to the door of the building, where he tapped on the glass. Manolo scrambled to his feet and opened the door, and the cop disappeared down the stairs, heading for the lavatory in the basement.

After what seemed an interminable few minutes, he finally saw Evelyn coming. She pulled the car up, and he quickly opened the back door. He began struggling with Irving and was near collapse from fright. What if the cop returned and happened to be one of the "good-guys"? He'd probably stroll over and offer to lend a hand. And the cop would surely know a stiff when he saw one. How would he explain Irving? . . . Uh, well, you see, Officer, we found him on East Sixty-second Street, rolled up in a rug . . . And you didn't call the police? . . . Uh, my wife was afraid you'd take the rug.

Somehow he managed to get Irving into the back seat of the car and into an upright position. He collapsed the wheelchair and placed it in the trunk. Then he ran around to the driver's seat and climbed in as Evelyn moved over. As they drove by the guard shack, Morty looked but could see no activity in the little structure. Had they been watching him? Maybe it was only the one cop. Or maybe, if there was another one, and if God was with them, the other cop was cooping, taking a little snooze for himself.

Morty drove to the corner of Lexington Avenue and stopped a bit abruptly for the light, and as he did, Irving heaved forward, slipping out of sight.

"Where are we taking him?" Evelyn asked. "You said you had a place all picked out."

"It's a fitting place for so special an occasion. A high and significant place." Morty was gradually calming down as he drove, and his sense of macabre amusement with the whole business was returning. "It's a place with a marvelous view," he added.

"A view? Morty, where are we taking him?"

"Wait and see."

A light rain began to fall as they cut back to the East Side, headed north on FDR Drive, onto the Harlem River Drive, and up to the George Washington Bridge. They crossed the bridge into Jersey, went immediately north on the virtually deserted Palisades Parkway, then pulled off at the first over-look, the Rockefeller Overlook, which provided an inspiring view of the Hudson, the opposite shore, the bridge, and beyond it, the skyline of Manhattan. He knew the spot well from having grown up in Jersey, and as he expected, there were no cars in sight. Who comes to an overlook at five in the morning? Especially when it has started raining.

"Is this perfect?" Morty breathed, feeling pleased with himself. "We'll leave him here to be the master of all he surveys." To which he added, "He can watch the dawn come up like thunder over Yonkers 'cross the way."

He pulled the car over parallel to the row of large rocks that provided a barrier to the bluff overlooking the river, and then, out of nowhere, lights flashing, a highway patrol car pulled quickly over next to him. Morty let out a tiny moan of dismay. His life, as he knew it, was over. All because of a lousy rug. He was ready to collapse into tears.

But Evelyn prodded him. "Morty! For God's sake, be cool. He fell down, in back. He's out of sight."

The trooper rolled down his window and shined a flash-light in Morty's face, signaling to Morty to roll his window down. Morty slowly did as he was told. The trooper studied Morty and Evelyn for a moment, and his expression changed. It softened, as if he couldn't possibly suspect this innocuous-looking couple of anything illegal. "Are you two all right?" he asked.

"We're fine, Officer, fine," Morty managed to get out.

"It seemed an odd time for anyone, like yourselves, that is, to be coming in here."

"It's our anniversary, Officer," Evelyn said. Morty turned and looked at her.

"Anniversary?" the officer asked. An amused smile.

"Fifteen years ago we got engaged on this spot. And at just about this time, believe it or not."

The officer looked as if, with that bit of information, he'd finally heard it all. "Well, congratulations. You two take care, hear? I wouldn't hang around this spot too long at this hour."

"Thank you, Officer," Morty said. And they watched as the patrol car roared away toward the exit and disappeared.

"Did he check our license plate?" Morty asked.

"He didn't check anything," she answered. "He didn't look at anything but our innocent faces."

"Good. You know something? You've got the makings of a great criminal mind."

Morty got out of the car and hurried around to the other side. He opened the back door and dragged Irving out, pulling him between two of the large rocks that formed the barrier to the high, steep bluff. Then he propped Irving up against one of the rocks, facing the river, in position to enjoy the view. "Stay loose, friend," he muttered to Irving. He hurried back into the car and headed for the exit, and home.

★ ★ ★ ★ ★

The rain grew heavier, and it pelted Irving's face, but Irving did not flinch. The ink on the sticky tag on his lapel was not waterproof, and the rain caused his name to streak, and finally to wash completely away.

★ ★ ★ ★ ★

Monday morning. In an elegantly appointed town house in Boston's Back Bay area, Mrs. Ira Waterman answered the phone. ". . . no, I don't know where Mr. Waterman is . . . no, I don't know how to get in touch with him . . . no, I, please let me explain. Mr. Waterman and I are separated. We are not in touch and have not been for quite some time, and I frankly have no idea as to his whereabouts, nor do I wish to have . . . yes, he could be in New York, I suppose. We did live there at one time when we were still together, and I think he still has business there. But he could also be most anywhere, and I assure you, I haven't the faintest notion where . . . you're very welcome."

★ ★ ★ ★ ★

Monday afternoon. Jack Sandifer entered the plane for his flight back to Chicago, went to his seat, and got comfortable. He was a tall man, lean, blond, athletic, striking in appearance.

After completing the project for which he'd flown east, he'd enjoyed a pleasant weekend in the Big Apple. A stay at the Pierre, a meal at Le Cirque, a couple of tough-ticket shows, *Les Miz* and *Phantom*. And this was in addition to the satisfaction of having been paid for a job properly done. The fifty thousand in bearer bonds was in his luggage. He always specified bearer bonds. Asking for cash always seemed a little lacking in class.

As the plane-loading process continued, he riffled through the *Post* he'd bought in the terminal. He studied the article about an unidentified man being found at an overlook off some parkway in New Jersey. A parkway in Jersey? And wearing a white turtleneck? "How in hell?" he said to himself. He glanced at the young woman who had taken the seat next to him. She was beautiful. She could easily be a model.

He reached into his shirt pocket and took out the little tuft of carpet fringe, examining it briefly and then putting it back. This business of keeping mementos of each of his projects was definitely a dangerous one, but it gave his work a quality, an edge of excitement, actually, that pleased him.

He'd liked his client. A very feisty lady for being so educated and polished. He smiled as he thought about her emphatic instructions. "I want you to remove all identification from him, and then label him in some way with his name before he changed it twenty years ago. And then deliver him back to our old address. That should do it for me."

And then she'd added the part about the rug. "Oh. And could you get that horrid Navajo rug of his out of the library? I've hated it since the day he bought it. Maybe you can think of some way to use it on this assignment. That would indeed be a nice touch."

The flight attendant came around to take drink orders. He asked for a couple of Scotches and then asked the woman next to him if she'd like a drink.

"Sure," she said with a disarming smile. "Thanks." And as their continuing conversation established that they were both returning to Chicago, where they both lived, she asked, "What sort of work do you do?"

"I'm a paid assassin."

"Gimme a break. Seriously, what do you do?"

"Actually, I deal in unusual antiques, specifically in primitive art. For example, I just delivered an authentic hand-woven, one-of-a-kind, antique Navajo rug to the City for a client. For which I was extremely well paid, I might add."

"Extremely? May I ask how extremely?"

"How's fifty-thousand? And to help me celebrate, have dinner with me when we get to Chicago."

Again that marvelous smile. "I'd love it," she said.

My first crack at trying to write an update of one of my favorite short stories, O. Henry's "The Ransom of Red Chief," kept getting longer and longer until it was book length and became my first novel, Taking Gary Feldman, *so I decided to try once more and have the kidnapee be a Jewish Princess, Retta Chiefman.*

The Ransom of Retta Chiefman

They watched her get out of the taxi, pay the fare, and hurry into Bergdorf Goodman. They quickly told their own cabbie to stop and then climbed out. "You go in and keep an eye on her," Harry said. "I'll stay out here."

"Why don't you go in and let me take the outside watch? I don't know how to act in a place like that."

"Just act natural. Act like you might wanta buy something. But don't let her notice you. Now move!"

Bert walked uneasily across the street and into the store. He spotted her in the shoe department, trying on some sandals. A solicitous young salesman was waiting on her. When she held out her foot and shook her head decisively, the salesman jumped up and hurried into the back, reappearing a moment later with three more boxes. Bert circled the shoe department and came to a good vantage point by a rack of expensive blouses.

"Can I help you with anything?" An elderly woman, tall, slim, bluish gray hair, elegantly dressed. She looked at him disdainfully. He obviously didn't belong, despite his suit and tie.

"Just kinda shoppin' around," Bert said. He lifted a blouse

off the rack and held it up by the hanger. After looking at it with great aplomb, he placed it back on the rack. "If I see somethin' I like, I'll let ya' know."

"Please do." She walked away.

Bert took another blouse off the rack. He delicately examined the hem of the fragile, silken fabric with his rough fingers and nodded in appreciation. He fumbled with the tag and read the price. "Jesus H. Christ!" The words were practically a gasp.

Bert glanced back at the shoe department; she was gone! The heat of panic engulfed him. He began looking frantically in all directions but she was nowhere in sight. Had he blown it? Harry'd kill him. He whirled around and suddenly found himself face to face with her. Up close she seemed older than twenty-seven, middle thirties at least, and a little heavy.

As she glanced at him, her expression suggested that she wondered what he could be doing there. A Bergdorf's customer he wasn't. She took a blouse from the rack and studied it.

As Bert backed away, the elderly saleslady approached. "Mrs. Chiefman. So nice to see you. Can I help you with anything today?"

"Oh, hi. I'd like this blouse, please. And wrap it as a gift, it's for my mother. Be sure and take off the price, of course. And could you please hurry, I have an important appointment in ten minutes?" Her voice had a nasal whining quality. She took her charge card from her wallet and handed it to the saleslady.

Bert moved into handbags and leather goods and watched from there.

After the saleslady returned with the package, Mrs. Chiefman added it to the shopping bag with the two pairs of shoes. Then she left the store. Bert followed her out.

When she reached the sidewalk, she headed uptown. Bert crossed Fifth Avenue and returned to where Harry stood waiting. "There she goes," he said.

"Walk ahead of me. She notice you in there?"

"I don't think so. Like you told me, why should she?"

"Let's go," Harry said.

They walked up Fifth Avenue, watching her from a distance. She crossed Fifth at Fifty-eighth and went into the lower level of the GM Tower to Vidal Sassoon.

"What now?" Bert asked.

"We wait."

"You got any idea how long?"

"This should take about an hour," Harry answered.

★ ★ ★ ★ ★

"Here she comes now," Harry said. He nudged Bert, who was thoughtfully observing people and traffic and things.

"She looks a little different," Bert said.

"That's the idea," Harry said. "Let's go."

They followed her back across Fifth Avenue and into the Plaza. She went into the Palm Court and was led to a table.

"Now what?" Bert asked.

"We eat lunch."

"In here?"

"We gotta eat somewhere." They followed the maitre d' between tables toward a far corner. As they moved across the area, Bert looked down at the food being eaten by people already served. Definitely not his idea of a good meal. Harry asked for the farthest table and they sat down, facing her back.

After the waiter had left them with their menus, Bert began studying it. "Jesus, look at these prices for this stuff!"

"Relax. It's an investment."

"There's nothin' to eat here."

33

"F'Crissakes, just pick somethin' and eat it!"

"What're you gonna have?"

★ ★ ★ ★ ★

They managed their finger sandwiches with fruit garnish and coffee and then trailed Henrietta Chiefman back down Fifth Avenue, taking turns following her into store after store. First it was Tiffany's, where she bought several pieces of expensive costume jewelry and dropped them into her shopping bag as casually as it she were buying groceries. She also bought a large sterling tea set and asked that it be delivered. Then off to Bendel's, where she found a blouse she liked and took one in every color. Then I. Miller for three more pairs of shoes, and finally Saks, where she made purchases on every floor.

They almost blew the whole thing when she left Saks by the side door and hailed a cab. Bert raced after her, heard her say Grand Central, and then ran to the front of the store to get Harry. They caught up with her as she was boarding the train for Scarsdale with her two shopping bags.

They sat a few seats behind her and when the train reached Scarsdale, they also got off. Then they trailed her Cadillac Seville in their panel truck and when she pulled into the long circular driveway, they were right behind.

As she was getting out of the car and the garage door was descending, they dashed under it, wearing their rubber masks, each carrying a gun.

She threw up her hands. "What is this?"

"You're coming with us."

"You mean, you mean this is a kidnapping?"

"Call it what you want. Only, let's get moving." Harry grabbed her arm roughly and pulled her toward the door. He pressed the wall switch and the door began to rise.

"You'll live to regret this," she said. "My Harvey'll see to that."

"If we do, lady, at least we'll regret it with money. Now do as you're told and you won't get hurt. Let's go."

★ ★ ★ ★ ★

The apartment was small, the upper floor of a tiny duplex house, isolated, the lower floor vacant. Henrietta Chiefman sat on a sofa in the living room, a set of crude manacles fastened around her ankles. Another lengthy section of heavy chain went from the manacles to a radiator pipe. The whole business was fastened together with a couple of bulky padlocks and was sufficiently long to give her range to reach the bathroom. The chains made dreadful noises when she moved around. And so did she. She didn't like the arrangement at all.

Harry had been watching the Chiefman house, studying their habits for weeks. He'd seen Harvey Chiefman come and go each day in his Maserati. He had also observed that Thursday was the maid's day off. He'd even followed Henrietta Chiefman on some of her past shopping trips to the City, as well as other places she routinely went—her clubs, local shopping, her friends' homes.

He'd decided it was time for them to make their move. Since it was Thursday, she'd be home alone. They would speak to her through the intercom, getting her to open the door on the pretense that they were deliverymen, and would simply grab her when she opened the door, pulling on the rubber masks at the last possible moment. However, when they reached the house, she had already started driving out, a little earlier than usual, to go to the station. Harry chose to follow her rather than wait for her return. He didn't think it wise to have been parked in front of her house all day on the day she was taken.

"You'll pay dearly for this, I'll promise you that." She hadn't stopped since they picked her up. "You've done a stupid thing. A stupid thing. You're in big trouble."

Bert tried to ignore her as he sat across the room and watched television. Some of his favorite shows were on Thursday nights. He said to her finally, getting hot under his mask, "Look, why don'cha just knock it off and watch the TV, whatta'ya say?"

"You just call my Harvey so he can start arranging to have you put where you belong."

Harry checked his watch. "Now that she mentions it," he said to Bert, "I think it is about time for me to go and make the first call."

Bert glanced at Henrietta Chiefman. "Why don'cha stay here and let me go make the call?"

"Just take it easy. I'll only be a few minutes."

★ ★ ★ ★ ★

"Is this Harvey Chiefman?"

"Yes it is."

"We're holding your wife."

"What do you mean you're holding my wife? Holding her how? Who is this?"

"Chiefman, we grabbed your wife today and we're holding her for ransom."

"Retta? You're holding Retta for ransom? So that explains where she is."

Harry scratched his head in confusion over the tone of Chiefman's response. "Chiefman, your wife's safe return will cost exactly one million dollars."

"Well, you'll never get it from me!"

"Then don't expect to ever see her alive again!"

"Look, whoever you are, if you kill her, you're in a lot of trouble. As a matter of fact, you're already in a lot of trouble, you know? But don't expect to get any money out of me."

"Isn't she your wife?"

"She is at the moment. Listen, I might as well let you have it straight. I'm planning to leave Retta. And when I do, what you're asking could turn out to be peanuts compared to what she and some lawyer are liable to come up with."

"Chiefman, how much *are* you willing to pay?"

"I won't pay anything. I thought I said that."

"Chiefman, you won't get away with this!"

"What are you going to do, call the police?"

"Chiefman . . ."

"One thing, though," Chiefman said. "Whoever you are, do me a favor and don't tell her I'm leaving her. Okay? I think the least I can do is tell her myself. Wouldn't you agree?"

"We'll be in touch, Chiefman." Harry hung up the phone and left the booth. He drove back to their flat and called Bert into the kitchen. "I think we may have a problem, pal," he told Bert.

★ ★ ★ ★ ★

How long do you expect to be holding me here?" Retta Chiefman demanded plaintively.

"It's hard to say for sure," Harry answered. "I'm trying to negotiate with your husband and frankly, he's not too . . . too cooperative."

"Well, if you plan to keep me in this, this place for another night, I'm going to need some things."

"What kinda things?" Bert asked.

"Some beauty aids. And some special foods. I cannot eat what you eat. I need certain special items."

"Such as?"

"Why don't I just write you a list?"

"Forget it. We can't be bothered."

"Don't tell me to forget it," she said with a raised voice. "I insist that you go and get what I ask for. I will not stay in this

37

house another night unless I have the things I need!"

Bert scowled.

"Get her a pencil and some paper," Harry said quietly.

Bert went into the kitchen and rummaged around, returning with a stump of a pencil and a scrap of paper. He gave them to her.

She wrote industriously for several minutes, compiling a rather lengthy list. She handed it to Bert. "I made it very neat so that even you would have no trouble reading it. Please go right away as I'm already a day off schedule."

Bert studied the list for a moment and began to read it out loud. "Skim milk, dried prunes, brewer's yeast, raisins . . . raisins? Whadda'ya gonna do with raisins? Bake cookies?"

"I'm going to eat them," she snapped.

He glanced back at the list. "Unprocessed coarse bran? You're gonna eat that too? I thought that's what they fed to hogs. Perrier water?"

"You can get all of those things at the health food store on White Plains Road."

"And what about all these other things you got written here? Charles of the Ritz?"

"I do not intend to explain and defend my need for everything on that list. I simply will not be without them. You can get them all at Lord and Taylor in White Plains, or go to Bloomingdale's or Saks."

He looked at Harry. "I'm gonna feel like an idiot goin' in those places to buy all this stuff."

"Don't complain," she muttered. "Idiot would be a step up for you."

Harry held up a hand to tell Bert to restrain himself. "Just go get the stuff on the list. Maybe it'll keep her quiet. And take it easy."

After Bert had left, she turned to Harry. "Do you know how to play gin rummy?"

"Of course I know how to play gin rummy."

"We're apparently going to have lots of time to kill. Would you like to play some?"

He shrugged and smiled beneath the mask. "Why the hell not?"

"Why don't we play for money?"

"You don't have any. We took yours. Remember?"

"You'll be giving me a chance to win it back. If I lose, I'll have Harvey take care of it."

He shook his head. "What the hell. Let's see if I can find a deck o' cards."

★ ★ ★ ★ ★

Harry met Bert in the kitchen when he returned from his shopping trip. "She won all her money back," Harry said.

"She what?"

"We played gin rummy while you were gone and she won all her money back."

"You gonna let her keep it?"

"I don't know yet. I'm tryin' to decide what's the right thing to do."

★ ★ ★ ★ ★

"Harvey Chiefman?"

"Yes."

"I'm calling back to see it we can't do a little negotiating and come up with somethin' acceptable to both parties."

"I've already told you I won't pay you one red cent."

"Have you called the police yet?"

"No. I'm hoping it's not going to be necessary. I'm a reasonable man. Look. You're in a lot of trouble. But if you just let Retta go, then we'll consider the case closed, no questions asked. Period. How does that sound?"

"Harvey, either you call the police or I'm gonna call 'em."

"You? Why would you call them?"

"I want 'em to know your wife's been kidnapped."

"I'll deny it."

"I'll warn 'em you'll probably deny it. Where are you gonna tell 'em she is, that they can check it out? What if they start thinkin' that maybe you're an accessory? And even if you convince the cops you're not in on it, how's it gonna look when the story gets into the papers and television that a man in your position and with your kind of dough isn't willing to put out a few bucks to determine whether your wife lives or dies? And I'll see to it that they know. And another thing, Harvey, how's this story gonna look when your case comes up in divorce court?"

Chiefman was quiet for a prolonged moment. Then, "I can see you've been doing a little thinking since the last time we talked."

"We're businessmen, just like you, Chiefman."

"Let me discuss it with my lawyer. Call me back tomorrow."

"Tomorrow morning, Harvey. And Harvey, we don't want to drag this thing on indefinitely. Understand?"

"Is she beginning to get to you a little?" There was a trace of knowing chuckle in his voice.

"Chiefman, I never said I didn't appreciate your position. But think of the newspapers and the divorce case and everything. Talk to your lawyer and come up with something reasonable. Okay?"

★ ★ ★ ★ ★

Bert was standing at the door when Harry returned from making the call. "She wants me to go shopping again," Bert said.

"What for this time?"

"She said she absolutely refuses to go another day without

40

fresh underwear. And another thing. She says the chains have to come off."

"For what?"

"For one thing, to put on the underwear. And another thing, she wants to take a shower and she refuses to take a shower if she can't close the bathroom door all the way. And besides, she'd never be able to step over the edge of the tub with the chains on her legs."

"So take the chains off for a while. She ain't going nowhere."

"There's more."

"What else?"

"She's got to have clean towels."

"Anything else?"

"She says the tub's filthy. Says she wants us to scour it before she takes her shower."

"Give her the soap powder and let her do it herself."

"I already tried that. She said she's allergic to soap powders. She can't do it without rubber gloves."

"Then we'll get her rubber gloves. Go to the nearest store, get her a towel, a clean pair of pants and a pair of rubber gloves."

"Incidentally, did you do any good with Chiefman?"

"He says he wants to talk to his lawyer. I think I got him thinkin'."

★ ★ ★ ★ ★

"Hello?"

"Chiefman?"

"Yes."

"You talk to your lawyer?"

"Yes, I did. He agrees with me. Right down the line. You let Retta go and I won't call the police and we'll consider the case closed. You have my word on it. It'll have been a nice adventure for her to tell her children about some day . . . if she

41

ever has any . . . which I frankly doubt . . . I know one thing. If she ever does, they won't be mine . . ."

"Chiefman," Harry said, trying to make his voice heavy with menace, "let me tell you something. This is a negotiation. Hear what I said? A negotiation. We don't intend to just let you call the shots. Now you come up with something interesting or we put her away. And we go to the papers and TV and make it known you refused to talk to us."

"Listen, guy, I respect your threat as a good tactic. As you said yesterday, we're both businessmen. But face it. You've committed a federal offense. That's heavy stuff. And stupid. Don't you know the Feds'll find you? And I'm giving you a chance to walk from this with a whole skin. Besides, who will the media believe, me or you? Think it over, pal. Learn to recognize a sweet deal when you hear one. As a matter of fact, I should really make you pay me a little something."

Harry hesitated a moment. "We'll be in touch." He got back in the truck and returned to the apartment.

Bert met him as be entered the kitchen. "Well?"

"He says he's sticking to yesterday's offer."

"You're kidding?"

"But don't worry about it," Harry said resolutely. "He ain't gettin' away with it. I don't give up that easy."

Retta Chiefman called to them from the bathroom door. "Will one of you please do something? We just ran out of hot water."

★ ★ ★ ★ ★

Harry dropped in a dime and dialed. The light bulb was out in the phone booth and he needed a match to see the numbers on the dial.

"Hello?"

"Chiefman?"

"Yes."

"Chiefman, we've decided to go along with your deal."

"I think you're being smart. I really do. You're saving yourself a lot of grief. How do you want to handle it? Are you going to drop her off near the house, here, or what?"

"Jesus, come on, Chiefman. What do you take us for? Here's our side of the deal. Without callin' the cops, you have to go get her yourself where we left her. I promise you she's okay. We got a deal?"

Chiefman hesitated.

"Come on, Harvey. You're gettin' it your way. You're winnin' out. What more do you want?"

After a slight pause, "All right. Where is she?"

"There's this park in Darien, Connecticut, that's completely deserted this time o' year and to get to it . . ."

"Darien? You want me to go all the way to Darien? At this time of night?"

"It ain't that far, Chiefman. Go by the Merritt Parkway. Take Exit Thirty-six, North, go about two miles, you'll see a big stone archway on the right. You can't miss it. Follow the main road in and you'll see a big deserted house. Behind the house, there's a shed. She's in the shed. We left a little electric lantern burning in there but it won't burn too long so you oughta get moving. And take a knife or something. We left her tied up and gagged."

"I like the idea of my being the one to rescue her, but couldn't you put her a little closer to home? Besides, that's over a state line, you know."

"Chiefman, you were the one that set the deal. Right? How long's it gonna take you in that fancy sports car of yours?"

After another pause, "Okay."

Harry hung up the phone and stepped out of the booth, which was located at the intersection of Chiefman's street and the main road leading to it. He climbed into the truck where Bert was waiting. They sat in silence until they saw Chiefman speed by in his Maserati. Then they drove to Chiefman's house.

They pulled into the long driveway and backed the truck to the door. Using the keys from Retta Chiefman's purse, they went into the house, looked quickly around, and began loading the truck: five color television sets and a Betamax, some custom stereo equipment, a few antique pieces and some modern paintings, eight fur coats, lots of sterling, including a matched service for thirty-six, all of Retta Chiefman's jewelry, some of her fancier-looking clothes and perfumes, Harvey's clothes, a dozen cases of liquor and another dozen of dusty-looking French wines. And of course they took the Seville, with the two shopping bags still in it. And they had the money out of Retta's handbag or what was left after shopping for her . . . What the hell! Everything considered, the caper didn't turn out all that bad.

You look for ideas for stories wherever you can find them. One of my major problems has always been coming up with workable ideas. When a big money heist took place out at JFK Airport, I decided I would be able to do something *with that.*

I'm Sorry, Mr. Turini

The room clerk looked down his nose with considerable disdain at Pasqual, his rumpled black suit and his black oily hair. "I'm sorry, Mr. Turini, but we have no reservation for you. And we have no rooms. We're sold out for tonight."

Pasqual's knees sagged. He needed to get into that room and out of sight, quick. A cop could come walking in the door any second and spot the briefcase. "Hey! Don't make jokes," he said to the clerk. "We had this reservation confirmed for weeks. Weeks!" The creep! He was going to try and pull a fast one. He'd blow Harry's whole plan.

"Have you a written confirmation?"

The clerk examined the smudged confirmation slip and then checked it against his bookings. "I'm very sorry, but a mistake has been made. We're overbooked. I'm afraid I can't honor this confirmation. There's nothing I can do."

Pasqual glared at the trim-looking young man in the monogrammed blazer. He would have killed him under other conditions. "You got that reservation over there. We made it a long time ago. It's got to be there, so go look again."

"I'm sorry, Mr. Turini, but I've looked. We don't have a room for you." The young man showed no signs of being intimidated by Pasqual's menacing tone.

45

Pasqual changed his approach to that of a plea. "I'm positive it's there. We was confirmed. My friends are coming to meet me here and I gotta be in this hotel."

"I'm afraid I can't help you as far as a room is concerned. We'll be glad to hold a message for your friends."

"You can't pull this." The threat again. "Look, we got reservations and you go check again."

"I've checked, Mr. Turini. There's nothing I can do. Now, could you please step to one side and let the line move forward?"

"Find me a room and we'll make it worth your while, really worth your while. Unnerstand what I mean? But we got to have that room."

"I'm sorry, Mr. Turini."

Pasqual was perspiring heavily. What was he going to do if he couldn't get into the hotel? There was no way to contact Harry. They'd show up looking for him. He couldn't leave a message. Even if it was safe to leave a message, what message could he leave? What was he going to do? Sit there in the lobby with close to five hundred grand in that briefcase? "Look," Pasqual said quietly, "I got to have a room in this hotel. This hotel. I'll pay any price, but just find me something. We had a guaranteed confirmed reservation and I'm going to make a little noise around here if I don't get it. Now, do something about it."

"Why don't you speak to our assistant manager?"

"Good. Lemme talk to him. Where's he at?"

The clerk pointed at a door and then pressed a button on the counter. As Pasqual walked toward the door, a slightly older man in a business suit emerged from it.

Pasqual went through the whole thing again with pleas, threats and offers of bribes. The assistant manager walked over and talked quietly with the room clerk for several minutes. They each looked at Pasqual a time or two during their conversation. The assistant manager came back and informed him that they were very sorry but, confirmation slip or not, they had no reservation and no rooms. Pasqual repeated the threat to raise a little hell and the assistant manager said quietly, "Shall I call our security officer, Mr. Turini? Or would you prefer that we just go directly to the police?"

Pasqual looked at the man for a moment without speaking. He wanted to set the briefcase down and take the guy apart with his bare hands—but what would that do for him? He sponged his forehead with the sleeve of his jacket and turned and walked out of the hotel. He looked around, half-expecting a dozen cops to rush him.

He hurried into another, equally fancy hotel a few doors from the first one, and after standing nervously in the short line, learned from the room clerk that the hotel was sold out and that he didn't think Pasqual would find any rooms on Central Park South because of the boat show in the Coliseum. "I suggest you try farther downtown," the clerk said.

Pasqual walked out onto the street feeling helpless. His instructions were to get into that first hotel room and stay quiet until Harry, Artie and Charlie showed up, but the last guy said go downtown and he figured he'd better do it. He had to do something quick; the briefcase made him nervous. It was an ordinary-looking briefcase like you might see anybody carrying down the street, but he still had to figure that a description of the case had been circulated and any cop might spot it and ask questions.

He reached Seventh Avenue and headed downtown. He walked fast although he knew it wasn't smart. Harry had told him a million times never to rush. It attracts attention. He'd remind himself to slow down, but then he'd gradually speed up again.

He felt hot and steamy. He had been dreaming of getting into that room in that class hotel and really enjoying it, soaking in a fancy shower, stretching out on the bed, waiting for Harry and the boys to bring fresh clothes. He'd never stayed in a class hotel except in Miami a couple times, if he could count that. Had that first clerk turned him down because he looked so bad for such a class hotel?

He had to get the briefcase out of sight. It was going to get spotted. He passed a luggage store and thought about going in and buying a suitcase and putting the little case inside the big one. He could pick out one that looked completely different. Then he remembered he didn't have enough loose cash to buy a suitcase. He was carrying close to half a million dollars and he couldn't afford a lousy valise. Harry had locked the briefcase "to keep it from opening accidentally," and had kept the key. Even if he had the key, you don't just open a case full of half a million bucks in a luggage store.

Harry's plan had gone without a hitch. No rough stuff, no foolishness. Just like it had been laid out to go. The first time in history a job that size had ever been pulled at JFK. They knew where every person was going to be and what they'd be doing the minute they walked into the freight terminal on the fringes of the airport. The money was there, being transferred just like Harry said it would be, and everything worked—the telephone company truck, the uniforms, the toolboxes for carrying the guns, everything.

Harry's planned getaway had clicked too. "There's no way they can check every cab leaving the airport within ninety seconds of the heist," Harry had said. "So we get the money out quick by cab." Charlie was waiting by his taxi with the hood up at the spot Harry'd picked out—a crazy combination underpass and sharp curve. You couldn't see the spot from anywhere around. He had jumped from the moving truck and gotten into the cab. Charlie closed the hood and drove him straight to the hotel and disappeared. He had changed clothes in the taxi while on the way.

"We got to keep doing what they don't expect," Harry had said, "and they won't be looking for a bunch of stickup artists in one of the palaces along Central Park South. So that's where Pasqual goes with the money. And we'll meet there later." With the reservation confirmed, even Harry hadn't figured on the creep behind the counter at the hotel.

Pasqual crossed 57th Street and exchanged looks with the cop directing traffic. Harry had told him a million times never to look one straight in the eye. He had to stop doing it. The cop glanced at the briefcase. Had he already been checked out on the heist? It was less than an hour old but the cop was staring at the briefcase!

Pasqual almost started running but forced himself back into a walk. Unable to resist the urge, he looked around at the cop and saw that he was using his walkie-talkie. No! He had to get that case outa sight! He broke into a run and ran to the next corner, crossed while dodging traffic and ran another block.

He spotted a huge hotel and headed for it. Panting and soaked to the skin, he got into the line at the registration desk only to be faced with the inevitable question: "Do you have a reservation?"

Pasqual returned to the street and looked around. There were more hotels farther down Seventh Avenue toward Times Square. They couldn't all be sold out. He began to think of the briefcase as being festooned with neon lights that attracted the eyes of the world. Everybody was staring at him, first him and then the case.

Spotting another hotel across Seventh Avenue, he dashed into the street, almost causing a massive pile-up of the frenzied traffic moving toward Times Square. He ignored the glares and raised fists of the hacks and other drivers and hurried to the other side.

He entered the hotel and got into the registration line. Only two people were in front of him, an old lady with purple hair and a businessman, yet the wait seemed endless—and even before he heard the question, he knew it was coming. He could see it in the eyes of the broad handling registrations. "Do you have a confirmed reservation?"

"Yeah, sure."

"Your name?"

"Pasqual Turini."

She checked it out and returned with the look he had come to know so well; the look of a room clerk in a sold-out hotel. "I'm sorry, Mr. Turini." Of course, they were booked up for the night. He considered going into the whole "You musta made a mistake" routine, but he could tell she was a tough broad and it was a waste of time.

He turned and walked toward the front of the lobby and the street. As he approached the door, a police car stopped directly across the street and four of the boys in blue climbed out of it. They stood in a group for a moment and talked, then they fanned out, two going down Seventh and one up Seventh. The fourth cop stood on the curb, waiting for traffic to break so he could cross toward the hotel.

Pasqual turned quickly and went over to the bell captain.

"You got a checkroom?"

"Yeah, sure." The captain pulled a check from under his counter and scribbled something on it. He tore it in half and tied half to the handle of the briefcase.

Pasqual took a deep breath and then mopped his face with

50

his sleeve. "I'll pick it up later," he said. "Who needs to be lugging that thing around town? You know what I mean?"

"Pick it up any time. Just bring the claim check."

Pasqual glanced at the door leading out to Seventh Avenue. "Say, you got a way to get through here to Broadway?"

"Sure." The bell captain pointed at a door in the corner of the lobby. "Through there, out through the parking garage, turn right. You can't miss it."

"Thanks." Without looking back, Pasqual headed for the door.

"Hey, you forgot your claim check," the captain said, pointing at the scrap of paper on the counter.

Pasqual stopped and almost collapsed. What if he had left without it? He rushed back over, grabbed it and squeezed it in his hand. He pocketed it as he went out.

Pasqual walked down Broadway feeling more relaxed and much less conspicuous. The case was safely out of sight. They could pick it up any time. Now he had to think where to go and where not to go. What would Harry tell him to do if he were there? He'd better not go to his own place. No way was that safe. Still, it had to be someplace Harry would guess. Rosie's. His sister Rosie's. Her little kid loved him. Had to go somewhere and wait. The whole escape plan was busted, anyway. Harry would have to put together a new one—and Harry would think to call Rosie's.

He looked around him at the crowds. Times Square. What a zoo! He thought about the money and then the claim check. What if he were stopped and searched? He reached in his pocket and pulled out the claim check and looked at it. A half-million bucks! He turned it over and fumbled it and dropped it. A breeze carried it several feet and he chased it, covering it finally with his foot, not far from a sewer. He picked it up carefully and slid it into the heel of his shoe.

When they frisk a guy, they don't look in his shoes. He glanced around. A cop was watching him and chuckling. Pasqual walked another block and then ducked down the steps into the subway.

★ ★ ★ ★ ★

Pasqual was sitting by the phone at Rosie's when Harry's call finally came. He could sense Harry's frustration when he described what happened at the first hotel, but it didn't seem to matter too much since the plan to get rid of the telephone truck had worked so very smoothly. They had avoided the possible chase and there had been no need for the car switch in the parking garage or the overnight delay in the fancy hotel before leaving the city. All they had to do was get in the car and go. Then Pasqual told Harry about the briefcase.

After sweating a moment of silence, Pasqual thought Harry was going to come through the phone at him. He tried to explain but couldn't make himself heard over Harry's rage. He listened painfully until Harry got it all out. Then, on the basis that what was done was done, Harry told him they'd take him by the hotel and let him pick up the case. After that, they'd be on their way. Things had gone well and still looked pretty clean, but Harry made it quietly clear what he should expect if for any reason, ANY reason, they didn't get that money back. Pasqual shuddered and clutched the claim check tightly.

★ ★ ★ ★ ★

Pasqual walked into the hotel and found the place a mess. The floor was wet and there was a burnt smell everywhere. He went over to the night-shift bell captain and handed him the claim check.

"See da manager," the man said, handing it back.

Pasqual felt the blood drain from his face. He grabbed the

52

bell captain by the lapels of his jacket. "Do what? No! Gimme the case!"

"See da manager," the captain repeated, brushing his hands away.

"Here's the check, gimme the case," Pasqual said quickly.

"See da manager."

"What for?"

"See da manager, he'll take care o' ya'."

Pasqual looked around, expecting to see himself surrounded by cops with their guns drawn. Instead, everything looked perfectly quiet, except for the mess and the smell. He walked uncertainly over to the registration desk and asked for the manager.

A new broad behind the desk went to an open door and spoke to someone inside the room. A man came out of the office. He approached Pasqual, and seeing the claim check in his hand, said, "You had something in our checkroom prior to five this afternoon?"

Pasqual looked around again, still expecting anything. Finally he said, "Yeah."

The manager took the check out of his hand and examined it. Then he walked around the counter and into his office. He returned in a moment carrying a white sheet of paper, a printed form. "We had a fire in our checkroom this afternoon," he said, "and everything in there was completely destroyed. However, we do have insurance to cover the damage and if you'll fill out this form and carefully itemize your losses, estimating values of each item, we will file the claim with our underwriter and you should be able to recover . . ."

Pasqual turned and glanced toward the front of the hotel and Seventh Avenue where Harry and Artie and Charlie were waiting. Then he dashed for the back door in the corner of the lobby that led to the parking garage and Broadway.

When my wife, Marilyn, and I first moved to Connecticut with our then two children (now they are three, and five grandchildren), we built a house, and for two years, I did little in my spare time other than work on that house. After that got old, I looked for a new hobby. I signed up for a creative writing workshop, conducted in Strathcona Hall on the Yale campus by a lovely man, Dick Banks, who was Director of the Yale News Bureau and who had sold countless short stories to Liberty Magazine *in his earlier days. This story was my first published short story in the mystery genre and was written as an exercise in his class, and in the story, he's the clerk and I'm the customer.*

The Everlasting Jug

It was a trifling matter, and yet Ben floundered in the throes of indecision. The penetrating, half-smiling gaze of the clerk heightened the embarrassment he felt for his vacillation. He had noticed this particular package store many times but had never stopped before. It was on his usual route to and from work and there was something about the unusual decor of the front of the store that had always intrigued him.

Now, inside the shop, he was sorry he had stopped as he felt suddenly aware of his old reluctance to spend money for whiskey. He tried not to fidget. He feigned an academic interest in the matter, pulling bottles off the shelves, examining the labels studiously, returning bottles to the shelves. There were some fifteen advertised name brands within a price spread of fifty cents, several that were more expensive, and several unfamiliar brands that were a good bit less.

He glanced in the direction of the clerk, caught his watchful eye for an instant and looked away. He had to act, so he grabbed a bottle of one of the cheap off-brands and walked over to the counter. "This stuff drinkable?"

The clerk studied him a moment before answering. "Oh, can't be too bad. Bottled in Scotland." The clerk was perched like a Buddha on a high stool. He was small, balding, bespectacled.

"Well, isn't it true that quite often these off-brands are good surplus stock being unloaded by the big-name distilleries under different labels? Some of them are real sleepers."

"I guess that's true, sometimes," the clerk answered.

"But you're not familiar with this one."

"No."

"What about some of the other less expensive ones?"

The clerk shook his head again.

"Hell, I can't tell one from another. And I don't believe any of my friends can. Sometimes I pour this cheap stuff into a good bottle and then everybody's happy."

The clerk maintained his omniscient gaze without commenting.

"What I need is a bottle without a bottom in it," Ben said. "Hell, you invite a couple of people in for drinks and it seems before you turn around you're out another six bucks' worth of booze."

"What would you pay for such a bottle?" the clerk asked.

"Why?" Ben chuckled. "Are you going to try and sell me one?" Ben's eye was suddenly arrested by the clerk's gilt tie-clasp. A bizarre arrangement of stars, serpents, and sheaves of grain.

"Would you like to buy one?" the clerk asked.

"Sure."

"You needn't smirk. I can deliver."

"A bottomless bottle of booze?" Ben gave the odd little man a silly smile. "Come on now, friend. What's the gag?"

"There's no gag, young man, no gag at all. And I don't think you should make light of the proposition I'm able to offer. You stand to gain too much from it. I've seen so many like you come in here and wring yourselves out over the money you spend for booze. You've gotten yourself into a situation, a status perhaps, where you've got to drink it and serve it, and you curse the system because it seems such a waste.

"You buy cheap, off-brand stuff, and when you invite people in, you mix it in the kitchen. You measure with a light hand and a small jigger and you fill up with mixer. You ask who'll have another and you flinch at every yes you get."

"I must admit," Ben said, "you're making me feel undressed, you read me so well."

"I know my work. Do you know what one of these bottomless bottles will do for you? It's all twelve-year-old stuff, name brands. You bring the bottle out and put it on your cocktail table. You pour it with a heavy hand. You're a sport, a bon vivant, a charming and carefree host. You'll acquire a casual confidence you didn't know you had. You'll literally be a different person with this bottle."

"I wish I could buy your story, friend," said Ben. "It's the kind of thing I'd like to believe is possible."

"You empty one of my bottles and bring it back. I'll give you your money back. I'll give you an affidavit." He reached into a drawer and pulled out a sheet of rich, white paper inscribed in exquisite black script. A gilt reproduction of the clerk's queer, serpentine tie-clasp insignia appeared in startling brilliance at the top of the sheet.

"Let's see one of the bottles," Bell said.

"Back here." They went back into the dusty rear of the

store. The clerk led Ben to a shelf where there were four or five cases of different brands of twelve-year-old Scotch. Each case had the serpentine gold insignia imprinted on it.

"Let me see the Chivas," Ben said.

The clerk reached into one of the cases, pulled out a bottle and handed it to Ben. The label looked routine except that it had the gold insignia in the lower right-hand corner—unnoticeable at a glance.

"OK, I'll bite," said Ben. "How much?"

"Two hundred."

"Two hundred?"

"Don't you think that's a fair price for a lifetime supply of twelve-year-old Scotch?"

"Lifetime? Not eternal? Sounds like a threat."

"It's not meant to be. The bottles come without curses. It's just that the bottle will be yours and you must keep its nature in strictest confidence. Otherwise, I'm afraid the affidavit will be invalidated." The clerk's eyes conveyed complete authority.

"How can I put out two hundred dollars without bringing my wife into my confidence? We have a joint checking account. Hell, that's more than my mortgage payment."

The clerk's smile penetrated Ben. "That's your problem, but somehow I think you can."

Ben clutched his breast pocket. He wondered how the clerk could have known. He had just gotten a dividend check for two hundred and some odd dollars. Sally paid no attention to such matters. There would be no problem. It was so pat it was eerie.

"Let me ask you something," said Ben. "Aren't people going to notice that the level in the bottle doesn't go down? I mean, you say, 'put it out on the table.' Won't people notice?"

"They won't notice. However, if you find you're concerned, walk out of the room with it and then back in. They'll think it's another one." The clerk smiled.

"Won't my wife notice?" Ben asked.

"Will she?" The clerk's confidence was supreme.

"No, I suppose not," Ben admitted thoughtfully. "She's happy to leave me supreme commander of the bar. Let me ask another question. Isn't a man with such a bottle prone to alcoholism?"

"I can't be responsible for abuses of this kind. It's your problem. However, I've received no information of such developments." His statement crackled with certainty.

"What if I drop the bottle?"

"It's a glass bottle. But tell me this. How many bottles of Scotch have you ever dropped? Any other questions?"

"You sound as though you think I'm buying."

"Aren't you?"

"I must admit I'm intrigued to call your bluff. It makes such a story."

"But one you can't tell," the clerk said quickly.

"You'll back up your . . . your affidavit?"

"As long as you adhere to all its terms."

"I must be out of my mind but, what the hell, this isn't budget money, I've got to see how this thing ends." Ben took out the dividend check and endorsed it.

The clerk examined it and put it in the register. He paid out the difference and handed Ben the bottle in a bag and the affidavit. "Good health," he said, ascending his stool.

"Same to you." Ben felt a momentary flush of insecurity as he turned and walked out.

When Ben arrived home, he put the bottle down in the kitchen. Then he went to his desk, took out an envelope, slipped the folded affidavit into the envelope, and sealed it.

He thought a moment, smiled, and marked the envelope, "Dividend Certificate." He put the envelope in the bottom drawer of the desk beneath a stack of miscellaneous papers and bundles of cancelled checks.

"I see you bought another bottle of Scotch," came Sally's voice from the kitchen.

Ben walked into the kitchen. "Yeah," he said, smiling. "Let's have a drink."

"Sure," said Sally, a little surprised at Ben's sudden extravagance. "What are we celebrating?"

"Let's toast the mysteries of life," Ben answered. He took out some ice, carefully opened the bottle and poured two drinks. He replaced the cork and set the bottle on the counter. They went into the living room and sat down.

They sipped their drinks and made small talk about the day's activities but Ben carefully avoided any discussion of the whisky purchase. He noted the unquestionable superiority of the whisky over the off-brand stuff he usually bought.

He finished his drink and went back to the kitchen for another. He held up the dark bottle to note the level of its contents and then poured a stiff drink. He held up the bottle again. He couldn't detect a change in the level of the whisky, but then, it was a short, stubby bottle. He wondered what would be the operating level, so to speak, of the bottle. He wondered if the liquid level would go down and come back up. He thought about challenging the bottle by pouring off into other bottles. He could fill a bunch of empty booze bottles! Milk bottles! Gallon jugs! No. How could he explain it to Sally? Too, there was the affidavit in the sealed envelope. He'd play it straight. He put the bottle down and returned to the living room.

The next day Ben had a few of his office mates in for drinks as they were all en route from work to an organizational dinner meeting. When he arrived with his friends, he brought the bottle out and poured with a heavy hand. The clerk's prediction was materializing. Ben was a new and different kind of host. His casualness seemed to engender camaraderie. They were coming up to their third round and it was a great little spontaneous party. Ben had gone into the kitchen for more ice when he heard the sickening shattering of glass on the tile floor. Ben ran back into the living room.

"Oh hell, I'm sorry, Ben. That was damn fine booze, too. I don't suppose there was much left in it though, the way we were hitting it."

Ben felt queasy and had difficulty holding himself together for a moment. "It's okay," he said, finally. "Don't give it a thought, Alex. We've all had enough. Let me get a mop." Noting that he was visibly shaking, he added, "I guess the noise startled me."

Andy Langham reached down and picked up the fragment of glass and label that had the gilt insignia. He ran his thumb over the insignia and looked up at Ben. Their glances met. "Funny," said Andy, smiling quietly. "Mine got broken too."

Reviewers are those fearful monsters who look for all the faults they can find in the works of those of us who strive to be creative, and the most absolutely villainous of all reviewers are drama critics, so I decided to do an update on our Patron Saint's famous tale, "The Cask of Amontillado," in which the ultimate villain is John Fortunato, drama critic for the New York Times.
"For the love of God . . ."

The Case of Grand Cru

"John, come over this afternoon at three."

"But, Justin, this rare vintage you've told me of—can't I sample it tonight at your party?"

"I'll be much too busy being a host. And I certainly don't intend serving any of it to that mob. Come at three."

"Three it shall be. I'll be there with bells on."

"See you then, John." Justin hung up. With a sense of total resolve, he made his decision to proceed with his plan—a fantasy that had become a preoccupation and denied him sleep for months. He hated John Fortunato. Despised him! John Fortunato exemplified the saying: "Those who can't create become critics." He took great pleasure in inflicting heartbreak on those who strived to create by wreaking havoc with their creations. To the world of theater, the man was a plague.

However, Justin had had his successes in spite of Fortunato. After thirty years of hard work, enough of his mystery plays had enjoyed extended runs on Broadway and elsewhere to make him wealthy. Other playwrights had been hit so hard by Fortunato's reviews that their plays had closed after opening night. Months, years of effort wasted. Crushing disappointments. Moreover, who knew what greater heights he himself might have reached had it not been for the impact of Fortunato's brutally unkind, self-serving reviews. The man was absolutely taken with the ring of his own glib pronouncements.

But all that was soon to change. Justin had brooded about it for months and the moment was now at hand. As he would be borrowing a scenario from the master, he was wryly amused at the appropriateness of Fortunato's name. The theater would finally be freed from John Fortunato's scathing criticism.

The knock at the door interrupted his musings.

"Come in, John."

"Justin, my friend. Where is this rare bottle I shall be privileged to sample?"

The monster had already been drinking. Wonderful! "Come into the kitchen, John. Sit down, and let me get you a glass." He watched Fortunato drop into a chair as he placed the fluted wineglass on the table. He then took an orange-labeled bottle from the refrigerator, peeled the heavy foil, untwisted the wire, pulled the cork, and poured the shimmering wine into the tall, slender glass. "Here, John. Enjoy."

Fortunato took a large swallow. "Ahhh. Yes! . . . Justin, where are all of your house staff?"

"It's Sunday—their day off."

"But what about your little *soirée* tonight for some, what, two hundred?"

"The caterers come at six. The party is called for eight."

"The party to celebrate the success of *Murder Among Friends.*"

"One thousand performances, John. Despite your review," he said, smiling.

"You mustn't take it personally, Justin. I calls 'em like I sees 'em. You know that. Above all else, I must be true to my craft. Would you have me do otherwise?" He drained his glass. "That doesn't mean we're not still dear friends."

"Of course not." Justin refilled the other man's glass and watched him quickly take another large gulp. "We all do what we must. Right, Justin?"

"Right." Fortunato rolled a mouthful of champagne around on his tongue. "Ahhh. Superb. The bubbles literally frolic against the palate. And this is from a bottle of that legendary best vintage you've told me about?"

"From this vineyard, every vintage is legendary." Justin stepped into the pantry as he spoke, quickly emptied a small envelope of white powder into the mouth of the bottle, and returned. He again refilled Fortunato's glass.

Another double gulp. "Yes, Justin, this is superb. But that one special case you told me about . . ."

The glutton! Great champagne is sipped, not gulped. But in this instance . . . He refilled Fortunato's glass and watched him lift it to his mouth and pour. "I have such a case, John."

"I must sample it. I absolutely must!" He was beginning to slur his words.

"I have it in a special place. In the cellar. Come. And bring your glass." He refilled the glass once more and watched his guest gulp before getting to his feet. Very little of the powder was needed, especially when mixed with alcohol.

Fortunato struggled to his feet and followed Justin to a door and down some steps, stumbling and nearly falling. "I'm suddenly not feeling too well, Justin. Maybe I'm drinking too fast."

"With this wine, John, it's most difficult to practice moderation. But you've experienced nothing yet, my friend. Wait until you taste this vintage . . ."

"I must sample it," said Fortunato excitedly, despite the drowsiness that had begun to set in. He clutched his glass in one hand and gripped the handrail with the other as he moved down the stairway. When they reached the cellar, he said, "It's chilly down here, Justin."

"As a good wine cellar should be."

"And damp. Clammy. It's damp and clammy down here."

"I'm planning to get a dehumidifier. Over here, John. In this special little room. He led Fortunato through an unfinished opening and into a tiny chamber constructed of cement blocks. Inside there was a small refrigerator, a tiny table, and one chair. "Sit here, John, and make yourself comfortable."

Rapidly losing control of himself, Fortunato practically fell onto the chair. But his fingers were still tight around the stem of the wineglass.

"And, now, my friend." With Fortunato watching through half-closed eyes, Justin opened the refrigerator to reveal twelve dark champagne bottles with orange labels.

"Yes!" Fortunato gasped. "Yes! Open one of them!"

Justin took one out, opened it, and filled Fortunato's glass. He watched as Fortunato brought it to his mouth and poured. His eyes closed, some of it running down his chin. He filled the glass again.

But Fortunato seemed to be losing the motor skills required to bring the glass to his lips. He was slumping, his eyes still closed, his chin on his chest. "Superb, Justin. Superb." The slurred words virtually bubbled from his mouth.

Justin stepped outside the tiny cubicle and grabbed a kerosene lamp. He lit it and set it on the floor inside the cubicle. "It's not wired for lights, yet," he said. He turned the flame to maximum and lifted the glass chimney off the lamp.

"Superb, Justin," Fortunato repeated, sluggishly.

Time to move quickly. Justin came out of the cubicle,

seized a wheelbarrow of fresh mortar, and pushed it over to a stack of cement blocks near the opening in the wall. He grabbed the trowel, sloshed cement onto the floor, set two blocks into place, and mortared between them. Then two more. He neatly trimmed and pointed the joints. One of the many odd jobs he'd held while working his way through college had been apprentice to a mason.

When his new masonry had reached shoulder height, Fortunato had experienced a momentary flash of consciousness and looked at him. "What on earth are you doing, Justin?"

"Have more champagne, John. The bottle's on the table."

"Yes. Superb, Justin." Fortunato slumped again, his eyes closed.

He finished sealing off the opening and touching up all the mortar joints. A neat job, even if a little rushed. The block walls were right to the ceiling, and the open flame inside would consume the remaining oxygen . . .

A waste of a case of fine champagne? Not at all. It wasn't from any "special year."

★ ★ ★ ★ ★

"Justin, darling, what a simply marvelous party! As yours always are."

"Thank you, my dear." Justin walked among his guests, over two hundred strong, greeting them, chatting, accepting their warm congratulations, watching them enjoy an array of beautifully presented canapés along with champagne from the dark bottles with the orange labels. A day to remember. An occasion worth a celebration of the greatest magnitude. His elegant East Side town house was ablaze with light and festivity.

"A thousand performances, Justin. Wonderful. *Mazel Tov.*"

"And we're still selling out every performance. Not bad for a show without music."

He moved on, took a glass of champagne and sipped it. He loved being among creative—genuinely creative—people, and this was a brilliant gathering of talent. Writers, producers, directors, actors, artists, composers, and designers, along with devoted patrons of the arts, and even critics—all except one.

"Justin."

It was Captain Frank Bowles, Chief of Detectives for the district and a long-time friend. "Frank. How's my favorite cop in the world?" he said warmly.

"Delighted to be here, Justin. Some kind of bash you've got going here."

"It would not have been possible without the help I get from you, Frank. I don't dare offer my work for consideration until I've gotten your blessing on the details."

"Oh c'mon. Quit trying to blame me for your success. You're the best at what you do. Tell me. Where's your 'great friend' Mr. Fortunato, who's always so prominent at these little get-togethers? Or have you finally decided not to invite him anymore?"

"Oh, no, he was invited. He's around here, somewhere."

"I haven't seen him. To tell you the truth, I can't believe one of you playwrights hasn't killed the bastard by now."

"That's an interesting comment, coming from a policeman."

"Well, he's an animal. I read his stuff. What else can I tell you?"

At around two, after the last guest had finally left, the significance of what he'd done earlier suddenly began to dawn on him. He nervously opened the door to the stairway leading to the cellar and listened for a full minute. Nothing. Had he really done what he'd done . . . Yes, he had—***Requiescat in Pace***.

But still. He had to walk down there and see. He took one step, then another, and suddenly felt a tremor of fear. He paused. What did he have to fear? Who was better qualified than he, the internationally celebrated creator of perfect murder scenarios, to detail and execute the perfect crime? Especially with a basic plan borrowed from one of the legendary masters.

Still . . .

He took another step. Then another . . .

"Justin?" A muffled voice from below . . .

He froze.

"Justin, is that you?"

It was Fortunato.

"Justin, COME DOWN HERE!"

He grabbed the handrail and moved downstairs to the new wall. One of the blocks at the top of the opening had been dislodged.

"Justin, if you didn't want me at your party, why didn't you just not invite me? Is this some kind of huge joke? What am I supposed to say to you? 'For the love of God, Montresor'?"

Justin stood frozen before the wall.

"Or were you actually trying to kill me?" said the muffled voice. "For God's sake, you're no killer. If you were, I should think you'd have had the sense to use poison instead of sleeping pills. I use them regularly. They're like candy to me. So I was lucid enough to put out the lantern or I might have suffocated. I've been here in the dark for what, now? Twelve hours?"

Justin remained tongue-tied, staring at the hole near the top of the wall.

"Enough's enough, Justin! Do something will you, please? Now!"

Justin was still too shaken to respond.

"Okay, if you'll just set me free from this . . . this . . . dungeon, I swear I'll never give you another bad review. Have we a deal? And I promise I'll never tell. Who'd believe me? We'll call it a private joke of classic proportions. Just between us . . . JUSTIN, LET ME OUT OF HERE!"

Justin walked to where he'd left a heavy, long-handled maul, picked it up, returned to the wall, and began to swing away at the newly added blocks. When he'd made a large enough opening, and Fortunato had started through it, he proffered, "John, why don't you take a bottle of the champagne?"

Fortunato stopped and turned back to the refrigerator. "I'll take two." He took one in each hand. As he walked through the jagged opening and headed toward the stairs, he added, "Would you be so kind as to order me a cab?"

At some point shortly after the title, "Missing in Manhattan," was chosen for another anthology by the members of the Adams Round Table, I was in Manhattan on a very cold day and, thrashing around for an idea for a story, saw a bunch of freezing Santas . . . I wonder how many people have noticed that some Santas in New York wear white belts and some wear black? I learned this during my research for the story.

Just Another New York Christmas Story

December 23, mid-morning

Cold. Bone-cracking cold. Cold? Oh, Jesus, Mary, and Joseph, too cold for any human being to be standing in one spot. Even for ten minutes. All day? Forget it. But there he was. And he was there for all day.

He'd just have to take it. For the first year after nine years in the corps, he got to pick the spot he wanted. Right in front of Macy's. And he intended to hold on to it. No question one of the best spots. Year after year, one of the biggies for payoff. And even close to home. When he'd heard that the big guy who'd had it wasn't around this year, he'd made his demands on the basis of seniority and gotten it. But this day he wasn't so sure he liked it. The wind blowing down Thirty-fourth Street was a wind tunnel. Gusting probably forty-fifty miles an hour, the wind-chill probably forty below. Hell! More like fifty. If you're moving, out fighting it, maybe five-ten minutes, that's one thing. But standing still? All day? It could freeze the balls off a brass monkey.

He knew he should have listened to Murphy. She was always right. He could still hear her talking in his ear. "Francis,

71

didn't you hear the forecast? What's the matter with you? You want to freeze? Wear everything you own out there today." So what did he answer? "Sweetheart, you don't know how warm that red suit can be out there. I'm tellin' ya. Red velvet, or whatever the hell it is. It can be roasting. I'm wearing my longies and a flannel shirt." And then he'd added, "Besides, I've got the pillow." That'd just made her madder. "Francis, the pillow's on your belly, not your back."

She'd finally just dropped it with a "You're gonna be sorry, Francis." And she was really pissed. Something he didn't need right through this stretch. Not with all her talk about what her daughter in Jersey wanted. That was scary. He didn't know what he'd do if Murphy left him. She was about all he had in the world.

An old lady came by and stuffed a dollar bill into the slot in his chimney and he gave her one of his best "Merry Christmas's" and got a big grin and that reminded him of how much he loved being in the corps.

He especially loved the kids. The little ones. He'd never had his own. He remembered once a whole busload got off right in front of him and every one of those soapy-smelling kids had to hug Santa. Now that was a payoff! But not the big kids. Not those bastards. "Hey, Santa, straighten your beard. There's kids around." Or "Hey, Shrimp, you're losing your tumtum. Pull it back up there." Or, "Why ain't you somewhere making toys for my kid brother?"

But the little kids . . . huggin' 'em, talkin' to 'em, posin' for pictures . . . how could there be any better kind o' work? And he was good at it. He had one o' the best Ho-Ho-Ho's in the corps. Even if he was the smallest Santa they had. One hell of a voice for such a scrawny little Santa. Ask any of the others.

And it was a good job for a person with time on his hands. He liked to think of himself as one of the temporarily jobless.

Which he had been for some years now. He didn't like to think about how many. And damn good pay. Thirty-five bucks a day plus fifteen percent of anything over a hundred. At least from Thanksgiving to Christmas, he didn't have to think about Murphy carrying him. He looked across the street at the clock. Just past eleven-thirty. It was about as warm as it was going to get all day. Come late afternoon and he was going to see some real cold.

Then he caught the eye of a man stepping from a long gray limousine. This man was no loser. Homburg, overcoat with a fur collar, silk scarf, shined shoes, the whole megillah. And a very fancy-shmancy brass and alligator-skin briefcase. You didn't see too many briefcases like that one. And the man was coming straight at him with a smile.

"Merry Christmas."

"Here you are, Santa," the man said, holding out a bill between his second and third gloved fingers.

Franny eyed it quickly and grinned. It had the number 100 in its corners. "Merry Christmas, Chief. You just made me my deductible, and that makes my day."

"My pleasure, Santa. It's the least I could do. I just closed a deal that made my day. And many thousands more of these, I might add. Literally."

"Well, all the best to ya, friend, and a very merry Christmas," Franny beamed as he kept stabbing at the quarter-inch slot in his padlocked chimney. But he wasn't missing the slot. He knew exactly what he was doing. The second he saw the number in the corner of that bill, something happened in his head, and he knew he had to do what he had to do. As soon as Mr. Homburg moved on, he deftly relaxed the lengthwise crease in the bill and folded it in half the other way, burying it in a pants-pocket inside his Santa suit. And he did the whole thing with just one of his frozen hands in its too-thin glove. He glanced around to see who might have been watching. He couldn't find anybody staring at him cross-eyed, and if somebody'd noticed, they would have been.

He looked across at the clock again. Almost twelve noon. The relief man would be coming soon to give him his lunch break. He had his lunch in his canvas shoulder bag with his smokes, and he could go into Macy's, have a smoke with some coffee, and warm up a little.

Actually, he didn't feel all that cold anymore. Money in your pocket tends to keep you from feeling the cold. He had very definite plans for that bill, and what the hell, he could pay it back. He was a working man. Right? Right. The last thing he'd do was steal from his own collections. Right? Right. He'd put it back after payday.

* * * * *

December 23, early evening

As soon as the van came by and picked up his chimney to take it to headquarters and empty it, Franny started walking with deliberate steps toward the destination he had been thinking about throughout the bitter cold day. A couple of short blocks and he was there. It was also only a couple of blocks from where he lived. He could have grabbed a subway down to Houston Street to the Rehabilitation Center for a hot meal with the rest of the Santas, but Murphy said she was putting up something special for him to eat before she left for her job.

He stood in front of McAnn's Bar and stared at the door for a long time. Should he go in? Of all the doors on God's earth he was forbidden to pass through, this was the most forbidden. Not because it was McAnn's, but because it was a bar. Any bar. He'd been struggling with it all afternoon, standing there, freezing his ass off, and now came the moment of truth. Did he break the pledge? Did he fall off? He yanked the beard and mustache and stuffed them into his shoulder bag. Then he pulled the door open and stepped into the enveloping warmth.

He tried to walk as if he knew what the hell he was doing, but he was shaking like a leaf in a windstorm. How long had it been? He wasn't sure, exactly. A few months, anyway, since before signing up with the corps for another year. It *had* to be that way with them. You *had* to be clean. Most of the Santas were "recovering alcoholics." Homeless. Living at the rehab center on Houston Street. Going regularly to the meetings. He'd gotten special permission to stay at the hotel with Murphy because of his years of service. He'd moved out of the Center when Murphy'd agreed to take him in.

He looked around and decided he had to stay. He had to have a couple. Just a couple. A little something to give him a mild glow. Just a bit of a buzz, a quick pick-me-up, a little help in thinking about how he would present his case to Murphy to keep her from moving to Jersey without him.

If they found out, they'd strip him of his red suit and whiskers. And the job. And the money. But what the hell, they wouldn't find out. They only did random testing and they'd had him pee in the bottle and breathe in the gadget just two days ago. They wouldn't check him again for a while. And even if they did, he'd be clean by morning.

He hoisted himself onto a stool and fumbled in that pants pocket inside his Santa suit for what was left of the C-note. The stupid pillow was always in the way of something. He finally withdrew a fifty and a couple of singles. He laid the fifty on the bar in front of him and smoothed it out. The singles went back.

The bartender came over. "Hello there, Santa. What can I get ya?" He had a friendly smile.

Franny began to tremble. It wasn't too late. He could always have a cup of coffee and get the hell out of there before he blew the game. Yeah! Why didn't he do that? He'd promised Murphy.

"What'll it be, Santa?"

It was no use. "Bar Scotch, neat."

The bartender studied him. "You're sure, now?"

"You see my money, don'cha? Start me a tab."

After looking at the fifty, the bartender set the shot-glass in front of him and poured the drink. He poured it past the white line, right up to the rim.

Franny listened to the barely audible bubbling sound of the liquor passing through the little chrome nozzle atop the bottle. Of all the wondrous sounds the universe had to offer, that was at least among his top ten, and he hadn't heard it in a while. He picked up the glass, and as he watched the bartender start a tab, he nodded, breathed a "Merry Christmas," and took a sip, then a bit more, maybe half the shot. As the delicious heat rocketed to the farthest limits of his body and his soul, all the months of restraint and meetings and pledges and promises to Murphy went down the tube. He was back.

He looked around. Now back, it felt good to be back, and the scene was to his liking. The place wasn't empty and it wasn't crowded. He didn't like drinking in empty bars or in the middle of a noisy crowd. He thought about what he'd say to Murphy, and then reminded himself that by the time he got back to their room, she'd have left for work. So what did he have to worry about? He'd have slept it off before he'd have to face her.

He looked at the man next to him and felt a sudden pang of fear. The man was large, but lean, with dark hair and eyes, and a dark, thick mustache. A big-ass mustache. Like a walrus, or something. He and a partner, both big men in heavy mackinaws and stocking caps, were nursing drafts, and the man was studying him, looking first at his face, half-shaven under the silly Santa hat, and then at the fifty-dollar bill on the bar. Once he'd made eye contact, he could tell the man was going to make conversation.

"Hey, Santa, looks like the Christmas business is pretty good," the man said, smiling.

Franny didn't want to deal with this. The man scared him. Franny picked up his glass and drained it. Then he nodded at the bartender and pointed at his empty glass. He watched the bartender refill it.

"Cat got your tongue, Santa?" the man said, a trace of annoyance in his voice.

The bartender turned on an over-the-bar TV to a Rangers game just about to get under way.

"So let's go, Santa. Talk to me. How's business?" the man said, becoming more annoyed.

"You talkin' to me? I'm just one o' the collectors for V.O.A."

"V.O.A.? What's V.O.A.?"

"Volunteers of America. You know, those red brick chimneys they got out there with a Santa by each one?"

"So what do you do? Collect one for them and one for yourself?"

"Hey, are you crazy? Those things are padlocked. We don't ever touch that money."

"Yeah?" The man chuckled. "Looks to me like you're doin' pretty well," he said, nodding at the fifty on the bar.

"Oh, they pay me a little something, but not very much." Franny was frightened of the man. He'd picked the wrong bar on the wrong night.

"So I see," said the man. "They pay you in fifties. Right?"

His partner grabbed his sleeve to get his attention. Franny

did not see the partner wink at the man, nod at Franny, and smile a smile of total communication. "Let's watch the game for a while," his partner said.

Franny picked up his glass and took about half. Jesus, it tasted great. For sure he wasn't cold anymore. Then he thought about the present he'd gotten Murphy in Macy's. It was the kind of thing he knew she'd like to have, really like to have, but could never buy for herself. But, what the hell, that's what Christmas was about. Right? Right. Comes Christmas you don't think about practical stuff. Dream wishes. That kind o' stuff. Right? Right.

He hoped she'd like the particular one he'd picked out. He didn't know one from another. It was the only one he could ever remember hearing about. And it was expensive stuff! How could they charge so damn much for such a little-ass bottle? Nearly half his C-note. The saleslady wrapped it real nice for him.

He patted the side of his canvas bag where he had the gift-wrapped perfume, and as he did, he glanced at Mr. Mustache next to him to find the guy had taken his eyes off the hockey game to watch him pat his bag. This sent another shiver of absolute fear up his back.

"Whatcha got in your bag, there, Santa? Toys for tots?" Mr. Mustache asked with a grin.

Franny tried to think of something. A quick answer. A good solid counterpunch. But he couldn't think of anything decent, so he finally said, "Just my smokes. And the brown bag from my lunch." And with that, he unbuckled the bag, reached in, and took out what was left of his cigarettes, which turned out to be a crumpled, empty pack. He wadded it up and laid it on the bar and asked the bartender to get him another pack of Camels. "Just put it on my tab," he instructed. He liked saying that. Made him feel like somebody of means.

Then he drained his glass. When the bartender returned with his cigarettes, he pointed at the glass.

As he watched the amber liquid being poured and listened to that haunting little bubbly sound, he went back to thinking about Murphy. How was he going to keep her from skipping out on him and moving to Jersey to live with her married daughter and child? And that S.O.B. husband of hers.

"What kinda life are you gonna have in Jersey? What? You gonna be happy baby-sitting and cleaning that dinky little house o' hers?"

"It's better than living in one room in a hotel for the homeless and cleaning offices at night, Francis. And it ain't dinky. It's a nice little house."

"And what about putting up with that rotten husband o' hers? You're gonna have to watch the way he treats her, the bastard. Cardozo. What the hell kinda good Irish Catholic name is Cardozo? She'd be a lot better off coming to live with us, Chrissakes."

"He'll treat her a lot better with me around, Francis. I guess you know that . . . He really doesn't treat her all that bad. Matter of fact, he takes pretty good care of her. Gets her anything she wants."

"When he's not knockin' her around. And what about me, Murphy?"

"What can I tell you, Francis? You're just not invited."

"I mean, what about me? You're gonna be sleepin' on a couch there. You're sleepin' in a double bed now. If you know what I mean. And you know what I mean."

"That's a problem for me. I have to admit."

Yeah, that's a problem for her, all right. Some things he did pretty well, and this was one department where he delivered the goods. 'Course, when you don't do nothing for a living, at least you're rested.

"I do care about you, Francis. A lot. But I'm sick and tired of living in that smelly hotel and working nights. Maybe if we could make things a little better for ourselves. If you could get some kind of job. A regular job . . ."

Job? What kind of job? What? What did he know how to do? Other than being Santa Claus.

"Maybe if I could get on at the hospital, I could learn to do brain surgery."

"How about being an orderly?"

"What? And carry around bedpans all day?"

"As long as you washed your hands before you came home."

He wondered what she'd left him to eat back in the room. She could work miracles with that little hotplate. A scrap of cheap meat, a couple of potatoes, a carrot or two, and it was a banquet. A stick-to-your-ribs feast. Soups. Eggs. Something great out o' nothing. The hotel rules said no cooking in the rooms. That's a joke. The smells in those hallways? It was like a Chinese restaurant in the barrio.

Franny picked up his glass, brought it to his lips, breathed "Merry Christmas," and downed it. He was drinking them in wholes, now, not halves. He needed the impact of that full belt. He savored the shock waves of the drink for a moment with his eyes closed and then glanced to his side. Mr. Mustache was watching hockey with one eye and him with the other.

* * * * *

December 23, mid-evening

Franny had held off for what seemed to him to be an eternity, at least an hour, well, maybe a half-hour, anyway, because he couldn't figure out where he was going to put any more. But it was definitely time for another, so he motioned to the bartender.

"Don't you think you've had about enough there, Santa?"

"Me? I'm just fine. Getcha bottle there and fill me up. Still got a lotta stuff to think about. Need all the help I can get." *Still got a lotta stuff . . .* Even Franny could hear that he couldn't get it out. One long slur.

"I think you've had about enough, old-timer."

"One more."

"Well, if you're gonna take any more, you're gonna have to add to your deposit there on the bar. You've about drunk that all up."

"Then, do it. I got plenty money. Plenty money."

"On second thought, forget it. I'm not serving you anymore. Want me to go out there and get you a taxi?"

"Taxi? What the hell do I need with a taxi? I just live around the corner . . . right around here, somewhere."

The bartender picked up the tab and the fifty, rang it up, put two dollars and change on the bar. "You take it easy, old-timer."

"Old-timer, shit!" he smiled. "But, Merry Christmas to you anyway, pal." He tapped his knuckles on the bar next to the money and slid off the stool. He moved uncertainly toward the door, pushed it open, and made his way through it. He did not see Mr. Mustache and his friend pick up their change off the bar.

Once outside he found the cold bracing and pleasant, something he badly needed. The bartender was right. He didn't need any more. No place to put it. The old hollow leg was full. He stood, weaving just slightly, trying to get his bearings, and then trudged toward Sixth Avenue. He tripped and fell, skidding on his palms on the frozen sidewalk and, with considerable effort, struggled back to his feet, rubbing his hands on his Santa suit. To the corner, turn right, a

81

couple blocks and then cross Sixth. Or cross Sixth and then a couple blocks.

When he got to the corner, the light was just turning green and traffic was sparse, so he crossed and then turned right. Greeley Square. Just two blocks and home to the hotel. He moved along in that direction, Merry Christmas-ing anybody he passed.

He came to an alley between buildings and was suddenly lifted off the ground by his upper arms and carried, running, into the alley. He twisted his head around and there it was. The black mustache! "Hey! Hey! What the hell is this? Put me down! Put me down!"

"We're gonna put you down," the mustache said.

The other one had a silly giggle. "Hih, hih, hih, yeah, Santa, we just thought we'd let you put a little something under our tree, first. Where've you got all those fifties, Santa?"

"I ain't got no money, guys. I swear. Two bucks."

Mr. Mustache slapped Franny ferociously. "Don't fuck with us, Santa. Where's your money?"

"I ain't got no money! I'm tellin' ya."

Another brutal slap that turned Franny's head sideways. Then a fist to the body that landed just above the pillow, knocking all the wind out of him, blacking him out momentarily.

"Where's your money, Santa?"

He hardly heard the question.

"Where's your money, Santa, or do we have to break you in half?"

Franny struggled to get the words out. There was no air in his body for speaking. "No matter what you bastards do," he breathed, "I got no money. No money, you bastards."

A crushing fist to the temple and Franny dropped like wet laundry.

"Jeez, you really gave him a shot," said the other one.

"I got sick and tired of his mouth. Let's find his money and get the hell out of here." He jerked Franny's limp body out flat, opened the big white belt, and ripped open his Santa coat, looking for pockets. The Santa suit had none, inside or out. He looked in the pocket of the plaid flannel shirt. Nothing. He yanked the pillow out of the way, rummaged through Franny's pants pockets, and found the two singles and change, a rusty old pocket knife, a wilted, half-used book of matches, and a ragged wallet that was empty. Annoyed, he tossed Franny's body around to see if there was someplace else he hadn't checked.

"What about his bag, there?" the other one said.

The flap was unbuckled on the bag. He didn't find anything of value. The Santa's beard and mustache with elastic straps, a folded brown bag, the Camels, and a *Daily News* Franny had picked up. "Nothing."

"Guess he wasn't lyin'," the other one said.

"Let's get outa here."

"Poor sumbitch gonna freeze left here like that."

"Guess that's *his* problem, isn't it?"

They walked back to Sixth Avenue, leaving Franny out of sight from the street, only a few yards in, but obscured by a pile of empty drums.

★ ★ ★ ★ ★

December 23, late evening

Nicky Varrone was walking up Sixth Avenue, heading back toward Forty-fifth Street where he lived and thinking about how cold it was, when he saw the chauffeured gray Cadillac move west across Sixth and then stop in front of an office building. He'd been hanging out at this little restaurant on Twenty-sixth where there was a young beauty working as a waitress, and she really rang his bell. Unfortunately, she wasn't having any part of him, and he was a little down. His problem was, he decided, that he didn't have anything. If he had real bread, he'd be Mr. Big with the ladies.

Nicky watched from a distance as the chauffeur opened the back door and allowed his passenger, some hotshot-looking type with a fancy hat, to get out and walk to the door of the building. Now, *there* was money. Why, hell, even the man's chauffeur probably drew three times what he was making. But what the hell were they doing showing up there at near midnight?

A night watchman opened the door and the man entered, signaling to his driver to come with him, and as the door closed behind them, Nicky decided he had to see the car up close, so he walked over and began admiring it, inside and out. Some piece of machinery. One of those thirty-footers. Hell, you could almost set up a table and four chairs in the back of that car.

A briefcase lay on the backseat, light glinting off the hardware. Had to be brass, of course, but Christ, it looked like gold. Rich-looking case. Was it alligator? Looked like the kind of case that could be filled with money. Neatly banded bundles of high denomination bills. What if it was?

Nicky looked into the lobby of the building. The night watchman had apparently gone somewhere with the man and his driver. Nobody in sight. The street was quiet . . . Then his heart suddenly began to pound. What the hell, he'd done worse. He was going for that briefcase.

The case was on the side toward the street. He looked in the lobby again and then walked around to the street side of the car. As soon as he touched the door handle, a voice came from the car: "Please do not come near the automobile." He jumped back and then smiled. One of those high-tech alarm systems. Nevertheless, he was still going for the case.

He peered into the lobby once more and then up and down the street. Quiet. The car door had been locked when he'd touched it; he'd have to find something to take out the window. He looked around and found just the ticket. A few yards away the curb was busted and he could lift out a section of it. A big solid chunk of concrete. After glancing around, he picked it up. Heavier than he expected, but he could handle it.

He checked the lobby again, and as soon as he put the concrete through the window, the car's alarm began screaming. He reached in, grabbed the briefcase, and was off. He didn't look back. He sprinted to Sixth and headed north, running with the briefcase under his arm. There were few people walking and they paid him little attention. This was New York. Still, he knew he looked conspicuous, so he slowed to a walk and tried to look natural. But he found that he couldn't, so he started running again. He still didn't dare look back. After running another block, he dashed into the middle of Sixth Avenue, dodging the light traffic, and crossed, continuing north on the opposite side.

He felt that he had to get out of sight, so when he came to an alley between two buildings, he plunged into it, deciding to take his chances. He didn't want to surprise anybody. Only crazy people went into alleys in New York, day or night, but this was special circumstances. He hadn't gone very far before he came to something that reminded him once again that, hell, nothing surprises you in New York. Nothing! Here was a man in a Santa suit, half-undressed, lying there asleep. Asleep? Sleeping one off? In a Santa suit? At that temperature?

He kept plunging ahead, figuring if he could make it Fifth, he was home free. Then he stopped, out of breath, and turned around. He just stood there, looking toward Sixth,

catch his breath and to see if he was in fact being chased. He waited motionless for several minutes. Dead still. He squatted on his haunches and waited another minute or so. Poor Santa back there would be dead before morning. A piece of ice. He stood up and started walking slowly back toward Sixth.

When he reached the Santa, he said, "Man, what the hell're you doing here? You're gonna freeze."

The Santa, in a state of near unconsciousness, managed, "Think I already have."

"How'd you get here?"

"Did I get hit by a truck? No, coupla guys . . . musta been longshoremen, I think. Big bastards . . ."

Nicky spotted some weather-beaten corrugated boxes. He put the briefcase in one of them, squashed the box flat, and stuffed it behind the empty drums. Then he bent down and easily picked up the scrawny little Santa.

"Put me down, dammit! Leave me. I was just beginning to feel good." Then he went limp and quiet.

Nicky walked out of the alley carrying the little Santa, who now seemed totally unconscious. A canvas bag dangled from the Santa's shoulder. Nicky found a grate with warm air rising from it. He placed the Santa down on the grate. He yanked the pillow dangling from the belt around his waist and put it under his head, noting the bruises and swelling. He pulled the Santa's clothes together as best he could. Then he went to a refuse basket and lifted out a thick *New York Times*. He blanketed the Santa with it, tucking the edges under.

When the wind began to loosen and blow away the sheets of newspaper, Nicky went back into the alley and picked out another corrugated box. Returning to the street, he split open one side, and wrapped it around the newspapers over Santa, tucking it under. The little Santa's feet protruded from the

end of the box. "Best I can do for you, Santa," Nicky said. "The cops'll come pick you up. They won't leave you here long."

No answer.

Nicky headed back to the alley.

★ ★ ★ ★ ★

December 23, around 11:30 P.M.

"Nine-one-one. Where is the emergency?"

"I want to report a missing person. My, uh, husband."

"Your name, please?"

"Bridget Murphy."

"Where are you located?"

"The Martinique Hotel."

"At Sixth and Thirty-second. Right?"

"You know the lovely place?"

"Deed I do, Mrs. Murphy. Mrs. Murphy, a missing persons call is not considered an emergency call to be responded to by the nine-one-one switchboard. You need to contact your local precinct. Call Midtown South at 555-9811. They'll take the call."

"Can you connect me? I don't have a quarter."

"Just dial Operator and give her the number. She'll connect you. Tell her I told you to call. That number again is 555-9811."

"If she doesn't connect me, I'm calling you back."

"She'll handle it, Mrs. Murphy."

Murphy dialed Operator and asked for the number, saying it was an emergency.

"Midtown South. How may I help you?"

"I need help. My husband is missing."

"Hold on. I'll connect you with the detectives' squad room."

"Detective McGonigal here. How may I help you?"

"D'ya say McGonigal? Good."

"Good? Why good? Do we know each other?"

"My name's Murphy. That clear it up?"

"Well, sure an' it does, Mrs. Murphy. How c'n I help ye?"

"McGonigal, my husband is missing."

"For how long has he been missing, Mrs. Murphy?"

"He should have been home by seven o'clock."

"Mrs. Murphy, we don't normally consider a person missing until he's been missing twenty-four hours. Now there are three exceptions, but they wouldn't seem to apply here."

"What are the three exceptions?"

"A small child, a mentally incompetent, or an EDP. That's an emotionally disturbed person. Any of those apply?"

"He's never late home, McGonigal. Something's got to have happened to him. I know."

"Have you been home all evening? Could he have tried to call?"

"We don't have a phone, but if he'd tried to call, they'd have called me from security. Been home all evening." She felt safe in this lie because the pot on the hotplate was still untouched and there were no dishes in the bathroom sink. "McGonigal, you gotta help me. Don't give me no song and dance."

"We'll put it out and see what it brings in, Mrs. Murphy. Okay? Where are you calling from?"

"The Martinique Hotel. You know it?"

"We know every hotel in this precinct, Mrs. Murphy. Be assured. And especially the Martinique. We've been in the Martinique, my partner and I, more than a few times over the years. Tell me, the kids still play stickball in the hallways?"

"That should be the worst that goes on in those hallways."

"I'm aware. Mrs. Murphy, what's your husband's name?"

"Francis Gilhooley."

"I thought you said he was your husband."

"Don't start with me."

"Can you give me a description of him?"

"About five-foot-four, maybe a hundred 'n twenty, twenty-five, mixed brown and gray hair, and beautiful blue eyes."

"How old?"

"I'd say between forty-five and fifty, fifty-five."

"Don't you know?"

"He says forty-five. He said that last year, too."

"When did you last see him, Mrs. Murphy?"

"When he left for work this morning."

"And where does he work?"

"In front of Macy's."

"Doing what?"

"Collecting money. He's a Santa Claus. How about that?"

"Oh! So we're looking for Old St. Nick. And a wee one at that. White belt or black belt, Mrs. Murphy? V.O.A. or Salvation Army? See? I know a couple things, too."

"White belt. They pick up his chimney at around six-thirty and he always comes straight home. I'm sure something's happened to him."

"Mrs. Murphy, what are the chances he just decided to go with a couple o' the other Santas and down a few and talk it over?"

"They're absolutely forbidden to touch a drop. They even test the men. One trace and they're outa there. Through. You should know that, McGonigal. And the same thing applies here with me, I might add. He goes off the wagon, he's out the door."

"Now that you mention it, I did know that about the Santas and the juice. We'll get on it, Mrs. Murphy. We'll see if we can't find that blue-eyed little Santa of yours. But listen.

If he shows up, you get back to us and let us know. Okay? I'll be here all night. Okay?"

"Something's happened to him, McGonigal. I'm positive. And I'm counting on you. Y'hear me?"

★ ★ ★ ★ ★

December 24, 12:45 A.M.

The Sector C (South Charlie) NYPD prowl car moved slowly north on the Avenue of the Americas (Sixth Avenue), approaching 34th Street and Herald Square. Officer Al Aliem Shabeez sat on the passenger side, his head back on the seat, his hat pulled down as if to shade his eyes, when actually the hat was simply a bit too small. His partner, Officer Vinnie D'Amico, looked left, watching the quiet traffic coming down Broadway as he drove. They were enjoying the lull, knowing full well that it could get to be a very busy night before this graveyard tour was over.

Suddenly Shabeez did a double-take and sat bolt upright as he looked back at something to his right they'd just passed. "I could swear I just saw a pair of feet."

"A pair of feet?"

"Sticking out of a box back there on the sidewalk."

"Somebody threw away a perfectly good pair of feet? Gimme a break, Shabeez. Next thing you'll be telling me, Muslims have perfect night vision."

"Back there, just before Thirty-fourth. Vinnie, humor me. Okay? Go around the block and let's take another look. If I'm right, he's gonna freeze."

When they came back around, it was clear there was a body in the box on the subway grate, and the occasional pedestrians were walking quite wide to avoid it.

"Looks like Santa fell off his sled," D'Amico said as they peeled back the box.

"I think he had himself a private party and decided he'd

sleep it off here," Shabeez said. "Let's get him up and moving before he freezes stiffer than he already is."

They attempted to get the little Santa to his feet and quickly surmised that they were wasting their time. This one was more than just preserved in alcohol, judging from the battered face. "We're gonna need a bus for this one," D'Amico said. He walked quickly over to the car and the radio. "South Charlie to Central K."

"South Charlie proceed."

"Central, we need a bus. Unconscious male on the street. Broadway, a hundred feet south of Thirty-fourth, east side of the street . . ."

★ ★ ★ ★ ★

December 24, 1:10 A.M.

"South Charlie to Central K."

"South Charlie proceed."

"One unconscious male en route to Bellevue. Dressed in a Santa suit. No identification possible at the scene."

"Ten-four. Resume patrol, Charlie."

Inside the ambulance, E.M.T. Wong Lee determined that the unidentified male in the Santa suit had good blood pressure and clear respiratory function.

★ ★ ★ ★ ★

December 24, 1:20 A.M.

Nicky Varrone sat on the side of his bed, looking at the briefcase. He was glad his mother had been long asleep when he got home so he didn't have to explain the case. Fancy leather. Not alligator, though. Something else. He looked at the business card in the matching leather card-holder attached to the handle. Mr. Ramon Henriquez, President. Peerless International Textiles Importers. West Twenty-ninth Street. Big bucks in that case?

How to get it open. He didn't want to bust it apart. No use

91

messing it up. Nice case like that? No keyholes to try and pick with a bent hairpin, either. Each catch had a three-digit combination lock. He tried several random combinations, which of course didn't work, and finally concluded that what he had was time. The thing to do was start at 001 and go up one number at a time until it opened.

It was boring but he stuck with it, annoyed that the son of a bitch couldn't have used a lower number. The lock opened when he got to 975. He set the other lock on 975, but it didn't open, either. Smooth operator, Senor Henriquez. Back to 001 and up. The second catch opened at 579. With a deep breath and a tremor of intense anticipation he lifted the top of the case . . .

Papers! Letters. To Henriquez, from Henriquez. Folders of papers. Contracts . . . Shit! He thumbed through the papers. Boring stuff. A small cloth label sewn into the case caught his eye. Genuine Ostrich Leather. Too bad for the poor fucking ostrich. He slammed the case shut and tossed it across the floor.

He threw himself back on his bed. Well, at least he had himself a nice briefcase. Not that he knew what he'd ever do with it. Maybe when *he* got to be president of something, like Henriquez. From where he was in Shipping, he had a ways to go.

He thought about the little Santa. What if he'd saved the man's life? If it turned out that way, what the hell, he would hardly say the evening had been a total waste. He'd have to check the *Daily News* for the next couple of days. Maybe it'd get a mention. Then again, maybe it wouldn't. This was New York.

★ ★ ★ ★ ★

December 24, 1:30 A.M.

McGonigal looked through the directory and then dialed.

"Police Headquarters."

"This is Detective Harry McGonigal calling from Midtown South. I dialed Missing Persons. None of them in right now, I guess."

"Not for a while. Try first thing tomorrow."

"I'll get whoever's catching here tomorrow to give 'em a call first thing in the morning. Thanks."

"Don't mention it."

★ ★ ★ ★ ★

December 24, 2:20 A.M.

The E.R. at Bellevue was a zoo when the ambulance carrying the little Santa arrived. The doctor in charge, on being advised that the little Santa had good blood pressure and normal respiratory function, along with a truly remarkable level of alcohol concentration in his blood (determined from a single whiff of his breath), advised his staff to treat his hands and feet for acute exposure and place him in the recovery room. "We'll admit him when he wakes up and can explain himself." The doctor then turned to consider the next patient, who was bleeding from a stab wound in the lower abdomen, in fact, very low in the abdomen.

★ ★ ★ ★ ★

December 24, 8:30 A.M.

Home from her night's work, Bridget entered the phone booth in the lobby of the Martinique, dialed Operator, and was set to raise some hell if she got an argument when she requested Midtown South. The call was put through and she asked for McGonigal.

"He went home. He's on nights."

She patiently explained who she was and why she was calling.

"There's a note here, Mrs. Murphy, now that you mention it. McGonigal left a note. We'll call Headquarters right now

93

and check with Missing Persons and see if we can't get them right on it. We'll get back to you as soon as we know something. Okay?"

Murphy went up to their room and fell onto their bed.

★ ★ ★ ★ ★

December 24, early afternoon

Nicky waited until his mother had left for the grocery before dialing the number.

"Peerless International."

"I'd like to speak to Mister—I guess it's—is it Henriquez?"

"That's close enough. He's left for the day. As has most everyone else. Christmas Eve. Half-day."

"We had that today, too. What are you still doing there?"

"Somebody's got to sit here on the stupid phone till five."

"Too bad. You sound pretty cute. You married?"

"Yes, I am."

"Too bad, again. Listen. I'm calling because I found something that belongs to Mr. Henriquez."

"Is it his briefcase?"

"Yes, it is."

"Please hold."

"Do you have Mr. Henriquez's briefcase?" Another voice. It sounded like an older woman, like a tough old broad.

"Yes, I do. I found it."

"Is it still intact?"

"It's still locked, if that's what you mean. I'm hoping there should be some kind of reward for it. It's a nice-looking case."

"I'm sure he'd be interested in getting it back. Give me your name and phone number. I'll see if I can reach him and get back to you momentarily."

94

The phone rang in what seemed to Nicky like a minute or less.

"Mr. Varrone?"

"Yes, ma'am."

"Can you take the briefcase to Mr. Henriquez at his home? It's on Fifth Avenue. Central Park East? Ten-eleven."

"Sure. Any apartment number, or anything like that?"

"Just ask the doorman. Ten-eleven Fifth Avenue. When do you expect to be there?"

"About an hour or so okay?"

"He'll be expecting you."

★ ★ ★ ★ ★

December 24, around three P.M.

Nicky knew he was uptown when he entered the lobby. This was the real thing. Polished brass everywhere, *clean* Oriental rugs, marble floors, classy-looking furniture. The doorman's uniform looked brand-new.

The doorman made a brief phone call and then led him to an elevator, pressing the button for the eighth floor. When the elevator door opened again, Nicky was not in a corridor but in the foyer of the biggest, fanciest layout he'd ever seen. Large picture windows overlooked Central Park. He gazed around tentatively, the briefcase in his hand.

"Come in, young man," the man on the sofa said to him. He was heavily built but not fat, a large head and full face, lots of streaked gray hair swept straight back. Another man in the room, apparently the driver, walked toward the door as if to make sure Nicky couldn't cut and run.

"Mr. Henriquez?"

"Yes. Come in. You have my briefcase, I see. Good. Good. Let me have it."

Nicky walked over and handed it to him.

Henriquez quickly set the locks and opened the case. He

looked relieved as he riffled through the contents and everything was apparently there. "Where did you find this, young man?"

"I happened to spot it an alley. Sort of over behind a bunch of old steel drums. Couldn't figure out what it was doing there. Brought it out, saw your card on it, and decided I should give you a call. Figured you might give me a reward."

"An alley where?"

"Over off Sixth Avenue."

"What were you doing in an alley in the middle of the night? Only a stupid fool would go in an alley in this city in the middle of the night."

"Not last night. This morning. I sometimes cut through there on the way to work." Nicky was pleased with himself for coming up with that one. A question and answer he hadn't even thought about on the trip over.

"Well," Henriquez said, and his expression suddenly hardened, "thank you for returning it. And now, get the hell out of here."

"Huh?"

"I said, get out! Go! Before I call the police!"

"But, sir, don't you think I should get some kind of reward for bringing it back?"

"Just be glad you're not going to jail. Your story doesn't hold, young man. You must have taken the briefcase. If someone else had taken it, they wouldn't have left it intact. They'd have broken it open to see what was inside before discarding it. You obviously broke into the car to get it, very patiently opened it, and when you found nothing of value, at least not to you, you decided to go for the reward. Fortunately. Because the contents happen to be very valuable to me."

"Wait, sir," Nicky protested. "Really. I cut through that

alley this morning, taking a shortcut to work, because I was running a little late. I wouldn't'a even seen the briefcase except it was stuck behind some drums right where I found this little guy in a Santa suit about to freeze to death. I brought him out and I think I may have saved his life. This is no shit."

Henriquez chuckled. "Now I'm sure I've heard it all. The children of the world will be eternally grateful that you've saved the life of Santa Claus. You and I have both had encounters with him during the last day or two, and I think mine made out a little better than yours. Thank you again for returning the briefcase, and now get out of here. Roger, show him to the elevator."

★ ★ ★ ★ ★

December 24, 3:30 P.M.

It took Marvella Robinson three calls to finally get the number of Security at the Martinique Hotel. She called and it rang a dozen or so times before somebody finally picked it up.

"Yeah?"

"Is this the Martinique Hotel?"

"Yeah."

"Who's this?"

"Security."

"I'm calling from Bellevue Hospital. I need to reach Bridget Murphy in room 1213."

"I'll look around here'n see'f I can find somebody to send up there. I can't leave the desk here."

"This is important."

"May be. But so's this. Somebody's got to be here'n this office. The other man didn't come in today."

"Who's this I'm talking to?"

"There's 'nother man comin' on at four. Maybe when he shows up, we can get a message up there."

"Don't you have some kind of intercom?"

"We did when it was workin'."

"Jesus H. Christ! What'd you say your name was?"

"My name's Abraham La Fontant, not that that'll do anything for ya."

"Well, Abraham, do you think you can get a message to Bridget Murphy as soon as possible? Room 1213? Tell her to get in touch with me right away. Right away, now. My name's Marvella Robinson, and I'm at Bellevue Hospital, the number's 555-4141, and I'm at extension 2114. D'you get all of that?"

"Call Miz Robinson at Bellevue. Say, what time d'you get off from there?"

"In time to go home to my husband. Jesus! Abraham, will you please get Bridget Murphy back to me? Her man's here in one of our wards. Now will you please do what I'm telling you?"

"Call Miz Robinson at Bellevue. Okay?"

"Marvella Robinson. Marvella Robinson. Don't let me down, now, Abraham. You hear me?"

"I'll get on it as soon as I can." As he hung up, his replacement, Slick O'Reilly, a little silver-haired man, came walking in, and almost before they'd so much as exchanged greetings, a skinny twelve-year-old with some lady's expensive-looking pocketbook clutched in his hand came running into the lobby, chased by a uniformed cop. LaFontant and O'Reilly watched the excitement and then LaFontant left. His shift was up.

★ ★ ★ ★ ★

Christmas Eve, a few minutes before midnight

"Midtown South. How may I help you?"

"Detective McGonigal, please. Is he there?"

"Hold on."

"Detective McGonigal here. How may I help you?"

"McGonigal?"

"That you, Bridget Murphy? I was just thinking about you."

"Thinking about me's one thing. Doing something's another. Did you do anything?"

"Absolutely. Missing Persons got it and is working on it."

"When're they gonna have something?"

"When they find him. They'll find him, Mrs. Murphy. I doubt he's left the city."

"McGonigal, I'm worried sick something's happened to 'im."

"I wish I could tell you more. Sit tight and hope for the best. What else can I tell ya?"

"It's Christmas, McGonigal. And I've gotta go clean offices all night, worrying about him."

"No fun working all night Christmas Eve, is it? I don't like it either, I can assure ya. I got a wife and family."

"At least none of 'em's missing. You better have some good news for me tomorrow."

"I hope we will. What else can I tell ya?"

★ ★ ★ ★ ★

Christmas morning, around five A.M.

"Detective McGonigal, here. How may I help you?"

"McGonigal, this is Sergeant Gotti over at the Borough office. I need some help. You got somebody who can cover the phone there for you for a little while?"

"I'm catching here alone right now, sir, but I can probably get one o' the guys downstairs to come up for a while. Whaddaya need, sir?"

"Sorry to have to bother you, but I can't seem to find a warm body on the East Side at the moment to handle this. Run over to Bellevue and get a statement from a shooting victim. He's in the E.R. right now, but he should be able to talk by the time you get there. The victim's name is Walker. Cass Walker."

"I'll take care of it, sir."

★ ★ ★ ★ ★

Christmas morning, around seven A.M.

McGonigal walked out of Bellevue and was about to get into his car when something caught his eye. He went over to it to take a closer look. In one of a long line of clear plastic garbage bags waiting for pickup was a red Santa's hat. McGonigal went back into the hospital.

★ ★ ★ ★ ★

Christmas day, around noon

Bridget Murphy entered the ward at Bellevue and saw Francis in the far corner of the room. He was propped up in bed, his hands and feet in loose bandages. As she started toward him, she noticed that the other beds were also occupied, all with older men, all surrounded by family. Too bad. She'd have to keep her voice down.

When she reached his bedside, she saw the side of his face and wanted to cry. But there was no way she could allow herself to do that. Not with the things she had to say. He was looking at her with his crazy, disarming smile. It wasn't going to be easy.

"Hello, love," he said.

"You all right?"

" 'Course I'm all right. Whaddaya think? Mild concussion, one broken rib, a little frostbite. Day or two, I'll be outa here'n as hot after my sweetie as ever."

"Francis, I'm afraid we're going to have to have a talk."

"Not now, sweetie. It's Christmas."

"Now!" She glanced around at the other people in the ward. She didn't want to attract attention. "What happened to you?"

His wacky smile. "Tellya the truth, I'm not sure I hardly remember. It's all kinda hazy."

"I'll tell you what happened. You tested positive is what happened. Very, very positive."

The smile. "Good thing, too. That stuff's like antifreeze. Otherwise, I might not be here now."

"If you'd come straight home like you were going to do and not gotten yourself stupid drunk, you wouldn't be here, either. Where'd you get the money, anyway?"

"I'm gonna pay it back."

"I figured. Francis, I came here to tell you something. I've decided to move to Jersey and live with Kathy."

"You can't do that, sweetie. What kinda life are you gonna have living with them? You know you'll hate it. And what about me, who loves ya?"

"You're on your own, Francis. I'm sorry. But I'm not tying myself to no Irish suicide. I've had it. I warned you last time. Remember?"

"Murphy, this time's different."

"Different? Why is this time any different? Would you like to tell me why it's different?"

"Look at me. Look what I been through this time. Don't you think it's different? I was nearly all finished out there. No more, Murphy. Not after this."

"It's no use, Francis. I've made up my mind."

"Wait. Got a Christmas present for ya. It's in my bag, hanging here on the bed. You'll have to dig it out." He held up his bandaged hands.

"You got me a present?"

"Wait'll you see. Something I think you'll really like. I wanted to get you something you would want but wouldn't ever buy for yourself. That's what Christmas is for. Right?"

She went into the bag and felt around, searching among the whiskers and newspaper. She finally came up with the tiny package. "This is for me?" She had to smile just a little.

The package was beautifully wrapped.

"Open it."

She opened it and found a tiny bottle of real perfume. Not cologne or toilet water or any of those. Real perfume. "Francis!"

"Hope it's one you like. You know me. I don't know shit about stuff like that."

"Francis, it's lovely. I'm sure I'll like it." How could she not smile? "Thank you." She leaned over to kiss the good side of his forehead, and when she did, he quickly tilted his head back and caught her smack on the mouth.

"So whaddaya say, Murphy? One more chance? C'mon. You gotta. Never again this business. Okay? I'll get a job. Somewhere. They'd probably take me on at McDonald's. They always got signs in the window. I'll work nights. When you work . . . Whaddaya say, Murphy?"

"You rotten little bastard." But she could feel the water forming in her eyes. And she could feel her lips bending into a smile. And she could see his face lighting up. "I'll give it a little more thought, Francis. Okay?" What the hell . . .

At the time I wrote this story, bank computers that operated by riffling punched cards were in use. I'm sure that today, punched card computers must be like slide rules and buggy whips. When I first got the idea for the story and began doing a little research, a couple of the bank computer whizzes I approached wouldn't talk with me, but finally, one of them decided I didn't look like a bank robber, and doubted my story would lead to a crime spree.

Those Who Appreciate Money Hate to Touch the Principal

He fingered the white card thoughtfully for a moment, studying the rows of repeated digits which ran its full length. He touched the corner of the card to his lip and then nodded. He'd hesitated long enough. The advance preparations had been made for quite a while. Time to put the plan into motion. Fascinating toys, computers. At least to those who knew how to use them. Really use them.

He glanced around the computer room at the technicians doing their thing. They weren't paying any attention to his contemplative posture in the chair in front of the keypunch. Why should they? It was a most familiar sight to see him there. He ran the operation. He was their mentor, their trainer, their confidant and father confessor, the renowned wunderkind and genius who taught them everything they knew about the role of the computer in modern banking, the mastermind who had toiled all those brutal hours, often far into the night, and had established and de-bugged all of the super-streamlined procedures that made the bank the envy of all the others in the city.

Even if they were to wander near and stand behind him and watch over his shoulder, they would not grasp what he was about to do. Because they knew their specific jobs and not too much more. They knew what he had taught them and what he felt they had a need to know in order to carry out their work with crisp efficiency. But they would not understand the complex, yet ever so simple little operation he was going to perform. And even if they thought they did comprehend it, they wouldn't believe it. Not after all his lectures about the legal aspects of the work in which they were involved. Absolute adherence to the law. He had trained them well.

His hand trembled slightly as he inserted the first card into the keypunch. He hoped no one noticed because he wasn't supposed to ever show even the slightest manifestation of having nerves. He was Rich Hamzer, the whiz kid. His veins were copper wire and his head was transistorized. He glanced around once again; rubbed his hands together a few times, took a deep breath and then began to hit the keys.

He completed the eight new cards and touched the corner of each with a red felt tip pen. His pulse accelerated. He opened the appropriate drawer and began inserting the eight cards in their proper locations, lifting out those he was temporarily replacing. Then he lifted a few other cards at random and dotted them with felt tip pens of other colors, green, blue, brown, before slipping them back down into place. The red dots would then be less obvious.

With all of the new cards in their proper places, he riffled the deck, watching the marked cards disappear like a drink poured over the side, into the sea. Then he closed the drawer. Done. The cards were a part of the vast system and the system would make no judgment but would do as it was told.

Rich picked up a phone and dialed Linderkorn's number.

★ ★ ★ ★ ★

Harry Linderkorn's ruddy face was ruddier than usual against the meticulously groomed silver temples and the custom shirt and he sat very erect. Hamzer slouched in the "client's" chair in front of the huge desk.

"Did you say resign? Rich, I won't hear of it."

"Harry, you already have."

"But why?"

"I'm sick of working."

"Take some time off. How about a month? Two months?"

"How about a year, Harry, or two years? Why not five?"

"You serious? You won't like it, Rich. You'll hate it."

"Let me try it and decide for myself."

"All right, Rich. How about a raise? A fat one."

"Harry, you haven't been listening. A little money won't change my life-style. This is Monday morning. Two weeks notice means a week from Friday. That's it."

Linderkorn paused and his eyes reflected a change in strategy. "Rich, this place is a miracle of modern banking efficiency because of what you've done here. It's a living tribute to your achievements. We're the standard by which others are measured. Don't walk away from it and let it run the risk of even the slightest loss of its vitality and perfection. We can redefine your job so that you can enjoy a change in life-style without leaving."

"Harry, I've checked and re-checked the program and it's bug-free. Get one of your head-hunters to find you a bright young D.P. manager-type and I'm sure he can keep things running without problems."

"Rich. how about unlimited privileges at the Midtown Tennis Club? Play every day. As long as you wish. I'll even line you up a parade of worthy opponents. And just come around the bank once in a while to see how things are going."

"A week from Friday, Harry."

★ ★ ★ ★ ★

Rich stood in the main banking room and watched the lines of depositors inch forward, reach the tellers' windows, complete their transactions and walk away. Sixteen tellers were working. And there were over two hundred branch banks! With three to ten tellers in each. The effects of the new punched cards, like pentothal into a vein, had flowed silently into the system, been absorbed and produced the desired changes. Nine more business days to go, with extended banking hours on Thursdays and Fridays.

What would be the total for the two-week period? The total, based on all interest accrued on all funds deposited during that period. What would be the total amount of remainder involved when all interest computations were rounded off to even pennies? Not evened-off dollars; just evened-off pennies. And what sweet, young teller would notice that all the computations just happened to come out to exact cents and not fractions? And even if someone noticed, would it make enough of an impression to prompt that someone to question? And if that someone did question, could the cause of the unusual coincidence be uncovered, particularly within the period up to a week from Saturday when his plane lifted off the ground? A long series of if's. The likelihood of an accusing finger ever being pointed at him seemed remote. He had every reason to feel secure. Even if the coincidence was noted, he himself would be the one called in to investigate the quirk.

At the end of the two weeks of business he would simply locate and remove the red-dotted, outlaw cards and put back the originals. Then things would return to normal. The surface of the bank's monetary waters would remain undisturbed. The tiny tremor of illicit activity that had occurred deep beneath its surface would quietly subside and life would go on as if no renegades had ever made their subtle raid on First National's remote vaults.

The outlaw cards would program the system to take all those rounded-off interest payments, those millions of fractions of pennies, and funnel them quietly into his own account. The system was omnipotent. But it was docile. It had no power to challenge a command.

And weeks before, Rich had set up an arrangement whereby all monies in his account in excess of what he had set as a suitable operating balance would be automatically transferred to an account in a Swiss bank. Two weeks of business. And two weeks was enough. Hundreds of thousands of dollars' worth of pieces of pennies. Possibly a million if it proved to be a good two weeks for banking. And no one would have to suffer. Who would miss it? And he would have bought his escape from his squirrel-cage existence to the idyllic life of the richest tennis and ski bum on the Continent. He mused for a moment about his return to the slopes he'd discovered on his last vacation in the Alps. Exhilarating runs that challenged even his considerable skills with their vastness and unexpected hazards and their unspoiled desolation. So different from the mountains in southern Vermont which always seemed reduced to slush by the impenetrable crowds.

And he could live off just the interest the money would earn in Switzerland, hardly touching the principal at all. A most pleasing thought. Because those who appreciate money hate to touch the principal.

Rich fidgeted for the rest of the day. He knew there was no need for concern but simply knowing wasn't enough to keep him tranquil. He called a friend and arranged a tennis match at his indoor club for that night. A little strenuous exercise would take his mind off things and help him get into some good sleep, which he began to feel might become an elusive commodity.

They played hard and he enjoyed it. He was a tiger, really on his game, and for the first time ever, he completely overpowered his friend. After more than two hours of enervating play and a quick shower, he emerged from the club into the chill night air and promptly sneezed two, three, four times. It had been stupid to rush out into the cold. He should have killed a little time before leaving, hung around, had a drink, taken time to fully cool down and unwind. He felt a drop of rain, then a drop or two more and then rain. He looked around for a cab but there are never cabs when it begins to rain. He sneezed again and wiped at his nose with his sleeve. He began hustling toward the subway, still watching for an empty cab. By the time he reached the subway, his nose was dripping steadily.

A double scotch and two aspirin had little effect on anything and he lay awake most of the night, sopping at his nose with tissues and throwing the little balls of shreddy wet paper at a waste basket in the corner of the room. He crawled out of bed the next morning with a whopper of a cold. But with only nine days of his professional career left, he was determined to show up at work.

He made it through the day but his cold grew steadily worse. By mid-afternoon his head was clogged solid. Excessive amounts of various antihistamines made him groggy but failed to penetrate the total blockage behind his nose and eyes. He went home early, dosed himself up with a little of everyone's recommended guaranteed remedy and went to bed, feeling certain that only long hours of sleep would help. But somehow, a dancing line of computer cards with tiny red dots in their corners always seemed to stay between him and unconsciousness. When he dragged himself out of bed again the next morning, his head throbbed. But he was once again determined to make it to the bank.

By mid-afternoon his entire body ached and everyone remarked that he looked terrible and shouldn't have come in. When Harry Linderkorn snapped that he should get the hell out of there before he infected everybody in the place, he finally left the bank and returned to his flat. Desperate for sleep, he resorted to sleeping pills, something he had somehow gone without the two previous nights, and took three instead of the prescribed one. The dancing computer cards moved quickly aside and total sleep engulfed him.

He was awakened by the phone.

"You any better?" It was Harry Linderkorn.

"I don't think so, Harry."

"I called you yesterday and you didn't even answer. Where were you?"

"I'm not even sure there was a yesterday."

"When I called you yesterday, I was merely being concerned about you. Today we've got a problem."

"What kind of problem, Harry?"

"One of your crew dropped a deck of cards."

"Tell him to pick them up."

"Rich, they're afraid to put things back together without you there."

"The cards are encoded sequentially. I've taught them better than that. They can do it."

"They insist that they need you."

"Harry, I'm not sure I'm going to live."

"Rich, this bank has got to pay continuous interest on all its accounts. We compound daily. Remember?"

Rich hesitated. "Why had they pulled that drawer, anyway?"

"I don't know. I only know that we've got to get that deck back in place. Correctly. Rich, I'm sending a car for you."

"When?"

"Be ready in an hour."

Rich walked slowly as he entered the bank, heavily bundled up, his entire body in pain, his head feeling ballooned all out of proportion. He had been awake very little during the two days just passed. He had awakened once and called his physician. He got up once more to answer the door and receive the medication the doctor had arranged for. The new medication had kept him heavily sedated. He felt he could lose control of himself at any moment.

He entered the computer room where his staff of helpers led him to a desk and he dropped himself into the chair. They clustered about him and talked earnestly about how the mishap occurred and why they had the drawer out and how sorry they were and how terrible they felt and all the reasons why they were afraid to try and restore the system to operation without his supervision. But he found be was unable to concentrate on anything they were saying.

Spread out on the desktop were the drawer, partly filled, and the rest of the deck, a few of the cards organized into neat stacks, most of them still loose. He spotted two or three of the ones with the red dots. He picked up a handful and looked at them, trying to make out the print at the tops but the printed characters blended into the cards. He strained to focus his eyes at the hazy, little block letters which faded and swam and spiralled and darted about. "It's no use," he said. He slumped back into his chair. "I can't see them. I can't do anything. It's no use." He closed his eyes and slumped further and then fell forward and laid his head on the desk and as his consciousness faded, he heard one of his girls say that they had better get help.

★ ★ ★ ★ ★

Rich awoke amid the muffled sounds and special smells of a hospital room. He glanced around briefly at the washed-out pastel hues of his institutional surroundings and then out the window at the familiar skyline. He closed his eyes and fell back asleep. He awoke again when a nurse came in to check his temperature and pulse. He watched her take the thermometer from his mouth and then jot notes on his chart. "How long have I been here?" he asked.

"It's Saturday. You came in yesterday."

"Who is paying for such a fancy room?"

"That's not my concern." She smiled without looking up from the chart.

"Am I getting better or worse?"

A nurse's smile of assurance. "I'd say better. But try to sleep some more. It's the best thing for you."

He watched her leave and then shifted his weight slightly and eased back into sleep.

A hand touched his am. He looked up and saw Harry Linderkorn and behind him, a stranger! Who was the stranger? Rich's pulse began to quicken as he looked at the other man's expressionless face. Young, bright, interesting face, but no sign of anything.

"How are you feeling?" Harry asked.

Rich studied Harry's face for a clue. Nothing. "The nurse told me I'm getting better." He looked past Harry at the other man. Who was he?

"They tell me you'll be fine," Harry said. "It'll just take a little while."

"How long?" Rich asked.

"What's your hurry? You've got plenty of time."

What did that mean? He looked at the other man again. Still no indications. "Harry, what about at the bank? You get things back together?"

"Business as usual, Rich. Our depositors won't lose a penny. I brought in Jennings here on a consultant basis to get the system straightened out and back in operation. Rich Hamzer, Clint Jennings."

"Nice meeting you, Rich," the young man said. "Quite a program you've set up. It's becoming the standard for the whole industry. I was delighted to have the opportunity to look at it."

Rich scrutinized his expression, searching for an off-beat reaction. "Did you have any problem getting the system back together?"

"No problems. The cards were sequential."

"And you were impressed with the way it's set up?"

"Very much so," Jennings answered. But there wasn't so much as a wisp of a smile as he spoke. He apparently had not deduced the significance of the eight cards with the red dots.

"I'm glad everything is okay, again," Rich said.

"We'll leave now so you can go back to sleep," Linderkorn said. "Besides, I'm late for my golf date. Just wanted to bring Clint by to meet you. And, of course, to show you that I care."

"Nice meeting you, Rich," Jennings said with a completely guileless smile. "Take it easy."

★ ★ ★ ★ ★

It was late evening when a hand touched Rich's shoulder again. Visiting hours had passed and the nurses had made their evening rounds. Rich rolled over and looked up through the haze of his medication. He saw Jennings, who was smiling broadly. And as he tried to concentrate on Jennings' face, he noticed even in the dim light that the smile had changed and taken on a new dimension.

"How're you doing, pardner?" Jennings asked with a

broad grin. He leaned over and snapped on a small light.

"Wha'? What're you doing here?"

"Wanted to bring you something."

"Bring me something? Wha'?"

"A present for you." Jennings held out a small object.

Rich took it and examined it. A red felt tip pen.

"Tell me, pardner," Jennings said softly, significantly, "how're we going to spend all that interest?"

For a brief moment the thought of losing everything he had worked so hard for, struck Rich like a blow! No more Alpine snow, now, with its blinding, dazzling brilliance; no more flirting with danger along the dizzying slopes, or challenging fate along the edges of those hidden chasms; no more defying gravity in those unexpected plunges . . . He paused, thinking a moment, and then looked up at Jennings' grinning face. "Tell me," he said, "do you ski?"

"That's a rich man's sport. Never could afford it." Jennings paused; his grin broadened. "Until now, that is. Yeah. Sure. I'd like to learn it."

"Good," Rich said with deep satisfaction. "I'll teach you myself."

For many years now, Marilyn and I have been spending a couple of weeks a year in Jamaica, where her brother owns a house by the sea. It's been a great place to write because there's no TV or other such distraction, and I don't even have to help with the dishes. There's really not much to do but swim, drink rum or Red Stripe Beer, read, and write. And one year when I wasn't in the middle of any other project, I decided to write a story that took place there. We met a colorful young Jamaican one day whose name was Neville and who tried to sell us ganja.

Neville

My mind was totally preoccupied the day I met him. I had been dealing with a particularly disabling case of writer's procrastination and had resolutely decided that I had to get something started. And being in Jamaica, where I'd spent so many winter months over the years, I'd also decided to have the action take place there and even include an element of the voodoo allegedly indigenous to the island.

I had driven into Port Antonio to walk around the farmers' market and replenish our supply of fresh fruit when I first saw him. Something about him made him appear a little different from most of the other Jamaicans that crowded the narrow streets and sidewalks. Perhaps it was his coloring, which was a shade lighter than the typical Jamaican, or maybe it was his bright red attire, the grossly oversized red cap, the red pants, and the matching red shirt imprinted with a vague design that resembled script but was not easily read.

Something else about him came across as different when

he approached me. His speech was articulate and free of the patois of the average Jamaican. "Pardon me," he said, "but do you think you could help me with getting some transportation into Kingston? I want to go and visit some friends there. They have invited me, you see."

"Sorry," I answered. "I'm not going to Kingston anytime soon." I continued walking on my way. Did he really expect a total stranger to take him to Kingston?

He looked away as if considering turning elsewhere for help, for greener pastures. I was obviously offering him no encouragement. Then he took several quick steps to catch up with me. "You can still help me," he said with a broad smile. His teeth were brilliantly white and flawless.

"How?" I asked.

"It is not my usual practice to ask for money," he said, "but—"

"Then don't," I said, cutting him off. This disappointed me. I didn't expect it of him, somehow.

"But economic conditions are not good here in Port Antonio," he continued, ignoring my interruption. "There is no work, and I must get to Kingston to see my friends who have invited me, and there are buses if I had the fare—"

"Look," I said, pausing to confront him, "I'm afraid I can't help you." But as I said it, looking into his disarming smile, I too smiled, and he knew he had at least a toehold.

"Maybe you need something, mon," he said. "Tell me, what do you need? I can probably get it for you." His teeth were truly spectacular, the kind that show up in toothpaste ads. His thin mustache was carefully trimmed, and with his giant cap thrown back, he was a charmer. He was slimly built and appeared to be in his early twenties.

"I need fruit," I said. "I'm going over to the market to buy fruit."

"The fruit is very good in Jamaica," he said. "The best in the world." And with that he made a world-sized gesture. "Mango season is almost here. Jamaican mangoes are sweet as honey."

"Yes, I know."

By this time I had stopped walking and had turned to face him.

"Fruit you can find in the market. Surely you need something else which Neville can get for you."

"Who's Neville?"

"I am Neville."

"You're Neville? Neville who?"

"Neville Churchill."

"Neville Churchill?" This made me really grin at him. "Why not Neville Chamberlain? Or Winston Churchill?"

He grinned right back, making me wish I could trade teeth with him. "Why not Neville Washington?" he said. "Or Neville Reagan? Because it is Neville Churchill. You see? What can I get you, mon? What do you need?"

"All I need at the moment is some fruit."

"How about some ganja? Jamaica's best, mon. I can get it for you. Cheap."

"Thanks, but no thanks."

"Would you like to go rafting? I can arrange it special."

"I've been."

"Then what do you need, mon? You name it. Everyone needs something."

"You're right. Everyone does need something. And that does include me. Okay. What I need is some very special information."

"What kind of information, mon?"

"I'm a writer. I write mystery stuff. Do you know what I'm talking about? And I want to write a story that takes place here in Jamaica. And in order to write my story, I need to know all about Jamaican voodoo practices. Can you help me with that?"

The smile left his race. "Voodoo? You want to know about Jamaican voodoo? What makes you think there is voodoo here?"

"I've heard there is. And I want to know about it. In fact, I want to see it in action. Can you help me?"

"Are you not well? Do you want to see the obeah man for a cure?"

"I'm fine. I want to learn about the other side of it. The evil side."

He looked a little unnerved for the first time. "You're talking something else now, mon. That part of obeah, that is dangerous business to try and find out too much about."

I drew my money clip from my pocket and pulled a Jamaican ten-dollar bill from it. "You interested or not?"

"For that? You expect me to teach you all about the obeah man for that? Mon, the exchange rate is nearly six dollars to one. That is barely worth two dollars U.S."

I peeled off a couple of twenties and held out all three bills to him. "How's this?"

"Not enough. Not for what you ask."

I added three more twenties. "Okay?" He shook his head.

I pulled a fifty from inside and added that. "This is it," I said with finality. "You interested or not?"

He took the money. "Where can I find you?" he asked.

"Do you know the San San area?"

"Of course." He was practically insulted by the question.

"The road down to the Blue Hole?"

"Of course," he said.

"The sixth house? Silver Cove?"

"Of course." Then he said, "San San is a most beautiful

area. Many famous people have lived there. Errol Flynn? The Aga Khan? Many famous writers, as well. Do you know Joshua Moore?"

"I've met him," I said.

He carefully tucked the folded bills into the pocket of his tight red pants. "I'll be in touch with you," he said. And for the first time I deciphered the message imprinted in the obscure script letters on his red shirt. "Life is but a mirror image." And directly beneath this line, the mirror image of the line. He turned and walked away, adjusting his big red cap

★ ★ ★ ★ ★

It was early evening of that same day at one of those typically San San cocktail parties that I next saw Neville. The party was in one of the gracious homes set into the steep green hillside looking down on San San Bay. Many of the noteworthy denizens of the San San area were there, including rich Britons and Americans who were enjoying the season in their winter homes, the wealthier of the local business people, a few political figures out from Kingston for the weekend, a sculptor, an artist, and the managers of several of the resort hotels in the vicinity. Liquor was flowing, talk was mostly glib and superficial, and several tables laden with finger food were being ravaged.

Most of the activity was outside the house on a spacious verandah in the deliciously warm tropical night air. The verandah afforded a truly stunning view of the steep terrain leading down to the sea. The San San area is a rain forest, and the downward slope was virtually choking with varied tropical growth, dotted here and there with a house and its lights.

I had made my way to a table of food and begun eating a beef patty, wishing I had a drink, when I saw Neville. He wore the black pants, white shirt, and black bow tie of a houseboy, and he was carrying a tray, serving drinks. He looked a little surprised on seeing me but quickly recovered.

"I see you found some work," I said to him. "I thought you'd be in Kingston by now."

He signaled with his eyes to quit speaking as if I knew him. "What would you like to drink, sir?" he asked.

"A scotch with lots of soda."

"Very good, sir." Then furtively, "I'll come and see you."

I continued eating, mostly the delicious Jamaican beef patties, a few stuffed eggs, bits of barbecued chicken, and the like, and sipping the drink Neville had brought me. My wife was in the living room, making conversation with a group of women, and as I moved about the table on the verandah, I suddenly found myself in the presence of a heated discussion between two of San San's most familiar individuals. The subject was the perennial question of bringing gambling to the island, particularly to the Port Antonio area.

"It will destroy life as we presently know it on this island. Can't you get that through your bloody skull?" Cedric Evans was a wealthy Englishman with a large winter home in San San.

"On the contrary, it will have the opposite effect. It will bring prosperity. It will create an influx of tourism and a great number of new jobs for the local populace." Hanford Gibbons was a Jamaican, a tall, burly man with light brown skin and a mustache. He owned the principal supermarket in Port Antonio and was also a major landowner in the area.

"We'll be overrun," Evans said. He was a puffy middle-aged man with flowing white hair and a very pink face that grew pinker when he drank or became agitated. "What we can look forward to is an influx of organized crime."

"The economy of this area is one of abject poverty. Increased tourism is Jamaica's best hope of economic survival."

Gibbons was from the educated minority of the islands. His diction was precise and careful. As large as he was, his presence was intimidating.

But Evans stood his ground, becoming pinker as his emotions grew in intensity. He'd had a bit to drink. "We have something lovely here in this remote spot. Bring in gambling, and we'll soon have a bloody strip. Another Vegas. Let them have it in Montego Bay, but keep it out of here."

"This area needs it more than Montego Bay. There's more unemployment *here*," Gibbons stated with quiet, overbearing intensity.

"Oh, Lord," Evans said, "next we'll have a jetport, and high-rise hotels as far as the eye can see."

"Would that be so bad? If there were no shortage of jobs?"

"And could it be that you'd like to sell some of your shorefront holdings for some of those hotels?"

Gibbons' face grew dark and brooding for a moment. Then, in a severely quiet manner, "Do I take it that you condemn the honest practice of business? Tell us, how do you afford to live in London and spend your winters here if you're so opposed to making money?"

"I don't earn my keep by destroying something beautiful," Evans said.

Then, in a plaintive tone, "Come now, you don't really want them here, do you? The mobsters? And the tourists by the thousands?"

I'd heard it all before. The endless debate. Saving Jamaica by legalized gambling, and the many side effects it might have. The scarf at Evans' throat caught my eye. It was a fragile silk crepe thing, a bright shade of red-orange, streaked with abstract lines of even brighter yellow. It was typical of Evans' "island attire." It went perfectly with his spotless white suit with the pearl buttons and the flare-collared, sky blue shirt. Back in London, he probably dressed in banker's grays.

"As a landowner and member of the Association," Gibbons said to Evans, speaking as if he was trying to put Evans straight with a final comment, "you may ultimately have a vote on this issue. I hope you don't plan to use it to perpetuate the poverty around here."

"I think you know bloody well how I'd vote," Evans answered.

"I'm most sorry to hear that," Gibbons said, looking away.

Neville reappeared, carrying a tray of drinks. I took mine and returned to the table that held the beef patties.

★ ★ ★ ★ ★

A week went by. I was sitting on the patio at Silver Cove, holding my pencil and blank pad and gazing out to sea, when Neville came bounding down the steps from the road, wearing his all red outfit including the giant cap. I had no idea by what mode of transportation he'd gotten there. He just seemed to materialize.

"You putting words on paper, mon?" he asked, flashing his brilliant smile.

"I'm waiting for an inspiration," I answered, showing him the empty page. "One that you were paid to arrange for me."

"You shall get it tonight, mon," he said. "If you are ready for it."

"You mean the obeah man?"

"I got the word from my sources that he will perform a ritual at his secret temple at midnight tonight."

"I'd like to witness that."

"I can take you there. I will come here at ten thirty. Do you have a car?"

"Yes."

"And do you have a thousand Jamaican?"

"For what?"

"For Neville, mon. For me."

"I already gave you over a hundred and fifty."

"I'll credit that against the thousand. What you are asking for is not without risk, mon."

"You're a thief, Neville," I said with a smile.

"No, mon. I'm a businessman." He glanced around him at the elegance of Silver Cove. "As the risk increases, so does the price."

"Okay, okay. You'll have the money."

"And wear dark clothes, mon. Pants, not shorts. And a shirt with long sleeves. All dark. And shoes in which you can run very fast."

"Hey! Where the hell are you taking me?"

"You want to see the obeah man? He does not do obeah on busy street corners, mon."

"Are you going to get me killed?"

"It is not without some bit of risk, mon. I told you that." Neville paused. "I think I can bring you back safely, but it pays to be properly dressed for any emergency." He paused again. "You still interested?"

"I'll see you tonight."

"You'll have the money?"

"I'll have the money."

"Could you also have a bite of food for me? Something good. Tell Ursula it is for me. She will know what to fix." And then he smiled his handsome smile.

Ursula was our cook. He obviously knew the territory.

I mentioned to my wife at dinner the plans I had made for late evening. Without thinking, I included the part about the dark clothes and the running shoes. I described it simply as an opportunity to observe a native religious ceremony.

She stared at me. "Have you completely separated your-self from your sanity?"

"Probably."

"For God's sake, when he shows up, tell him you've changed your mind. Tell him to go himself and come back and tell you about it."

"I'm going," I said. And then I turned away from her, ig-noring the look of total disbelief on her face.

★ ★ ★ ★ ★

Neville arrived on time, and again I had no idea how he had gotten there. After Ursula fed him a meal that appeared to be mostly red beans and rice, we left. We drove through Port Antonio and continued along the shore road until Neville had me turn left on a very narrow, winding, unpaved road leading upward, into the dense brush.

"I trust you know where the hell we're going," I com-mented.

"You can be sure of it," he answered.

The road grew gradually worse, becoming deeply rutted and quite overgrown. I wondered what damage the small rented car was going to suffer as we thumped and bounced in and out of holes and over the tenacious undergrowth. "I don't like the looks of this," I remarked, finally. "We're in the wrong kind of car for this."

"We will soon be where we are going," he said. And finally he said, "Let us leave the car here. Turn it around so we will be headed back."

"Turn it around where? There's no room to drive, much less turn around."

"Pull right in there," he said, pointing, "and back around. You will do fine."

I followed his directions and felt certain we'd damaged the car in some way. We got out of it to find we'd missed a ditch by inches, one deep enough to have totally disabled the car. But we'd missed it.

We began making our way through the underbrush with Neville leading. The night was clear and the moon brilliantly full and visibility was quite good, but the thick foliage was difficult. I began to feel I should have listened to my wife, but was pulled ahead by what I hoped to get to see.

It seemed we had gone quite a distance on foot, maybe close to a quarter mile, when Neville stopped me and pointed ahead. "There," he said.

I saw what he was pointing at, which included several men gathered in a small clearing. I also made out the flames on a cluster of maybe eight to ten candles, and there was a small source of fire near the ground. "Let's get closer," I said.

"We must be careful," he responded.

"I can't see what the hell is happening. This is what I came to see, and I want to see it."

"Careful," Neville said, cautiously leading me closer. He went a few feet at a time, picking objects to use for blind.

"Let's move up to right over there," I whispered, pointing at a clump of greenery quite near the action.

"It's too close," he whispered back.

"No, it's not," I said. "They're not giving a thought to anyone's being out here. It'll be okay." I immediately stood up and moved in that direction.

"Wait," he said. "Follow me." He caught up with me and led me in a slightly less direct path toward the spot I'd indicated, moving a careful step at a time in a crouched stance.

When we reached the spot I had picked, we were within fifty yards or less of the scene and could see quite well. Four men stood under a kind of crude canopy supported on four bamboo poles and held taut by ropes from its corners to stakes in the ground. A small table in the middle held an array of short candles. On the ground next to the table stood a dark receptacle containing a fire.

One of the men, apparently the obeah man, was lean, gaunt, and stoop-shouldered. He was dressed in a priestly white full-length robe, trimmed in bright colors. His grayish hair was in long braids, dreadlocks, and as he held his hands above the candles, he was chanting some sort of incantation, a barely audible sound from where we were crouched. His dark-skinned face gleamed in the reflected candlelight.

Two of the others in the group were typical Rastafarians. They wore suntan-colored pants and no shirts. They were tall and very black with shiny, muscular bodies, and they too had masses of coarse hair braided into unkempt dreadlocks. Each held a serious-looking machete in one hand.

The fourth man was large and stout and lighter in color.

He even looked familiar. He was dressed conservatively in slacks and a shirt and was apparently the client, having come to the obeah man for some purpose. As we watched, he pulled a brightly colored cloth object from his pocket. This, too, looked strangely familiar.

Suddenly, all the pieces fell into place, and my breath caught in my throat. The client was Hanford Gibbons. And the bright cloth object he'd produced was Cedric Evans' scarf. It was the one Evans had been wearing the night of the cocktail party where I'd watched them argue about bringing gambling to the area.

Gibbons held the scarf by two corners and waved it back and forth as the obeah man continued his incantations over the candles. The two bare-chested Rastas stood in stoic, almost bored silence as they watched. I focused my attention on the scarf. Bright orange, streaked with yellow. Visibility was good enough to be almost certain. Yes! It had to be Evans' scarf.

The priest motioned to one of the Rastas.

"Now, watch," Neville whispered.

The Rasta laid his machete aside and, kneeling down, reached into what appeared to be a heavy burlap bag. He drew out a live chicken by the throat. Then, still kneeling, he gripped the chicken's neck in both hands and stretched it flat on the small table near the candles. The other Rasta raised his machete, held it poised for a moment, and then brought it down with a heavy thud on the table. The Rasta holding the chicken stood up, his arms raised, the head in one hand, the rest of the wildly thrashing, headless chicken in the other.

The chicken slipped from his clutch and fell to the ground, where it flopped about. As the Rasta reached for it, it flopped away from him, almost as if sensing the presence of his grasping hand. He grabbed again and again, but the chicken stayed just beyond his reach. He finally turned and hurled the chicken's head into the darkness and then pounced on the flopping chicken with both hands, bringing it back to the table.

The obeah man took Evans' scarf from Gibbons and held it high over the fire. The Rasta held the chicken, now still, over the orange scarf, bloody neck down, allowing blood to drip onto the scarf. The obeah man resumed his strange noises, looking skyward, his voice raised slightly. After a few moments, he released the blood-spattered scarf, allowing it to fall into the fire. Then he dropped his arms to his sides and bowed his head in silence.

"I know whose scarf that was," I whispered to Neville.

"Yes, mon?"

"Yes. Is this obeah business really supposed to do anything?"

"Would you like me to take him your shirt?" Neville asked.

I thought about the question only for a moment because

on moving my foot to shift my weight I stepped into a small hole and turned my ankle sharply, enough to make me yelp in pain before I realized what I'd done.

Neville reached out and grabbed me. "Mon?" he whispered.

We both looked up. They had heard me and were staring into the darkness in our direction. The two Rastas, machetes in hand, took a step toward us, then another. I was suddenly possessed by total panic and, in spite of the pain, began moving in the general direction of the parked car.

"Mon!" Neville said in a hoarse whisper. Since I'd given him little choice, he followed. "This way, mon," he said. "Follow me. You're going wrong. And run!" He angled away in a slightly different direction, and I followed his lead, running despite my ankle.

I looked back and saw that the two Rastas were following us. We had a substantial lead, but they were powerful men, much younger than I, in much better condition, and much more accustomed to running through the tropical underbrush. Then I tripped and stumbled to the ground.

Neville stopped, came back, grabbed my outstretched hand, and pulled me to my feet. When he did, I sensed a wetness in our gripped hands, something more than sweat. But he began running again, and I plunged after him. The Rastas were gaining ground.

As we reached the car and climbed into it, I discovered that my hand was bleeding heavily. I'd cut it on something when I fell. I jammed my bloodied hand into my pocket and fumbled for the key. The Rastas were getting close.

The car started and I shoved it into gear, causing it to lurch forward. And just in time. One of the Rastas threw his machete at the car and I heard it hit with a thunk. I accelerated, bumping along the rutted little path, and we got out of there.

After we were safely away from them and nearly back to the main road, Neville asked if, having almost gotten his head cut off, I was satisfied with what I'd seen. I assured him, as I looked for something on which to wipe my hand, that I'd found the little excursion most interesting.

"Very good then, mon," he said, "I'd like the rest of the money."

* * * * *

I chose not to tell my wife all the details of the trip. I played the whole thing down and did not mention Gibbons' presence or Cedric Evans' scarf or the chase. I told her I got the cut hand when I accidentally slipped and fell. The cut required several stitches the next morning at the emergency room of the small hospital in Port Antonio. The wound would make it impossible to write for a few days.

Later this afternoon I was nothing less than stunned when Hanford Gibbons came walking down the steps into the patio at Silver Cove.

"I just happened by to see how you're getting along and how your hand is mending," he said with studied casualness. His presence was always rather imposing, and I was startled on seeing him because although I'd met him at many social functions in the area, we'd never really gotten to know one another. He'd never been to Silver Cove before.

"How did you know about my hand?" He could not have possibly seen who was running from the scene the previous night.

"It's a small community," he said. "Word gets around." Then he said, "I guess it will be difficult for you to do your creative work for a short while."

"Yes. For a few days, anyway."

"How are you enjoying your visit to our little island this year? Are you finding many interesting items of local color to weave into your stories, perhaps?"

That question had the almost undisguised chill of a threat about it. How should I answer? "You know how I love your island," I said, after a brief pause. "It is both beautiful and fascinating."

"I trust you will be discreet in your, uh, descriptions of the things you observe."

That comment carried the full impact of his intimidating manner. "I only write fiction," I said.

"A wise choice," he said.

"Based on whatever happens to really fascinate me," I added.

This remark annoyed him, and he stared coldly at me.

My wife wandered out onto the patio, and she too was taken by surprise to see Gibbons there. "Oh, hello, Mr. Gibbons," she said

He nodded at her. "Your husband and I were just exchanging a few pleasantries. He is a most sensible man, I trust." As Gibbons was leaving, I watched to be sure he didn't pick up anything of mine.

★ ★ ★ ★ ★

I saw Cedric Evans the following weekend at another social function, a show and reception at one of the resort hotels for a not very talented local artist, and Evans was clearly not well. "Just a tonic and lime, lots of lime," he said to one of the waiters serving drinks. "I'm a bit out of it today. I'd best skip the gin, regrettably."

And in conversation with me, he said, "I can't understand it at all. I've never had anything quite like it before. It just seemed to come over me rather suddenly. Some sort of tropical malaise, I suppose."

I didn't dare comment. How could I possibly? To begin with, I'd sound like an idiot. And if he should take me seriously, how could I explain not being in touch sooner? And going one step further, I refused to accept his condition as being anything more than coincidence, at least at one level of consciousness. However, at some other level, I was thinking self-preservation. Why look for trouble? I was relieved when Hanford Gibbons didn't make an appearance at the gathering.

"One of our servants referred to this condition as some sort of chicken fever," Evans added. "Can you imagine such a thing? Chicken fever? Something new for the annals of medicine."

I hardly slept at all the night after the artist's reception, and the next day secretly accepted the fact that the whole business had me totally unnerved. I told my wife I was driving into Port Antonio to pick up a supply of fruit and left to look for Neville.

He was not hard to find. He was near the corner where I first met him, wearing his huge red cap, a blindingly yellow printed T-shirt, and his marvelous smile. "You like the new shirt, mon?" he asked. "I bought it with part of my fee for being a native guide," he said, grinning. He posed for me to read the shirt's inscription, "Life is better with money."

"Neville, I've got to talk to you."

"What is it, mon?"

I told him about Gibbons' visit, and then about Evans' condition, and the fact that the scarf had belonged to Evans. I explained that while I was not inclined to take such things seriously, I wanted his comments as a native of the area.

"I don't know, frankly," he said. "They say black obeah can be strong medicine, but I have no firsthand experience, only hearsay. I'll keep my eyes and ears open."

★ ★ ★ ★ ★

News of Evans' worsening condition continued to make

the rounds. Whatever the strange malady was, he'd been suffering increasing symptoms of it for days. His wife kept frantically flying in all sorts of specialists in rare tropical diseases, doctors from the States and England, and even one from North Africa, but none of them could come up with a cure or even a certain diagnosis.

I saw Evans once during this time and had to agree I'd never seen a man look so ill and still be alive. I repeatedly considered going to Gibbons and confronting him and asking him to do something, but on the one hand, I refused to admit that such a thing was possible, and at the same time, I was dealing with an element, perhaps small but definitely real, of unmitigated fear.

From time to time, when in Port Antonio, I walked by Gibbons' supermarket and looked through the window at him sitting at his desk in the small enclosure near the front of the store, busily doing paperwork. On one of these occasions he happened to look up and our eyes met. His expression on seeing me made me very uneasy. After a moment, he nodded, waved with his pencil hand, and returned his eyes to his work. Business as usual.

And then it happened. I woke up in the middle of the night with a touch of nausea and some abdominal pain. I was unable to get back to sleep, and by morning the nausea was worse and the abdominal cramps had become severe. I tried to ignore the symptoms, to keep them from my wife, to assume that whatever had entered my body would leave. But as the day wore on, the symptoms persisted, and even intensified. And others began to appear, such as dryness of the mouth, and a strange, unpleasant taste there. Ursula, the cook, watched my condition develop and commented that it appeared "you have the chicken fever like the other man have."

I also began to wonder what object of mine, what article of clothing or whatever, had fallen into Gibbons' hands, and how he'd gotten it. I suspected everyone. All of our staff. I even began to watch my wife's actions for any sign of suspicious behavior. Then I thought of Neville.

Neville! Was he playing both sides of the street?

Anything for a buck? Business was business. Was that it? Although I felt rotten, I decided to go into town and confront him, to ask him what he knew. Since the sun was broiling hot, I looked around for the green hat I often wore in the sun. I hadn't worn it in a few days, but it could be almost anywhere, since I was inclined to leave it lying about.

But where was it? My search, slow and methodical at first, gradually became frenzied. Was it in the car? The living room? Upstairs in the bedroom? The dining room? The patio area? On the dock? I ran from place to place, frantically looking behind things, under cushions. I took a second look everywhere, retracing my steps. It was nowhere to be found. I tried to remember the last time I'd seen it. I was certain it was before I fell ill. Who took it? Who? The significant fact was that the hat was gone. I asked Ursula to find it, and even shouted at her, something I never did.

The dull cramps in my body grew fiercer. The pain suggested that something was inside me, thrashing and kicking, trying to get out. The nausea and dizziness grew stronger, and the abdominal pain became unbearable. I gave up the trip into town. I wasn't going anywhere. I could hardly stand up straight. I made it to the bathroom and found a bottle of strong painkiller. I took a double dose and then a little more. My wife was away somewhere with some of our friends. I crawled onto the bed and lay there, contorted in pain, praying the painkiller would work. The green hat. Where was the green hat? I had to get help. Neville. I had to find Neville. As soon as I had the strength to move . . .

★ ★ ★ ★ ★

My wife woke me with the news: Cedric Evans was dead. No one knew the cause of death. No diagnosis had ever been agreed upon. Except possibly the story among Isilda and her cronies that he'd contracted a really bad case of what the Jamaicans called "chicken fever."

Then my wife looked more closely at me. "Are you okay?" she asked. And as her face began to show extreme concern, she began talking about checking my temperature and trying to find a good reliable doctor in the area, if that was possible. She didn't dare even suggest that I might be coming down with whatever had hit poor Cedric Evans.

"I'm fine," I insisted. "Incidentally, where's my green hat? I want it. I'm going into Port Antonio, and I want it."

"It must be around here somewhere. And besides, I think you ought to stay in bed for awhile. You look terrible. I'm going to try to find a doctor."

"Where's the hat? I want the hat. And I'm going to town!"

"Okay. If you feel you must go, then go. You won't need the hat. It's gotten cloudy."

"Then I'll go without it."

★ ★ ★ ★ ★

I found Neville on his usual beat, on the sidewalk along the main road through Port Antonio. His attire this time was brilliant green, green pants and a green shirt imprinted, "Life is a bitch and then you die." But along with all the green he was wearing the outsized red cap. I decided I'd have to trust him. What choice did I have?

His eyes showed concern when he recognized me. "Hey, mon, you do not look very well at all today."

"Neville, I need your help, you hear?" I said, grasping at his arms in a helpless manner. "Listen. You've got to do

134

something. Evans is dead. Do you hear me? And whatever it is, I'm coming down with it."

"Not here, mon," he said, looking around at the Jamaicans who were staring at me, an American begging for help from one of them. "Come. Follow me." He led me down a narrow alley between storefronts to a small clearing, cluttered with garbage and debris.

"Neville, you've got to get me to someone who can stop this thing before it kills me, too. You hear?"

He looked furtively around and then nodded. "Tonight. I'll come for you tonight. Ten thirty. Okay?"

"Okay."

"One thousand Jamaican. Okay?"

I controlled the urge to call him a thief. "Okay."

"See you tonight then, mon." He turned and walked away, leaving me standing there.

When I returned to Silver Cove, my wife informed me that she had arranged for a doctor, a Jamaican who lived in the area and held an important position at the hospital in Port Antonio, to stop on his way home and take a look at me.

"I don't want to see him," I insisted. "It won't do any good."

"What's the matter with you? You're obviously not feeling well. How can you refuse help?"

"He won't know what's wrong with me."

"How do you know that?"

"Because I know."

"He'll be here in a little while. Honestly, I think you've been just a bit deranged ever since you took that crazy trip into the jungle that night with that young Jamaican."

"I'm going again tonight."

"You're what? Now I'm positive that you've separated yourself from your sanity. You said last time that you were going to research a story idea, and you've hardly written a word since then."

"I'm still going again tonight. Maybe after that I'll be able to start writing."

"The doctor will be here shortly," she said, as if ignoring my last statement.

The Jamaican doctor was well dressed, but his clothes were a little wilted from a long day of activity in the small hospital. His manner was brisk and businesslike, and his examination quite thorough. He made a point of letting me know that he had trained in the United States.

He admitted that he couldn't be sure of the diagnosis, but he suspected I might have developed an infection in the wall of my abdominal cavity. He'd seen a similar case once before. He felt an antibiotic should clear it up, and he gave me a healthy shot. He also gave me some antibiotics in capsule form and advised me to be in touch if I wasn't feeling some relief within a day or two. I was cooperative and agreeable. My major interest was getting rid of him. My thoughts were focused on going with Neville to a *real* doctor.

★ ★ ★ ★ ★

Neville showed up on time, and despite my wife's near-violent protests, I left with him. The animal within me was still thumping and clawing as wildly as ever.

After we had gone a short distance toward Port Antonio, I asked Neville to drive. It was a prospect he welcomed, and I was in too much pain to deal with the car. Besides, he knew where we were going.

We drove what seemed like several miles past Port Antonio and came to a fork in the road. He took the left fork, and we went up into the Blue Mountains on roads that curved and wound about, coming at times to what appeared to be unprotected dropoffs of thousands of feet. Finally we came to an intersection with another little side road, and Neville turned off, following the rutted little road deep into the underbrush.

We came to a tiny wood frame house. A small lantern burned on the wall of the porch, and the door leading inside was ajar. "You wait here, mon," Neville said. He got out of the car and went inside, and from where I sat, I could hear him talking with someone but could make out nothing being said.

When they raised their voices from time to time, I could tell they were conversing in Jamaican patois.

I was in pain. Their conversation seemed endless, and I wanted relief. I got out of the car, went up the steps to the porch, and entered the small house.

Neville was talking to a tiny man in a white robe. When he saw me enter, he left the little man and came quickly over to me. "I was just coming for you, mon," he said. "Come and meet the doctor." There was something nervous and hurried about the way he spoke that suggested they had been arguing about me, that maybe the "doctor" had been resisting having anything to do with me, a white American. But I was there.

Neville led me over and introduced me to "Doctor Bountiful Goodness," who was small, delicate, and very old, definitely not the same man we'd seen at the chicken ritual. The tiny man's black skin was heavily wrinkled, and his dreadlocks were a bluish-gray. He wore a badly soiled, full-length white robe, held loosely together around his waist by a snakeskin sash.

The doctor spoke to me in words that were largely patois, but I understood the message, which was "welcome." His expression and voice suggested polite reserve. I looked at Neville to let him know that I felt uneasy, and Neville said, "He welcomes you to his hospital." Hospital? I took a quick look around at the interior of the "hospital."

It consisted of one room, lit only by a small oil lamp on a desk against one wall. At one end of the room was a large iron woodstove with a fire going and several oversized black pots on it. The pots and the top of the stove looked filthy in the dim light, as if the result of a million spills never wiped away. At the other end of the room were four ragged pallets, lined up side by side on the floor.

The rest of the contents of the room included several chairs and some rough shelves near the desk cluttered with a variety of things: more pots, some bottles, bowls, crocks, some large tropical fruits, husked coconuts, tied bundles of weedy dried vegetation, and several pumpkins. A dead animal, appearing to be some variety of large tropical lizard, hung by its tail near the shelves. The air in the room had a fetid odor.

The doctor spoke again and motioned toward the pallets. I looked at Neville, and Neville said, "He wants you to lie down on one of the beds while he fixes strong medicine for you. Medicine for inside you and outside."

The doctor led me to the pallets and pointed to the end one as he spoke. "He wants you to lie down here, mon," Neville said. I did as I was told and stretched out on the hard pallet. As I lay there, my feet toward the wall, I could hear them behind me, talking and fussing with the large iron pots on the stove. I turned on my side, my arms pressed against my belly. Despite the pain, I think I must have dozed.

I do not know how much time passed before I felt Neville touch me on the shoulder. "Here, mon," he said. "Sit up. Sit up and drink this." The doctor held out a half of a coconut shell filled with a dark, thick fluid.

I took it and smelled it. The shell was warm, as was the liquid, and the vapor coming from the liquid had a sickening odor. How would I ever get it down? "What is this?" I asked.

"Strong medicine," the doctor said, along with a few words of patois. "Good medicine. Just for you."

"It's special for you, mon," Neville said. "To make you well. Go ahead, mon. Drink it."

I wasn't sure I would be able to, but it was what I had come for. I brought the shell to my lips, shut my eyes, and gulped it. The taste was many times worse than I had expected, extremely bitter with a fishy aftertaste. A wave of nausea swept over me, and I didn't think I'd be able to hold it down. But somehow I did.

Neville took the shell from me and told me to lie back down. Some minutes later, Neville and the doctor returned to me. Neville was carrying one of the large pots. The doctor unbuttoned my shirt and laid it open. Then he did the same with my pants and pulled down the elastic of my undershorts to bare my entire torso. What next? The doctor began taking sheets of what appeared to be banana tree leaves from the pot where they had been soaking in hot oil. He laid them on my body until I was covered with several layers. This oil, too, had an extremely disagreeable stench about it. The leaves felt neither good nor bad, merely hot and oily.

The doctor spoke a few words and Neville said, "The doctor says you must sleep now." I wondered if I would be able to sleep. But I didn't wonder long. When I awoke, it was midmorning. Neville and the doctor were sleeping peacefully on pallets next to me. I still had cramps but felt as if they'd let up a bit.

As we were driving home, Neville said, "The doctor saved your life, mon. You know that is true."

"I hope so," I said.

"He would like a thousand Jamaican also," Neville said.

"He'll have it." How else could I respond?

After we'd driven a little farther, I asked Neville what the doctor had put into that stuff he cooked up for me to drink.

"Very good medicine, mon. Many good powerful things."

"Such as?"

"Coconut water."

"Okay."

"Ripe papaya."

"Okay."

"Pumpkin."

"Those don't sound so bad, so far."

"Shark."

"People eat shark."

"Eel."

"Eel?"

"Sea urchin."

"And I drank it?"

"And a whole, live tarantula," he said finally.

★ ★ ★ ★ ★

When I got home in the early afternoon, my wife was absolutely beside herself. "We've had every policeman in this entire area out looking for you. What shall I tell them, now that you're back?"

"Tell them I'm feeling much better, thanks," I answered. And not wanting to get into it any further with her, I left her seething and went upstairs to the bedroom. I got the two thousand Jamaican and took it down to Neville. Then, avoiding my wife, I returned to the bedroom and stretched out on the bed. I still felt the need for a little more rest. I stared at the hypnotic movement of the slowly turning ceiling fan until I fell into a deep dreamless sleep.

I woke up the next day feeling completely recovered and wanting very much to know more about some of the events of the last couple of days, particularly the healing practices of obeah, I decided to go back and revisit Doctor Bountiful

Goodness and his hospital. I retraced the route as accurately as I could remember it from the previous trip, which was made in darkness when I was in intense pain. I'm reasonably certain that I made the right first turn from the main road, but after that it was hopeless. I spent a couple of hours wandering around in the Blue Mountains, trying one obscure little road after another, but I didn't see anything that looked like the doctor's "hospital." It was clear I'd never find it without Neville's help.

I made my way back to the main road and returned to Port Antonio. After parking, I went to where I always found Neville, on the corner in front of the bank, up the street from the farmers' market. He wasn't anywhere in sight.

I began to ask around for him, approaching various other young Jamaicans who would be his peers.

"Who?"

"Neville."

"Neville? Neville who, mon?"

"Neville Churchill."

I received no positive responses, only shrugs, a few comments in patois that I didn't quite understand, and several offers of ganja or good deals on rafting trips. A little discouraged, I got in the car and headed back to Silver Cove. The prospects for doing more research into obeah practices weren't looking too promising. But at least I had to admit to myself that a vague outline for a possible story was beginning to form in my mind . . .

★ ★ ★ ★ ★

As it turned out, I did write a yarn about a Jamaican thief, and I called it "Neville." And my agent got top dollar for it.

And the controversy over bringing legalized gambling to Jamaica seems to go on and on.

As for the green hat, I never found it. And I never saw

Neville again. Maybe he made his way to Kingston and stayed there. And as for the background detail for the story, well, I still shudder whenever I happen to recall the taste of Doctor Bountiful Goodness' strong medicine.

When we first moved into the house we built, in what I consider to be a lovely, suburban, middle-class Connecticut community, I began to notice that here were lots of battered mailboxes along the road. No foolin'. And over the years, ours took a battering or two, as a matter of fact. But, what the hell, teenagers have got to have something to do when they're out nights in the family car, with all that stored-up energy. Right?

The Battered Mailbox

The first Sunday Harry Warner found his mailbox lying on the ground, he thought little about it. The mail was still in it. He knew he'd only done a so-so job of mounting it on the rough-hewn cedar post, and he assumed the mail carrier must have knocked it loose. He braced it with light wood strips when he set it back in place.

A few Sundays later, he found the mailbox back on the ground, splintered braces and all. But this time it could not have been the mail carrier. He'd already brought in Saturday's mail. He called the town's police station.

"We're aware of the problem," the officer stated. "We get quite a few calls but we've never been able to catch them at it."

"These kids need to be caught and locked up," Warner snapped. "A town such as ours should be free of this kind of thing."

"We're doing what we can," the officer said patiently. "If we pick them up, we'll be in touch with you."

"Don't these kids know that tampering with a mailbox is a federal offense?"

"I really couldn't say," the officer replied.

Dissatisfied with the policeman's answers, he called the federal postal authorities from his office the next day.

"You're quite right, Mr. Warner. It is a federal offense. But we can't investigate these or that's all we'd ever do. I'm afraid we leave them to the local authorities. Have you called the police in your town?"

On the way to the lumber yard later that day, Warner noticed quite a few other mailboxes on the ground. He also noted that those still in place were well fastened to their posts. His would soon be also. He bought heavy lumber and long wood screws and when he'd finished re-mounting the box, he was certain it would never be removed from the cedar post again.

His apprehension about the mailbox eased after two or three weeks. He was pleased with the new installation, which was not only sturdy, but also rather appealing in design. Its lines were clean and trim, yet suggestive of strength, and the box was prominent among the others on the quiet suburban road, jutting out defiantly, provoking the Saturday night raiders to just try and knock it from its perch.

Two months later, as he walked out his driveway to get his *Sunday Times*, something about the mailbox looked strange. When he reached it, he found it had been crushed by a large rock which lay on the ground next to the post. One side of the sheet-metal box was completely caved in. He clenched his fists and stared helplessly at it for several minutes. Then he looked at the rock and fantasized about crashing it into the skull of the rotten, teenage misfit who was terrorizing him.

He wondered what man's son could have done it, what child in that pleasant, affluent community had grown up so totally without a sense of restraint that he found pleasure in that kind of destructive behavior. The child needed to be caught and his face slapped from one side to the other until he completely understood the sanctity of other people's property.

He calmed himself and spent a half-hour pounding out the collapsed side, re-shaping it so the door would still close. The box was a mess, but it was functional. As he worked on it, he wondered if any of the passing cars contained the kid who'd done it. He finished and decided he was not going to willingly let it be attacked again. If federal and local authorities couldn't be counted on, he'd catch the animals himself.

Much to his wife's annoyance, he began maintaining a vigil every Saturday night from midnight to daybreak. All social commitments were adjusted to meet this condition. He sat in total darkness in the breezeway of their house, staring through the glass louvres at the mailbox by the road. At dawn, he went to bed and slept till noon.

The break came sooner than he expected, on the sixth Saturday night of his campaign. He was dozing when he heard the rhythmic sound of a handsaw. It was almost 3 A.M. A shiny car stood near the mailbox. He tiptoed from the breezeway and grabbed the six-foot length of steel pipe he'd kept by the door. Then he ran toward the street, holding the pipe in front of him.

One boy was sawing at the cedar post and another stood and watched. They did not hear him until he was almost upon them. When they finally looked up and saw him approaching, they jumped into the car, but before they could pull away, he brought the pipe down across the hood of the car with all his strength.

"What the hell are you trying to do?" shouted the boy driving. He had been the one with the saw. The other one seemed totally frightened.

"When you get home," Warner shouted back, "just tell

your parents that the hood of their nice new car was wrecked by the man whose mailbox you were cutting down. Tell them to feel free to call me."

"Why, you son-of-a-bitch," snarled the boy. "I'm tempted to run over you."

Warner drew the pipe back and held it poised. "You want this through your windshield?"

The boy gestured with his fist. Then he started the car and roared away, his tires screaming. Warner walked calmly into the house, phoned the police, and gave them the license number of the car.

★ ★ ★ ★ ★

Warner relished the call he received from the town's police station the next day. Yes, he would certainly be more than glad to come to the station and make the necessary identification and sign the required papers to press charges.

The confrontation was quiet. The boy's name was Ronnie Gerardo and he was just eighteen. His father was present, and Warner was struck by the family resemblance. The boy's clothes were flashy and he stared at Warner as if he were being done an injustice. But a mistaken identity was impossible, since the car with the crushed hood was parked in front of the station. The father was indifferent toward Warner and the complaint. He was clearly protective of his son. The Gerardos lived in another, equally affluent part of the town, a mile or so away.

The boy's accomplice had not been identified but Warner didn't care about him, in view of the difference in behavior of the two the night before.

The police sergeant examined all legal aspects of the proceedings, including the federal offense overtones. And although he didn't say as much, it became clear during his comments that any action taken against the boy would hinge almost entirely on Warner's testimony, because they had no other case against him. Gerardo asked Warner if he would drop the charges if the mailbox was replaced to his complete satisfaction and he was assured the incident would never happen again.

Warner looked at young Gerardo. "Are you ready to apologize? Do you understand the significance of what you've done?" When it was obvious the boy was not going to give him any satisfaction, Warner said to his father, "I feel you need to be thinking about why a child of yours has been driving around nights pulling stunts like this."

Both father and son scowled at Warner.

The sergeant explained that the boy would be held until bail could be set and paid. After a moment of silence in which all present looked around at one another, the sergeant motioned to young Gerardo to follow him down the hall to one of the spotlessly clean, seldom used cells. Warner and Gerardo were still seated when they heard the cell door clang shut.

When the sergeant returned, Warner stood up and asked, as if he'd just thought of something, "Sergeant, may I speak to Ronnie alone?"

The sergeant turned to Gerardo who looked mildly surprised, but after considering it for a few seconds, shrugged indifferently. The sergeant led Warner down to young Gerardo's cell and let him into it, leaving it unlocked. The youth was sitting on the edge of the cot.

After the sergeant had disappeared, Warner said, "I would have considered going along with your father's offer but I don't even think you're sorry you did it. Are you?"

The youth remained silent.

"You're not," Warner said. "It's obvious. Why do you have to go around destroying other people's property? Would

147

you mind telling me what pleasure it gives you? Or what need it fills?"

The boy studied him but didn't respond. He appeared to be paying little attention to the questions.

"Well?" Warner said. "Aren't you going to answer? Let me ask you this. Have you ever thought about having the shoe on the other foot, maybe? Would you want someone to come and destroy your property? What if they wrecked something that meant a great deal to you?"

The boy maintained his silent, penetrating stare.

"Have you thought about the fact that what you're doing is sick? That's what unprovoked vandalism is. It's sick. You're not committing a crime out of need. Because you don't need anything. What you need is help. Do you know that?"

The youth's eyes glowed with hate.

"Well?" Warner said impatiently.

"Are you going to drop the charges like my father wanted or not?" young Gerardo asked. His expression was free of any emotion.

"You've got to be made to understand that what you did was wrong," Warner answered.

"Because, if you don't," the boy said quietly, "I'm going to burn your house down." Then he added, "And I won't get caught doing it."

Warner's knees sagged with fear. It could easily happen. The statistics on unsolved arson cases were staggering. He thought about the well-kept home he'd shared with his wife all those years, a house which showed the fruits or many hours of painstaking labor. He visualized it being consumed by uncontrolled flames. He saw himself standing before it, helpless, feeling the heat.

He focused his thoughts back on the boy's deep-set eyes,

148

which were still boring into him. Warner was frightened. He was deathly afraid the youth was capable of carrying out his threat. But he couldn't let him know it. Besides, the history of the world was an endless parade of events which proved that appeasement never worked. Never. He had to respond in kind to the threat. He had to try to frighten the boy or at least deter him. "Do you fully understand the significance of what you just said?" he asked, finally.

"I just hope you heard me," the boy answered.

"Then let me ask you one more question." Warner mustered all his strength and concentration in trying to appear as cool and assured as the boy seemed to be. "You care anything about your parents?"

A glaze of confusion moved across young Gerardo's eyes. "What's that got to do with anything?"

"Just this," Warner said, almost whispering. "If something like that happens to my house, I'm going to know you did it. Understand? And then I'm going to kill both your parents. And I won't get caught, either. So think about that before you start playing with matches."

The youth's eyes widened slightly but he didn't speak.

Warner turned and walked out of the cell. As he moved down the hall, he thought about what he'd said and began to shake. He'd wanted something big enough to stagger the boy, to totally and dramatically counteract any trace of serious thought the boy might have had about putting a match to his house. But from another standpoint, Warner had made a threat on someone else's life. He'd actually verbalized it. In apparent seriousness. Prior to that moment, he would have considered himself totally incapable of saying anything like that, even in jest.

He was trembling when he reached the room where the sergeant and Mr. Gerardo waited. "Do you know what your son just told me?" he said to Gerardo. "Can you guess? Your son threatened to burn my house down if I didn't drop the charges." Then he looked at the sergeant. "Did you hear that? I want you to make a note of it. Now, while his father is present. Make a note of it. Just in case."

"What did you say to him?" the sergeant asked.

"I told him he was sick and needed help."

★ ★ ★ ★ ★

Warner chose not to tell his wife about the boy's threat. He knew what effect it would have. She was easily frightened and would probably want to move completely away from the community. He called the police sergeant the next day and was advised that young Gerardo had been released on a small bail to his parents' custody. Warner had difficulty sleeping that night.

He called his insurance agent the following day and insisted on a complete reappraisal of his house and contents with the premium adjusted as necessary. He wanted maximum possible coverage in the event of fire.

"Okay, Harry, if you insist," the agent said. Then in a lighter tone, "You sure you're not planning to burn the place down yourself?"

"Don't even say it as a joke," Warner answered.

★ ★ ★ ★ ★

Several restless weeks passed for Warner. When he had almost succeeded in getting the incident out of his mind, a tiny news item appeared in his local paper. Among recent court cases, Ronnie Gerardo had been found guilty of vandalism, given a suspended sentence, and released on a short period of probation to the custody of his parents.

Warner read the article several more times. The boy had spent a total of one night at the local police station. Some might feel that one night was more than reasonable for one mailbox. Except that the size of the crime was not the issue.

Young Gerardo was disturbed and needed to be locked up and treated accordingly.

★ ★ ★ ★ ★

A short time later, Warner came abruptly face-to-face with the Gerardo boy in a local supermarket. After recovering from the momentary shock, Warner managed a slight smile and said, "Hello, Ronnie, how's it going?"

Young Gerardo regarded him for a few seconds and then said, "How's your furnace working? Getting plenty of heat?"

Warner felt weak and was unable to respond. The boy continued staring at him and walked past him down the aisle. Warner turned his cart and hurried after the boy. "You did wreck our mailbox. Right? And God knows how many others. For God's sake, Ronnie, stop and think about what you were doing."

The boy ignored him.

As soon as Warner arrived home, he called the police station. He wanted to tell the sergeant about the incident in the supermarket. But the Sergeant Rubano who had been on duty on the Sunday young Gerardo was brought in was no longer on the Town's force. He had recently moved to Pennsylvania and gone into some kind of business.

Warner tried to explain the background of the case and the significance of the supermarket incident to the new officer. The new man was polite enough, but Warner could sense that the story wasn't getting through to him. "Look it up in the file on the case," Warner said. "If you'll just look it up, I'm sure Sergeant Rubano made a note at the time."

"We'll check it out, Mr. Warner."

"I can assure you I'm not making this story up."

"Of course not, Mr. Warner. And we'll keep an eye on things."

Warner got off the phone. It had become obvious that the more he tried to explain the matter to the new sergeant, the more his own credibility skidded.

★ ★ ★ ★ ★

As the date approached for his company's annual expense-paid week in Florida, Warner found himself in a deep quandary. Although he had trouble sleeping in the house, he was even more apprehensive about leaving it unoccupied. When the date arrived, he chose to go. The last few months had left his wife very distraught and she needed the vacation. Before leaving, he called the police, as he had always done routinely when they planned to be away. He asked them to keep an eye on the house until he returned.

The chartered plane left on Saturday and they received the call at their hotel early Sunday morning . . . A fire of unknown origin . . . An investigation was under way . . . They repacked and took the next plane back. The flight seemed interminable, the longest they could ever remember.

His wife stood and wept as Warner paced back and forth on the lawn in front of the wet, charred remains of the house, tears streaming down his own face. His neighbor spotted them and came over. The town's volunteer fire department had responded promptly but the house just seemed to have been enveloped in flames so quickly that the firefighters had been able to do little more than keep it from spreading to other houses.

Warner strode into the police station house and demanded that the Chief of Police be called in. "You know who did this, don't you?" he shouted, after the Chief arrived.

No, the Chief replied, they didn't know who did it, or for that matter, if anyone had maliciously done it, although there were distinct indications that it might have been arson. They were presently investigating.

"Ronnie Gerardo set fire to our house," Warner screamed. "He told me he planned to do it."

The Chief studied Warner for a few moments and then stated that Warner's accusation was a rather strong one. He asked if there was any basis for it.

Warner calmed himself enough to relate the details of the mailbox incident and the conversation he'd had with the boy afterward. "Look it up in the file on the case. I'm sure you'll find it."

The Chief had the new sergeant pull the file and they went over it but found no reference to the boy's threat.

"Then contact the man who was the sergeant at that time. He'll confirm it. I don't know why he didn't write it down. I told him he should." Warner was quieter, almost plaintive.

The Chief asked the sergeant to try and reach Rubano in Pennsylvania. When they got Rubano on the line, the Chief turned on a phone speaker so all present could hear. He briefed Rubano on the fire and asked about the previous incident.

"I recall it quite well," Rubano replied. "Warner pressed charges and then asked to speak to the Gerardo boy alone. He definitely claimed at the time that the boy threatened arson."

"Wouldn't you say he's carried out his threat?" Warner shouted at the little speaker.

"I'm afraid I can't be of much more help than to repeat what I remember," Rubano replied.

The Chief ended the conversation with Rubano and then turned to Warner. "We'll certainly interrogate the Gerardo boy as part of our investigation," he said.

Warner and his wife checked into a motel. Their insurance coverage, which was rather complete, included living expenses for the emergency period.

Since both of their cars had been in their garage and consequently had been lost in the fire, they went out the next day and bought two new ones. Warner then began calling local contractors to discuss rebuilding his home. His wife felt strongly that they should sell the lot and move to another town, but Warner adamantly refused to consider it.

That evening Warner received two phone calls. The first was from the Chief of Police. He had sent two investigators out to talk to Ronnie Gerardo the previous evening. Young Gerardo denied ever making the threat on the house. As for his whereabouts on Saturday night at the time of the fire, he claimed he was with three of his friends. These three boys had also been interrogated and all three confirmed young Gerardo's story.

"Three friends!" Warner shouted. "Are you going to settle for that?"

"I'm sorry, Mr. Warner, but there's not much more we can do until we have a little more to go on. We're continuing the investigation."

Warner's second call was from his insurance agent. "Harry," he said, "I called because I wanted to let you know the insurance company that has your homeowner's policy is questioning why you wanted your coverage increased so completely just weeks before the fire."

"Well, didn't you tell them?"

"You mean, about the Gerardo kid and his threat?"

"Of course."

"Well, yes, Harry, I mentioned that. Then they called me back and said they checked with the police and apparently the boy denies making the threat."

"Then what are you trying to say?" Warner asked. "That they think I burned it down? Of course the little animal denies everything. What would you expect him to do? Look, I was in Florida when . . ."

"Now, take it easy, Harry. Everything's going to be all right. I just said they were asking a few questions. That's all." He paused. "One of their questions, Harry, did you have to buy two new cars the first day?"

"But we need two cars."

After Warner had gotten himself reasonable assurance that the company would stand behind the policy, he got off the phone.

His wife, who'd listened to his end of both conversations, said, "Can't we please move away from here? Let's move to one of the towns on the other side of the plant."

"No," Warner snapped. "Absolutely not."

★ ★ ★ ★ ★

Harry Warner spent the last two days of his week's vacation standing in his yard, watching the workmen clean away the charred rubble that had once been his home and all of the treasures and possessions he had accumulated in it. Occasionally the workers turned up something salvageable, a glass paperweight or the like. He thought of these objects painfully as "artifacts," found among ruins.

Despite his wife's continued protestations, he'd made a deal with a contractor to rebuild the house exactly as it had been, as quickly as possible. He'd sent his wife shopping for a new wardrobe to keep her distracted. His fellow employees were still on vacation in Florida.

Earlier in the week, he'd watched the police officers, two uniformed and two in plain clothes, go over the property for the third or fourth time, taking pictures and looking for leads of any kind. They'd been able to find nothing. They'd brought in a cop from the city nearby, an arson expert, and he'd stated that it looked like it might have been arson, done skillfully with gasoline, but he couldn't be sure. They'd interrogated everyone in the neighborhood, but the fire had started very late on Saturday night. They'd questioned the Gerardos and the parents of all the boys who supported young Gerardo's alibi. The boys had apparently been together, in one of their basement recreation rooms, shooting pool.

Warner went by the stationhouse to see the Chief again. "You've got to find some way to link that kid to the fire," he protested. "You know as well as I do that he did it."

"Mr. Warner, our entire department has been working on little else all week. I think you know that. But so far I'm afraid we don't have much."

"That kid is a public menace!" Warner said in a raised voice. "You've got to get him off the streets. God knows what he'll do next. Everybody in this town knows about him."

"We're doing all we can, Mr. Warner. We can't make arrests without some kind of case."

★ ★ ★ ★ ★

Several weeks passed. The new house was framed and topped out. Warner made his weekly visit to the stationhouse.

"I'm sorry, Mr. Warner, but once again we have nothing new to report. We consider the case still active and we keep hoping we'll come on to a new lead, but until we've something to go on there's really not much we can do."

"That's not good enough," Warner said quickly.

The Chief looked up. "What do you mean?"

"Nothing. Nothing at all," Warner said. He ended the conversation.

He left the station-house and drove to a nearby sporting goods store where he asked to see handguns. "Something for recreational target practice," he said. "Something that doesn't require a license."

The proprietor sold him a twenty-two semi-automatic with ammunition and then answered Warner's questions about loading and firing the gun. Warner was clearly inexperienced with firearms. When Warner presented a credit card to pay for his purchase, the proprietor noted the name on it and looked up momentarily. Their eyes met. Without comment, the proprietor made the call to check Warner's credit and then completed the sale. Warner took the gun to his room and hid it in a drawer.

That evening Warner received a call from the Chief of Police. "I understand you've bought a handgun."

"It's only a target pistol. I'm joining the pistol club at the plant."

"Don't they furnish guns?"

"I prefer to use my own."

"Mr. Warner, I must tell you that this has me very concerned."

"Chief, this gun does not require a license and I really don't feel I have to answer any further questions about it."

The next night Warner received another phone call, this time from young Gerardo's father. "I hope you're not planning to try something stupid," he said.

"I don't know what you're talking about."

"Look, my kid told me what you said to him that day."

"Mr. Gerardo, if he told you what I said, then he must have told you what he said that prompted me to say it. Right?"

"He's a kid. He just happened to say the first thing that popped into his head. Look, it's bad enough you made him spend a night in jail and have a record because of that little bit of mischief involving your mailbox. You didn't have to do that. I offered to replace it and see that it never happened again. I'm sorry about your unfortunate fire but quit trying to blame it on my son. The police have already established that he had nothing to do with it."

"Mr. Gerardo, I don't believe for one minute that you think your son had nothing to do with it. The boy is sick. Don't you see that?"

"I'll say it once more, Mr. Warner. I hope you're not planning to try something very foolish."

"You needn't worry, Mr. Gerardo. I don't do foolish things."

As Warner hung up the phone, his wife looked across the motel room and asked about the call in a somewhat disturbed tone.

"It was the boy's father," Warner said.

"I gathered that much."

"The man is an idiot," Warner snapped and would discuss it no further.

★ ★ ★ ★ ★

When Warner arrived in the room from work the next day, he found his wife getting her things together to leave. She'd found the gun.

"I'm planning to join the pistol club at work."

She looked at him in disbelief. "That's something new."

"It's true," he said.

"You've always talked about how strongly you feel that no guns should ever be kept at home. Am I right?"

"Times have changed," he said.

"You should have let the boy's father fix the mailbox," she said as she continued packing. "I'm going to stay with my sister Ruth for a while."

"But that's ridiculous."

"We can be in touch by phone," she said with a note of finality.

★ ★ ★ ★ ★

Warner's life fell into a routine. He lived alone at the motel and went to work each day exactly on time. Often during his lunch hour he went to check on the progress of the house. He ate his meals by himself and spent evenings watching TV in the room or going to an occasional movie. And every Tuesday and Thursday after work, he went to his company's clubhouse and spent an hour at the pistol range, becoming proficient at the use of his new gun.

He frequently called his wife, insisting that she come back. She stated that she would not return unless he got rid of the gun and gave up his intention of moving back into the house when it was completed. He refused to yield on either matter.

One Saturday night at around midnight Warner left his motel room and drove across the town. As he approached the Gerardo home, he turned off his lights, driving the last block in darkness. He pulled up and stopped across from the Gerardo home. He sat quietly in the unlit car, watching the house. When occasional cars drove past, he ducked out of sight.

Several hours went by. A car approached at greater than usual speed, braked, and cut recklessly into the Gerardo driveway. It stopped with a shudder just inches away from the rear wall of the spacious double carport.

Warner watched young Gerardo hesitate before going inside. The youth stood in the driveway and squinted at Warner's car across the street. He walked down the driveway, crossed the street, and approached it uncertainly.

When he came face-to-face with Warner, he gasped and dropped to the pavement where he lunged toward the back of the car. He ran a few zig-zagging yards on hands and knees and dove into the shrubbery on the opposite side of the street. He crept along the ground behind the shrubs until he approached his house and then dashed behind the cars parked there. A few seconds later, he slipped into the house.

Warner watched and smiled as he saw lights come on behind draped windows.

Within minutes one of the town's radio cars pulled up behind Warner, its revolving lights ablaze. The two cops got out and stood behind the opened doors of their car, their service revolvers drawn. They inched forward, watching Warner in the beams of their headlights.

When one of them reached Warner's open window, Warner asked, "What are you trying to do?"

"I think we're supposed to ask you that," the officer said. "Get out of the car."

"There is no law which requires me to do that under the circumstances. Therefore, I will not do it."

The cop looked across the top of the car at his partner. Then he looked back at Warner. "May I see your license? There is a law which requires you to show me that."

"Glad to," Warner said pleasantly. He took out his wallet and handed the cop his license.

The cop holstered his gun and examined the license with his flashlight. "Mr. Warner, would you mind getting out of the car while we search it?"

"Have you a warrant?"

"Under the circumstances we don't need a warrant."

"What are the circumstances?"

The cop hesitated. "Suspicion of carrying dangerous weapons."

"You won't find it. I didn't bring it."

"Mr. Warner, would you mind telling us what you're doing here?"

"I like it here."

"You can't stay here. You're going to have to move along."

"There is no law which forbids my parking here and sitting

in my car. And I don't intend to move."

The cop looked across the car at his partner who motioned to him. They walked to the rear of Warner's car and exchanged a few words. Then they got back into the cruiser. They left their revolving lights in operation.

Warner watched them in his rear-view mirror for ten or fifteen minutes, irritated by the pulsating illumination that flooded in and out of his car. He finally started his engine and drove away. They followed him back to his motel and, as he climbed the staircase to his room, he saw them pull into the motel's parking area and cut their lights and engine.

★ ★ ★ ★ ★

Warner received a call from the Chief or Police the next morning. "Would you mind telling me what that business was all about last night?" the Chief asked.

"I was keeping an eye on things." Warner paused and then added, "I wanted to see what time the kid got home."

"What business is it of yours? Leave police work to the professionals."

"That kid burned my house down. What did you do about it? Tell me that."

"We've been over that, Warner. We can't point any fingers at anyone without evidence. Meanwhile, you're getting a new house. Are we going to have to assign a man to follow you around?"

Shortly after receiving the Chief's call, he got a call from his wife. She was going to Florida for a week or so with Ruth and her husband.

"When are you going to come back to me?" he asked plaintively.

"I think I've already answered that question."

He hesitated. "Have a good time," he said with a soft voice.

161

★ ★ ★ ★ ★

Toward the middle of the following week a small item in the society section of the newspaper caught Warner's eye. Mr. and Mrs. Gerardo were leaving with several other couples on a cruise. That meant the boy would be staying home alone. There had to be a way. He sat in his room in the big leatherette chair, jotting notes on a pad of paper, scribbling, tearing off sheets, starting fresh. After a couple of hours, he began to smile. He flipped to a fresh page in the pad and composed a detailed list.

On the following Saturday he left the motel in the morning with his new pistol in his pocket and took a bus to the center of the nearby city, leaving his own new car parked in its usual place near his entrance to the motel. He went to his sister-in-law's house and, using his own set of keys, took his wife's car. He drove to a bustling discount store and bought a five-gallon gasoline can, a hammer, a package of large nails, and a length of plastic tubing. Before returning to his own town, he used the tubing to siphon gasoline out of the car and fill the can.

The rest of the day was tedious. Nothing more to do until late that night. He couldn't risk going back to the motel.

Well after midnight, he drove to the vicinity of his new home under construction. Taking care not to be seen by his neighbors, he parked his wife's car in an unobtrusive spot, took his gasoline can, hammer, and nails and walked to the new house. The night sky was clear enough; he'd need no extra light.

He found a plank of wood and drove a large nail into it. He placed the plank by the side of the driveway where he could easily find it later. He removed the top from the gasoline can and walked around the house, sloshing a ring of gas on the unpainted shingles that formed the lower perimeter or the house. He set the empty can near the board with the nail and put the nails and hammer inside the garage. Then he set out on foot for the Gerardo house, ducking out of sight to avoid being seen by the occasional car that drove by.

Young Gerardo didn't finally pull his car into the driveway until nearly dawn. As the boy got out of the car, Warner materialized from the shadows or the carport. "Hello, Ronnie."

The boy froze when he saw the gun. "What are you doing here?"

"How would you like to burn my house down again?"

"What are you talking about?"

"Come on. Let's go over in your car. Get in."

"What are you gonna do?"

"Just get in the car, Ronnie."

Warner kept the muzzle of the gun close to the youth's side as he had him drive slowly back to the house under construction. They pulled into the driveway and Warner directed him to get out of the car, keeping the gun aimed at point-blank range. Then Warner held out some matches. "Here, Ronnie. Go ahead. Light it. Have yourself some more fun."

"What's the matter with you? You sick or something? Wasn't once enough?"

"I thought you'd like doing it again. But if you wouldn't, listen, you don't have to. Go ahead home. I just wanted to have a little fun with you."

"If you're smart, you will let me go," the boy said.

"I said you could go."

Without further comment, young Gerardo got back in the car and started the engine. Warner grabbed the plank with the nail and jammed it, nail upright, behind a rear tire. When the youth started the car rolling backward, a hissing sound emanated from the tire and it went quickly flat, stopping the car. The youth jumped out to see what had happened.

"You came to burn it down again and you ran over a

nail," Warner said. "Too bad."

"What are you talking about?"

"Watch." Warner struck a match and touched it to the gasoline on the shingles. The fire quickly caught and began to move along the base of the house.

"You must be crazy. I'm gonna tell the cops you did it. I'm gonna tell 'em this whole thing."

"Think they'll believe you?"

Without warning, the boy shoved Warner, knocking him down, then dashed across the yard and broke into a dead run toward his home.

Warner got up and set the empty gas can on the floor in the rear of the youth's car. Then he hurried off to the other car and drove away as the line of flame continued traveling around the perimeter or the house.

Dawn was just beginning to break when he reached the motel and there were no signs of life anywhere as he pulled his wife's car into a corner of the parking lot. He tiptoed up to his room and entered quietly. Nothing left to do but wait for the phone to ring.

*In 1993, when the consensus of the Adams Round Table members
was that the theme (and title) of our next anthology was to be*
Justice in Manhattan, *I was at a loss to come up with an idea
for a story. Nothing came to mind. But then, one June
afternoon, when we were attending a picnic to celebrate the
high school graduation of one of our local friends' son, I was
sitting around the table, taking in a story about their
friend who lived in New York, and heard the line of dialogue,
"How Much Justice Can You Afford?" I snapped to attention. I
got the specifics of the story, and to quote the Bard in the past
tense, "Thereby Hung a Tale." Sometimes you just have to get
'em where you find 'em.*

How Much Justice Can You Afford?

When Matt Guinan began telling friends that he'd decided to
dabble in real estate investment and buy an apartment house,
his best friend, George Hebner, laughed. "Matt, what the hell
do you want to do that for? Why all of a sudden are you crawling
out on a crazy-ass limb like that?"

"Why?" Guinan responded. "Because, George, the time is
right. That's the reason."

"But, Matt, you're making a bundle in the business you're
in. And it's growing like a weed. Given a little time, you're
gonna be one of the richest guys I know. Now, from out of nowhere, you're talking about diving headlong into some real
shark-infested waters. Waters where you've got no experience whatsoever. None."

"What experience did I have when I started my office supplies business? The answer is also none. Right? Absolutely none."

"But, Matt, this is different. Real estate is different."

"You're right. It's quite different. No inventory."

"Where the hell are you going to get the money?"

"I've already been to see my banker. And he likes it. This building I've found is fully occupied. Hear what I said, George? Fully occupied. Using the business for collateral, I can have whatever I want. And the owner's got the building on the market at a very favorable price. Definitely below market."

"Oh?" George chuckled. "It's fully occupied and the owner is giving it away? Doesn't that have a slight smell to you?"

"The man says he wants to retire."

"Is he an old man?"

"Listen. People are retiring younger and younger these days when they can afford it."

"Matt, if I were you, I'd reconsider this very carefully."

"George, just wish your old buddy well. Okay? All I want to do is become the richest man in New York."

"Well, I certainly do wish you luck, Matt, because I've got a feeling you're going to need all the luck you can get."

★ ★ ★ ★ ★

The year was 1975 and Matt Guinan was right about some of the thoughts behind his planned move into the world of Manhattan real estate. Times were good. The Vietnam thing was over, but all the guilt and recrimination had not yet befallen the country, Nixon had resigned and Ford was president. New York City's financial collapse had not yet occurred, and real estate was considered a very secure investment. A great deal of the city's major wealth was in the hands of the Zeckendorfs, the Helmsleys, and their ilk.

It was also a time when much of the life in the city was still quite laid back, particularly below the midtown area. Cocaine had not yet become a major factor, and pot was enjoyed rather freely within even the more socially acceptable circles of the population. The Village was still the Village.

Matt was forty-three, a burly, easy-going Irishman, a handsome man with a lot of hair swept straight back, had a quick, self-effacing sense of humor and was slow to anger. He and his beautiful wife, Valerie, who had been "to the manner born" on Long Island, lived in a lovely house in the best block of St. Mark's Place.

Five days a week Matt wore a suit and tie and ran his office supply company with considerable business acumen. But successful entrepreneur that he was, when Matt returned home from the office, off came the tie and jacket and he, Valerie, and their many friends enjoyed a laid-back lifestyle that bordered on being Bohemian. One of Matt's favorite pals was a huge black cop, Big Mike to his friends, who often brought the very best grass available to Valerie's little *soirées* and impromptu gatherings, and on several occasions escorted Matt and Valerie and a few of the friends up to Harlem where they moved around like visiting dignitaries to the best music joints and soul food restaurants.

At the same time, Matt and Valerie enjoyed much of the other side of New York's night life, the "uptown life," so to speak, with its culture and frequent invitations to functions in middle-to-upper social strata. They were on some of best lists and were once even included in a photograph in *New York Magazine* which had been taken at a black tie benefit at the Metropolitan Museum.

The building that Matt had come upon for his first foray into real estate was The Albion, a decent but not fancy middle-class apartment house, a block south of the Flatiron

Building. Twenty-four units, six floors, four units to a floor, a single elevator, and a custodian on call, but no doorman. The neighborhood had just begun to undergo revitalization, a face-lift. And all twenty-four units in the building were occupied. Matt reviewed the prospects over and over again. A fully occupied building in an improving neighborhood? At a favorable price? How could he go wrong?

★ ★ ★ ★ ★

Matt and his lawyer sat across the table from the seller and his attorney. The seller was clearly a very smooth operator who appeared to be about Matt's age. His attorney was a sharpie from a small firm specializing in real estate. The meeting was relatively brief, the crossing of t's and dotting of i's having already been done by the two attorneys, and both parties signed the various documents in all the necessary places. And with those signatures, Matt became the new owner of The Albion, with a serious mortgage, of course.

After the business had been completed, Matt forced a little small talk with the seller, trying to get a handle on why the man was so anxious to sell.

"Let's just say that I've got bigger fish to fry," the man quipped. And that was about all he had to say on the subject.

★ ★ ★ ★ ★

Miguel Santana was the consummate New Yorker, a snappy dresser, always decked out in the best that Barney's had to offer, quick enough on his feet to be at ease in any circle, and blessed with more than his fair share of street smarts. He made a nice living as a manufacturer's rep for several electrical equipment suppliers, and had become a salesman's salesman, a highly skilled player in the world of business skip-rope and stoop-tag.

At the same time, Santana was a wily little man who was

always looking for an edge, an opportunity to pick up a quick buck, or just have some laughs, to score at someone else's expense by applying a little heat of some kind, within the law, of course. He was sharp-witted and could be quite funny at times, usually at the expense of others. Beneath the humor, his mind was always looking for that little chink in the protective armor of any existing or potential adversary.

Santana's oily brow sloped back from his dark, deeply set eyes, so that in profile, the line of his nose seemed to flow rather continuously up his brow and into his receding hairline, giving his face a rat-like appearance. Along with this look, he had a pudgy, roly-poly body. Thus, his presence was that of a fat mouse. A fat but scheming mouse. His eyes were in constant motion, giving the impression that his mind was never at rest.

Santana and his wife were among the newer tenants in the apartment building in which they lived, having only been there a year or so, and when he received the friendly letter from the building's new owner, announcing the change in ownership, he decided to test the man, to see how he was put together.

He reviewed the letter and dialed the phone number. The flushing mechanism on the toilet in one of the bathrooms in his unit had a tendency to occasionally stick and cause water to dribble continuously. And since water is much too valuable a commodity to waste, the toilet needed attention. Right? Right. Even though the slightest jiggling of the handle on the toilet put a quick end to the dribble.

After a receptionist answered, he asked for Mr. Guinan.

"Matt Guinan here."

"Mr. Guinan?"

"Yes."

"This is Miguel Santana calling. Number 4-D."

"I'm sorry. What's number 4-D?"

"Apartment 4-D. Do you recall sending out a letter to us poor, miserable tenants, telling us you were the new owner of our building? That ring a bell?"

"Oh, of course. Of course." He laughed. "Sorry, Number 4-D. And what did you say your name was?"

"Santana. Miguel Santana."

"Nice to hear from you, Mr. Santana. Sometime soon I'm having a separate phone line put in just for real estate work, but I don't have it, yet. Maybe then I'll take the time to call and say hello to all the people in the building. Try to know everybody by name. A bit of personal touch. I thought that would be nice."

Personal touch? What kind of a total asshole have we got here? With a soft chuckle, Miguel said, "Yeah. That would be nice. Very nice."

"Anyway, how can I help you, Mr. Santana?"

"We've got a toilet here in the apartment that needs attention. It's wasting water. Besides being a pain in the butt. You can hear it all over the place. It's kinda like water torture, if you know what I mean."

"You called Mr. Landini, the custodian? He should be able to take care of that."

"He's been up here a couple of times. Frankly, Mr. Guinan, I don't think the old guy's able to fix this or much of anything else. He keeps the lobby swept, but that's about it. We're going to need a real plumber up here. And I frankly think we'll need a new toilet. Or at least a whole new set-up inside the thing."

"I'll see if I can get somebody up there. Anything else?"

"The intercom's not working very well. You can't make out who the hell's down there."

"Did you tell Mr. Landini?"

"You're going to have to get a professional, Mr. Guinan. That old guy . . ."

"I'll look into it, Mr. . . . You said your name was . . . ?"

"Santana, Mr. Guinan. Santana."

"Mr. Santana, I'll look into these matters. I want all my tenants to be happy with things. Okay?"

You want to keep us happy, Mr. Guinan? You're going to be one busy sumbitch. "Thanks, Mr. Guinan. Sounds like having you as our new landlord'll be a definite change for the better around here."

★ ★ ★ ★ ★

Guinan made a few calls and found a plumbing firm that specialized in maintenance in residential real estate in the city. He dispatched them to the Santana apartment with instructions to do whatever was necessary to satisfy the tenant. It took Guinan even longer to find the right firm to deal with the intercom system in the building, but he finally did, and he sent them over with the same basic message he had given the plumbers.

He was a little startled when he got the plumbers' bill, and shaken when he got the one from the electrical contractors. The profit margin between his monthly notes on the building and the total income from the rents was rather substantial with full occupancy, but he'd be losing money on the Santanas' unit for a couple of months.

But of even greater importance, he'd wasted an afternoon fooling around with this problem, time he could ill afford away from his business. Would he have to hire a manager to handle his modest entry into real estate? Or possibly make a deal with some realty management firm? What would that do to the margins?

As he sat, pondering these questions, his receptionist put another call through to him, a Mr. Redelsheimer, in 4-A.

"What can I do for you, Mr. Redelsheimer?"

"Mr. Santana said we should call you, that you'd take care of a problem here. We have a window that won't open if we should need some air. And the door on one of our closets, the hinges have come loose from the wall."

"Did you call Mr. Landini, the custodian?"

"Long ago. He couldn't fix it. He scratched up the window trying to get it open. He even cracked one glass."

"I'll see what I can do."

★ ★ ★ ★ ★

The phone kept ringing. The wave of complaints picked up momentum. Guinan received calls from the other two tenants on the fourth floor, with Santana's name being dropped, and then calls began coming from tenants up and down the building, with Santana's name often being mentioned. What was the man trying to do?

Guinan began to feel the effects of this rather strongly. He was spending all his time and lots of money responding to these calls, making him afraid to pick up the phone, sending him home in a foul mood, pushing him into long periods of brooding, both at the office and at home—a condition Valerie found very irritating. This wasn't his style. And this change impacted their way of life.

He began to drink more and to lose interest in living their free-spirited social life. His venture into real estate was fast becoming a losing proposition, and all his negative thoughts about it seemed to focus on a single word: Santana.

The clincher came in the form of a letter, signed by all tenants, with Santana's name first, practically demanding that the "corridors" on all floors be redone, with improved lighting, new wall coverings to replace what was there but was still in good condition, and carpeting over the lovely old imported tile floors to reduce the noise of traffic. What corridors? With only four units to a floor? And what traffic? With only four tenants to a floor, going in and out, maybe once or twice a day?

He tried to satisfy this one by simply having old Mr. Landini put larger bulbs in the antiquated fixtures. He quickly received another letter, signed by all tenants, assuring him that this was not an acceptable improvement. And once again, lo, Santana's name led all the rest.

Guinan contacted his lawyer, Dave Goldman. Did he have to respond to this barrage of demands he was getting from the tenants in the building? Goldman reviewed the lease agreement form and advised him as to which demands he had to meet and how much time he was allowed in complying. There was certainly nothing in the leases that required him to refurbish and carpet the elevator landings.

Guinan looked up the number and dialed. Santana's wife answered and told him that Santana would not be home for two days, that he was away on a business trip. Guinan impatiently waited the two days and called back at around five in the afternoon. Santana wasn't home yet, but should be arriving from his office shortly. Guinan decided to go over and confront Santana, to try to find out what the man was trying to do.

He took a taxi from his office to The Albion. He entered the lobby with his passkey, rode the elevator to the fourth floor, and knocked on the door for 4-D. Santana opened the door cordially, inviting him inside.

Guinan glanced quickly around, finding the decor distinctly Southwestern, about as Mexican as was possible within the limitations of a typical two-bedroom unit in an old New York apartment house. The furniture was of a good quality "ranchy" character, and a large, authentic-looking Indian rug covered the living room floor. A huge sombrero hung on the wall above the sofa. The several paintings in the room all contained cactus.

But if the room smacked of Old Mexico, Guinan noted that Santana, although a bit Mexican in facial appearance was very much corporate American in manner and dress. Tassel-tie shoes, flannel slacks, a button-down shirt and repp-striped, silk tie, a veritable Ivy Leaguer. With an infectious smile, the man grabbed Guinan's hand and shook it vigorously. Mrs. Santana entered the room. She was definitely not Mexican, but WASPish in appearance, attractive and seemingly charming. She smiled and greeted him.

"Well," Santana said, grinning, as he looked Guinan up and down, "now we see the man that goes with the voice. A big, good-looking Irishman, just as I expected. Can I fix you a drink? Big, good-looking Irishmen usually like a drop or two this time of day. Right, Matt?"

Guinan might have liked accepting the seemingly good-natured offer, but he sensed that he was being manipulated. "Thanks, no."

"You sure, now? Don't get the impression that our liquor cabinet is limited to tequila, our national poison. Matter of fact, I'm not even sure I have any on hand at the moment. Who can drink the stuff? But we do have single malt Scotch, Beefeaters, Stoli, even Bushmill's for you Irish types, in fact, most anything you'd want. Or how about a cold Heineken?"

God, I'd, love one. "Thanks, no." But he smiled, something he hadn't intended doing on this visit. He hadn't expected Santana's personality to be so disarming, and wondered how he was going to be able to say what he'd come to say.

"Well, let me tell you, Matt—mind if I call you Matt?—we all think you're doing a great job here. A great job. First class all the way. Keep up the good work, and with my help, pretty soon you're gonna have one of the nicest buildings in the neighborhood."

That did it, you son of a bitch! "*Keep up the good work, and with my help . . .*" "That's what I came to speak to you about, Mr. Santana." Guinan felt the heat rising under his clothes but concentrated on remaining outwardly calm. "I came to ask you to stop helping me. And the rest of the tenants. Don't help them, either. You're creating a problem for me."

"Come on, Matt, baby, we all got your letter telling us what a stellar landlord you wanted to be. I've just been trying to be a good Samaritan. What's wrong with that?"

The grin on the fat little face was no longer an engaging playful grin. It was something entirely different, and Guinan's temperature continued to rise. He suppressed a strong urge to take a swing at that face. "Mr. Santana, my phone is ringing off the wall with tenants calling about all sorts of nitpicking little things. Things they should take care of themselves. As well as outrageous requests—no, not requests, demands—for stuff not covered in the lease. I want you to stop creating this problem for me or I'm going to be forced to take some sort of action—"

"Just what sort of action do you have in mind, Matt?" Santana interrupted.

"I'll talk to my lawyer. I hope I've made myself clear, Santana." He studied Santana's face. A faint smile persisted, but it wasn't a real smile. It was a look of challenge, of picking up the gauntlet. Guinan glanced in Mrs. Santana's direction, but she had disappeared. He turned and let himself out. He walked across the tiled landing to the elevator.

★ ★ ★ ★ ★

A few days later a call came in from Mr. Landini, announcing that the elevator wasn't working. Guinan phoned Goldman, his lawyer, who advised that this was a complaint he should act upon at once, but Guinan decide to drag his feet for a few days. Let Mr. Santana and the rest of them walk up and down the steps a couple of times. It would do them good. But when the complaints persisted throughout that day, particularly from an elderly tenant on an upper floor, Guinan felt a strong sense of urgency about getting it fixed quickly. He got the name of the company that routinely serviced the elevator in the past and dialed.

The next day he heard from them. "Mr. Guinan?"

"Yes."

"Mr. Guinan, I'm John O'Reilly, the service manager here at Standard Elevator. My guys checked out the elevator in your building yesterday, and they brought me out there today, and, well, to tell you the truth, there's something a little funny about your elevator problem."

"My first question is, were you able to get it fixed?"

"Oh, I'm afraid it won't happen that fast. Not this one."

"I hope it won't take too long. We need it fixed right away."

"That's an old unit in there, Mr. Guinan. It's going to need a whole new controller, and that could take some time. And some serious money. I felt you oughta be warned about this."

"How much time is it going to take?"

"Well, we've got to locate a suitable replacement controller and prepare a proposal, and get you to sign it, and then order the unit, get it shipped, and schedule a team over there to install it and check it out."

"Mr. O'Reilly, we've got to get it fixed. Some of the old people in the building are prisoners there without that elevator. How long are we talking?"

"Probably three, four weeks. Maybe a little less."

"Jesus! And offhand, how much is it going to cost?"

"Hard to say 'til we price out that controller. But like I said, we're talking a whole new unit, and it won't be cheap."

"Ball park figure?"

"Probably around thirty thousand."

"Shit! And Mr. O'Reilly, what's so funny about this situation?"

"Sir?"

"A few minutes ago you said there was something funny about the problem with our elevator. What's funny about it? I can't find anything to laugh about. I feel more like crying."

"Oh. Sorry. I certainly didn't mean funny that way . . . Mr. Guinan, do you know of anyone who'd have any reason to want to . . . how should I say this? . . . who'd want to sabotage that elevator?"

Santana! "Are you serious?"

"Well, lemme tell ya, it's an old unit, but it's been running just fine for a lotta years. But listen to this. When I went up top to the motor room with the mechanics, they opened the controller cabinet and showed me some small traces of water inside there. And as I'm sure you know, last thing you're wanting to find in one of those cabinets is any water. You understand that."

Santana! "You found water? Jesus H. Christ! Anyway go on."

"Well, after going over the unit with them, it looks to me like someone who knew what he was doing simply went there and threw a bucket of water on the wiring and stuff so it shorted everything out."

Santana! "Are you serious?"

"That's the way it looks. And then I guess he must have turned off the main power switch and tried to towel up the water, because it looked like someone had wiped around in there. You could tell from the way the traces of dust inside the unit had been wiped up. But not all of it. And he didn't get all the water. Because, as I said, we found a little in places he wouldn't have been able to reach with a towel. And the guts of that unit is a mess. It's an old relay logic unit. Nothing but relays. No solid state. And everything's burned up. You know how you can look at wires to tell they've been arcing? You know how the ends of wires can look burnt and melted?"

Santana! "Sure. Of course I do."

"Well, I don't have any proof of anything, and I know this sounds a little far-fetched, but I'm just telling you, I think somebody's been into that controller with a bucket of water. At least that's the way it looked to us."

Santana! "Well, regardless of what happened, we've got to get the thing running again. Will you work on it and get back to me as soon as you can?"

"We'll get on it, Mr. Guinan."

"I mean, soon. Absolutely as soon as possible. I can't leave those people without an elevator."

★ ★ ★ ★ ★

Guinan had received the call from the elevator company several days before the end of the month, when rent checks were due from the tenants, and by the fourth day of the following month, no checks had been received in the office. Usually, the checks began to trickle in a few days before the end of the month, and most were in by two or three days into the new one. A reaction to the elevator problem? Possibly, from a few tenants. But from all of them? It just wouldn't happen from top to bottom in the building unless there was something going on beneath the surface. *Santana!*

Guinan had rushed a letter out to all the tenants, apologizing for the inconvenience, and assuring them that the elevator service company was working diligently to get the thing back into operation as quickly as possible after its total and unexplainable shutdown. But, still, nobody was paying the rent. Nobody. This called for at least a couple of phone inquiries.

He scanned the list of tenants and called a family named Abelson in 2-B. Second floor. Only one flight up. And what's walking up one flight? Why, hell, most of the houses in the world were two-story houses out of choice! He called and Mrs. Abelson answered, and she seemed embarrassed when he identified himself and explained why he'd called.

"Tell me, Mrs. Abelson, is having to walk up one flight of stairs sufficient justification for not paying your rent? Just one flight, for a short time, while the elevator is being repaired as a result of its strange ailment? You'll recall when I took over the building that I wrote you and told you I wanted to do a good job of keeping everybody happy. But I can't afford to just sit around and do nothing if people don't pay their rent."

"To my husband you should probably talk. He did it to help the people on the upper floors."

"What? Help them how?"

"Well, from upstairs a man came around and asked everybody to help. He said it would get the elevator fixed a lot faster if everybody held back the rent money."

"Tell me who the man was."

"Well, I guess it's all right to say. Santana, I think his name was. Santana, or something like that. Fourth floor."

"A very persuasive man. Right?"

"I guess you could say that. Yes."

★ ★ ★ ★ ★

In his mind's eye, as he spent the rest of the day brooding, Guinan repeatedly watched Santana, wearing rubber gloves, creep up the stairs in the middle of the night, slip inside the motor room, which should have been locked, open the door to the cabinet, toss in the bucket of water, and then jump back and sit on his fat haunches and stare with his playful smile at the fireworks as wires and switches and relays sparked and fumed and sputtered, shorting out everything in the box. In some of his run-throughs of this fantasy, he had Santana even wearing the huge sombrero from his living room wall.

Then he watched Santana pick up a towel and meticulously wipe around, taking pains to get all the water. But he couldn't get it all. It's impossible to get every trace. And while he was sopping up water, he was also leaving wiping patterns in the accumulated dust inside the unit.

But, so what? Accuse the man? How could he establish that Santana had done such a thing? Tell the police to check for fingerprints? There would be fingerprints, possibly quite a few, from mechanics over the years, but none of Santana's. Santana would be too smart for that. So what could he tell the police? What would his story be? Santana didn't like me and didn't want to pay his rent, so he wrecked the elevator and then organized a rent strike because the elevator didn't work? How would the police react to a story like that?

He watched the second hand on a wall clock move slowly around. It was almost four and he'd wasted the whole day doing nothing, just staring at the clock and replaying the fantasy about Santana. He finally decided he had to have a showdown with his friend Mr. Santana. Face to face. He'd go over there at around five-thirty or six. Santana should be home by then. And he wouldn't call Dave Goldman first. Dave would only discourage him from going, and he was in no mood to be discouraged.

He walked out of his office, down to the street, and across to the dark stillness of his favorite little watering hole. He needed a bit of reinforcement before cabbing over to The Albion.

"You're awfully quiet today, Mr. Guinan," Paul, the shiny-domed bartender said to him.

"Yeah. I got a problem."

"And you don't wanta talk about it?"

"No." He'd planned to nurse just one double Scotch the whole time he was there waiting, but found he needed at least one more. And then, one more after that. But no sweat. He'd had some of his most productive afternoons after three doubles at lunch. Then he went out and hailed a taxi.

When he arrived at the building, he realized that he needed someone to buzz him in. He'd left his passkey at the office. Should he go back for it? No! Let Santana buzz him in. He pressed Santana's button on the intercom system.

"Who is it?" Mrs. Santana answered.

"Mrs. Santana, I need to talk to your husband."

"Who is this?"

"It's Matt Guinan, Mrs. Santana. Could you buzz me in?"

A short delay, and then, Santana. "What do you want, Matt?"

"I want to talk to you. Will you please buzz me in?"

"I . . . don't think so. I don't think I like the way you sound, right now."

"Santana! Press the goddamn button!"

"I'm afraid that doesn't seem like such a hot idea to me."

At that moment an elderly couple walked into the vestibule and eyed him apprehensively as the husband used his key to unlock the door. Guinan quickly stepped through the door with them, muttering that he'd forgotten his and forcing a friendly smile. He made small talk about weather with them as they walked up the steps together. They went into a door on the third floor and flipped the deadbolt behind them as he continued up the steps.

He reached Santana's door and knocked.

"We don't need any, today," Santana said.

"Mr. Santana, would you open the door? I'd like to talk to you." As he said it, Guinan realized his voice was a little louder and a little stronger than he'd meant it to be.

"Well, I've got nothing to say to you. If you've something you just have to tell me, write it in a letter and I'll take it under advisement." There was a trace of a chuckle in his voice.

"Santana, open the goddamn door! I want to talk to you."

"The feeling's not mutual. Go away."

"OPEN THE GODDAMN DOOR, YOU HEAR?"

The door to another apartment opened and a middle-aged couple walked out and toward the stairs. They paused, looked at Guinan, and then quickened their pace.

Guinan wanted to say something credible and friendly to them, but he was too far gone. He just stared back, and as soon as they had turned the corner and started down the steps, he pounded on the door with the side of his fist. "SANTANA, OPEN THE FUCKING DOOR! YOU HEAR ME?" The footsteps on the stairs paused for a prolonged moment and then resumed at a slower pace.

"We just left by the back door," Santana yelled. "See you around."

"THERE IS NO BACK DOOR! NOW OPEN THE FUCKING DOOR!"

"We're using our parachutes."

"OPEN THE DOOR! NOW!"

"Bye-bye."

Guinan threw his shoulder against the door, and it didn't give way, but he felt a slight splintering. He threw his shoulder again and did more damage. Then again, and again, and the upper panel gave way. He pushed through it with his hand, and saw Santana in the middle of the room. He reached inside and turned the doorknob, but the door didn't open. He fumbled upward from the knob and found a deadbolt. He turned it and the door opened, allowing him to stride into the room.

"You dumb knocker," Santana said, "you're gonna be going to jail. You know that? You just broke and entered."

"That's not all I'm going to break." He moved toward Santana. "Just who the hell do you think you are?" he yelled. "Wrecking the elevator and then organizing a rent strike because there's no elevator service. Is that your idea of some kind of a joke?"

"What is wrong with the elevator? Matter of fact, that's something I've been meaning to call you about. But you certainly don't expect us to pay rent when the thing's not working. This is not exactly some el cheapo, rent-controlled building you've got here . . . Hey, Matt, cool it, man. What the hell's with you? What are you doing coming at me? I wouldn't suggest coming any closer. You wanta be in real deep shit?"

"You slimy little bastard! I can't believe you'd fuck up that elevator like that!" Guinan kept coming, his eyes focused on the grin that was beginning to fade from the fat little face. Out of the corner of his eye, he saw Santana's wife standing in the doorway at the end of the room looking frightened, but he kept coming, in short but deliberate steps.

And when he got close, he yielded to an uncontrollable need and swung out with one of his clenched fists, hitting Santana flush on the side of the face. Santana's wife screamed as he staggered and cried out in pain but didn't go down. He swung at Santana's stomach with his other fist doubling him over, and then hit him in the face knocking him to the floor.

"You stupid asshole!" Santana yelled, gasping for breath from the shot to his belly. "You're in real deep shit now, sucker! Now you're really gonna be going down."

Guinan looked apologetically at Santana's horrified wife but couldn't manage to say anything. He turned, and as he walked out the door, he heard Santana yell, "You're mine now, sucker!" He'd made a bad mistake. A truly bad one. In all his adult life, he'd never struck another person. He hardly ever raised his voice. Suddenly trembling, he hurried down to the street and hailed a cab.

★ ★ ★ ★ ★

He knew exactly who was at the door when he heard the bell. He'd been home for a little over an hour and had had several more drinks. To Valerie's dismay, he'd recounted his afternoon's experiences and then started drinking. He walked uncertainly to the door and opened it.

"Mr. Guinan?"

"I'm Guinan."

"Mr. Guinan," the plainclothes cop said, looking at the glass in his hand. "I'm Detective Barone from the Thirteenth Precinct, and this is my partner, Detective Heinrich. We have a warrant for your arrest." Both cops flashed their shields. "We'd like to ask you to come to precinct headquarters with us."

"Don't I get to tell my side of the story, first?"

"Sure. If you've got a side to tell. We'll want to take your statement, whatever it is, when we get there."

Valerie walked into the room to see what was happening, and a look of shock crossed her face when the second cop pulled out a set of handcuffs.

"What the . . . ?" Guinan said. "Hey, guys, come on. Put those away. I'm not going to run or anything." And as he said it, even he could hear himself slur the words. He was sloshed.

"It's the usual routine," Barone said. "We might have made an exception in your case, but considering the charge,

184

and considering the condition you're in, let's stick to the routine."

"Can I call my lawyer to meet me there?"

"You can call him from there."

"How long will I be there?"

"You're guaranteed arraignment within twenty-four hours. Maybe tonight. Tomorrow, the latest. At that time, you should be able to post bail, or whatever. It'll be up to the judge."

"You mean you're going to . . . lock me up 'til then?"

"For this charge, I'd say you'll be retained until your arraignment. Yes."

Guinan looked helplessly at Valerie, who stood watching in total disbelief. He set his glass down. "Please, guys, do you really have to use handcuffs? Come on. I've got neighbors."

"I think we'd better stick to the routine."

"Shit!" Guinan held out his wrists.

"In back, please." Heinrich said. He grabbed Guinan's hands, pulled them behind him, and snapped on the cuffs.

As they led him toward the door with Valerie watching, he tried to think of something funny to say but couldn't come up with anything. He finally said, "Call Dave and tell him to come to the Thirteenth Precinct. Right, guys? You said the Thirteenth?" Then, he just listened as Barone began reciting the Miranda.

★ ★ ★ ★ ★

Guinan sat in front of the huge, clear desk and studied the face of Alexander Hammond, the ultra-prominent criminal defense lawyer, as the man quietly scanned the one file in front of him.

"Your attorney, Dave Goldman, said you wanted me to represent you," Hammond said.

"Yes."

"Dave and I reviewed the case at length. I hope you know that you're in serious trouble."

"What about my side of the story? Are you sure you're familiar with everything Santana did?"

"Organizing a rent strike is not a criminal act. You should have let Goldman help you deal with that through the various legal options open to you."

"What about the elevator?"

"If it could have been established that Santana did in fact do intentional damage to that elevator, that might have helped your case. But the police did investigate your claim that Santana was responsible for the elevator and could find absolutely nothing that tied him to it. You may as well face the music, Mr. Guinan. You're on the hook for an aggravated assault charge."

"Well, I want to fight the charge, anyway, Mr. Hammond. Anyone who looks at all aspects of the case has got to get the picture. Do you know what that elevator control system cost?"

"The prosecution has an open and shut case against you, Mr. Guinan. You broke the man's door down, you forced your way into his home, and you attacked him. In front of his wife. And they have other witnesses to your violent state who heard you screaming profanities in front of his door and who heard you start to break it down. And the cops who picked you up shortly afterward reported that you were heavily intoxicated. Here. Take a look at this. One of their exhibits. You probably haven't seen it." He handed Guinan a photograph from the file.

The photograph was of Santana with one side of his face bruised and swollen. Guinan winced and tossed the photograph back. "I still want to fight this. He's a rotten son of a bitch for doing what he did, and I want justice."

"Weren't you listening, Mr. Guinan? You're on the hook. My advice to you is to plead guilty and let me get you the best deal I can in negotiating with the prosecutor. You're obviously not a criminal type. You're a prominent businessman, a tax-paying citizen with an absolutely spotless past. You should get a very minimal, and probably even a suspended, sentence."

"But I'll still have a criminal record. Right? I don't deserve that. I want justice."

"What do you want to do? Go to trial? I can't guarantee that you'll be cleared. Dealing with a jury is always a crapshoot. And it'll cost you a lot more money."

"Mr. Hammond, Dave sent me to you because he said you were the best around, and I had the best chance of being cleared with your help. For what he did, Santana deserved a hell of a lot more than what he got from me, and I at the very least want justice for myself."

Hammond shrugged his shoulders, and then his demeanor changed, taking on a sudden intensity as he studied Guinan. "Well, it might not be impossible that I could get you your justice. But there's a major question involved here."

"Which is?"

"Mr. Guinan, just how much justice can you afford?"

Guinan stared at him in confusion. "What? What do you mean?"

"How much justice can you afford, Mr. Guinan?"

"I'm not sure I understand the question."

"Assuming you want *absolute assurance* that you will be cleared of all charges, and would not be satisfied with a brief or suspended sentence, or a little community service, your defense could cost you a great deal of money. How much are you in a position to pay for that defense?"

"I want to do whatever's necessary to be *cleared* of the

charges. Which I'm confident will happen with your help."

"Well, what can you afford? Give me a number."

"If it means going to trial, okay, I want to go to trial."

"A number, Mr. Guinan."

Guinan shrugged. "What do your services for handling my kind of case usually come to?"

"A number, Mr. Guinan."

Guinan sighed. "Oh, I don't know. Forty thousand? Fifty? Maybe sixty? Maybe a little more? That's about the limit of what cash I can raise, I suppose. You know. Without some kind of nasty lien on the business."

"And if I suggested that it might take three to four times that amount? Maybe more, for the kind of assurance you want?"

He studied Hammond. "Is that what your fee would be for defending me in a court trial? Or are we talking . . . something . . . else?"

"What I'm talking is my estimate of what it would cost to be absolutely sure we'll get you off scot-free. Do you understand? And there'd probably be no need for a court trial."

"You're talking something else." Guinan took a breath. "I think I get the message . . . well, I can't afford that, Mr. Hammond, but I still won't plead guilty. I want to go to trial, and win, and with your reputation for handling cases like this, I'm convinced that we've got a chance. I still believe no court would convict me once they have all the facts. Can I afford you for that?"

"To go to trial? I would think so. As long as you understand that I can't guarantee you the acquittal you expect. You're sure this is the course of action you'd like to take, despite the fact that it does not follow the advice I've offered you?"

"I want justice, Mr. Hammond, and what I need is your

representing me and all the facts known. Then, I'll get it."

Hammond studied Guinan at length before speaking. Then with a shrug, "Well, it's clear you don't 'get it.' Considering the case the prosecution has, I think you're more than a little optimistic. But it's your decision, and if you wish to move ahead on that basis, I'm willing to give it my best shot."

★ ★ ★ ★ ★

Guinan grew increasingly relaxed as the brief trial moved along in the sparsely occupied courtroom. The jury seemed benign enough. And no question about it, Hammond was good. He had a natural flair for the dramatic. He drove his points home with force: Matt Guinan was anything but a criminal, or even a violent person, but instead a highly respected member of the business community who had been goaded into a brief act of passion by the mean-spirited wiles of an unconscionable individual clearly intent on causing Guinan great trouble and expense. The aftereffects to this individual were minimal, a few well-deserved bruises which were gone in a matter of days. No permanent damage whatever.

On the other side of the room the prosecutor went about his work in a totally undramatic, strictly business manner, calling Santana and the other witnesses to the stand, and interrogating them quietly to establish the factual details of the case. Nothing more. The judge charged the jury and sent them out after reviewing the applicable details of the criminal code.

Guinan felt very much at ease as the jury went out, and he even looked forward to their return so that he could turn and smile at Santana, sitting near the back of the room. During the trial, he'd studied the prosecutor and the judge wondering if they would have been the recipients of the pay-offs alluded to by Hammond. Obviously, this wasn't needed.

The jury returned within an hour and the judge was called back to the bench. Guinan was almost grinning as the judge asked for a verdict and the foreman got to his feet. When Guinan heard the word, "GUILTY," he felt as if he'd been kicked in the pit of his stomach. He looked in anguish at Hammond who returned his stare without comment.

As Guinan was led out of the room, Santana walked over to the aisle, and when Guinan passed, he grinned and playfully jumped back, saying to the cops escorting him, "Be careful with him. He's dangerous."

★ ★ ★ ★ ★

Guinan's sentence was set at six months and he served four at Rikers Island before being released. During that period, Valerie returned to her family out in the Hamptons, and only came to visit him once, an event she found distasteful.

Fed up with New York because of all that had happened, Guinan quickly sold the apartment building at a loss and moved his business to New Jersey. He bought Val a lovely home and fully expected life to return to normal. But she soon found life in Jersey painfully dull, considerably less to her liking after the fun years in the city, and as a result of this, along with the fact that their relationship was already badly strained because of the ugly stigma of what had happened to him, she left him.

And so much for life and affordable justice in the Big Apple.

We spent a weekend in Vermont some years back with friends who own a ski chalet right on a mountain, and since I'd given up skiing for life after two lessons, I decided to just stay inside and see if I could write something. As I watched the activity out the window, seeing single skiers riding the T-bar lift to the top of the slope, a thought of unnerving horror occurred to me: what an interesting (and helpless) target they'd make for a sharpshooter at the top!

I'm Sorry, Mr. Griggs

Sighting through the heavy snowfall, he lined up the cross-hairs on her chest as the cable brought her into view. He focused on a brightly colored emblem on her parka, perfectly and conveniently located, and after following it for a second or two he squeezed off the shot. The girl heaved against the safety bar, then slumped back into the ornate seat. Another perfect hit.

How many was that? Eleven? An even dozen? Maybe even thirteen. He had lost count. All clean kills. Only one had required two shots. A big man who had shifted in the seat just as he fired. The man began struggling after the first bullet hit and he fired a second with greater concentration, instantly stopping the man's wild thrashing movements. But he'd hated having to fire a second time—it was a blow to his otherwise perfect score.

He leaned the rifle against the wall of the shed and pressed the handle of the chair-lift drive. A little farther. Another twenty feet or so. As the chair glided into the landing area beneath the shed he cut the power, just as the ski-patrol attendant would have done to help a skier out of the seat.

He moved quickly up to the chair, pushed the sagging body backward, raised the safety bar, and pulled the man onto the platform. Then, turning him over, he gripped the man under his armpits and dragged him along the planked floor to the back of the platform and toward the convenient little hollow behind the shed. When he reached the dropoff into the hollow, he gave the body a push and then a kick and watched it slide on its own, downward and into the pile with the others.

He hustled back into the shed and grabbed the ski poles out of the holder on the lift-chair. He wheeled and hurled them toward the array of bodies, skis, and poles. Then he returned to the lift drive control and started it again. Time to bring another nice live target into view.

The girl in the seat still some fifty feet out showed no signs of life. Why should she? Fish in a barrel. A human shooting gallery. A helpless human form moving slowly in a set path at 50 yards or less. And with a scope sight. Almost unsportsmanlike.

He thought about snipers who'd made the news in recent years. Kids with .22's, popping at cars on parkways near big cities, never hoping to score a clean kill. Or butchers, hauling an arsenal to the top of some tall building and blasting away at everybody in sight. Suicidal exhibitionists! Morons! With no hope whatever of walking away from it. No imagination. No planning. No class. He'd show the world how it was done by a master. A real master. And in the process he'd return a small favor to the ski community.

His mind riffled back through the countless interviews he'd had with the honchos of all the ski mountains.

"I'm sorry, Mr. Griggs, but we've completed our recruiting for this year's ski patrol."

"But, sir, I'm no ordinary skier. Look, I can make these

guys you've been hiring look like beginners."

"I'm afraid we're just full up at this time."

"All I ask is a chance. Before Vietnam I was the lead in-structor at Stratton. I taught the advanced classes. I even trained most of the ski patrol. All the college hotshots. Don't you understand? I'm a pro. The best."

"I can appreciate that, Mr. Griggs, but we're just not taking on any more men this season."

"Look, somebody's got to give me a break. Skiing's my life . . . It's because of my war record, isn't it?"

"I'm sorry, Mr. Griggs, we're just not hiring."

"You've been running ads, looking for guys."

"We've finished filling our roster."

"You know, this isn't a fair shake. I couldn't help all that publicity. I had no way of stopping it. I didn't want it. Be-sides, I was acquitted. Completely. They let me go clean. I was only a noncom. I was acting under orders at all times."

"I'm sorry, Mr. Griggs."

"Look, if you'd been over there as long as I was, you'd have reacted the same. All I wanted was to stay alive and get back. It got to where you couldn't tell the women from the men, or the kids, either, for that matter. There were even in-stances where our guys *did* get it from kids or women. That was a mess, over there. You've got to have been there to know about it."

"I'm sorry, Mr. Griggs."

"Look, I was given a clean bill and all I ask is to get back into skiing. I couldn't help all that publicity. You can't keep me out forever. I want to make my living on skis."

"I'm sorry, Mr. Griggs, I'm sorry, Mr. Griggs, I'm sorry . . ."

He set himself and took a breath and followed the next target that moved into view and fired and smiled at the whispered crack of the silenced rifle and at the way the young man lurched in the seat and then collapsed. Another clean hit. And he watched the chairs move closer. Almost time to stop the lift and take off the chick with the plugged emblem.

He was a master at two skills. Skiing wasn't his only area of expertise. He could shoot. And he liked shooting. Back in Nam he had become his company's cleanup man. As the unrelenting tension of the hide-and-seek fighting worked on him, he found he could best keep his head by taking pleasure in doing what he did well. If he was to kill to survive, he might as well be good at it. And to be good at it he had to like doing it.

His C.O. had recognized his instinctual capacity and had given him all the "special assignments." He soon grew to feed on them. He liked good clean kills because they were a challenge. Tough to pull off in the jungle. But he also liked those "special assignments," the closer-range "less competitive" jobs. And he had liked doing them with neatness and finesse.

He stopped the lift and began struggling with the dead girl's body. She'd been good-looking. A dish. He would have liked knowing her a little better before she decided to take the chair-lift up Old Imperial that particular morning. But too bad. There would be other chicks.

Since she was light and feminine, he put his shoulder into her waist and hoisted her up and carried her to the edge of the little pocket where he had been piling the bodies. He dropped her onto the incline and she slid down among the others. Too bad about her. She was nice. Really nice. She'd picked the wrong day to ski Old Imperial.

How many more should he take before skiing down and driving away? He probably had enough already to leave his mark on the ski world for a long time. How many people would start thinking twice and maybe just stay home and watch TV before planning a weekend of skiing? A weekend of being a helpless target, dangling from a lift-cable, moving slowly toward the top of a mountain? The operators were going to pay for keeping him out.

He'd returned from Nam in the summer and could hardly wait for the snow. But that one sticky morning when the story broke about the incident in the town by the river marked the beginning of a nightmare even greater than all those he'd had in the stinking jungle. Who the hell ever heard of locking somebody up for defending his country? "Everything I did I did under orders, sir."

"Some of our witnesses feel that you seemed to have more than just a desire to carry out orders on the morning in question."

"Sir, I was doing as I was told. We were at war, regardless what college kids might say. I was mainly interested in survival. It could have been them or me."

"That's for the court to decide."

The punishing uncertainties of the trial and the confinement dragged out for months, during which he was restricted inside the base, and he watched the season come and go, reading the daily ski reports when he could get a paper. He was finally acquitted and released. But his name, Wesley Griggs, had become a familiar phrase, almost a synonym for the senseless excesses of the war.

As soon as the next season approached, he began his tour of the Northeastern ski areas, looking for a job, a full-time skiing job, ready at last to begin living again, to buckle on the new boots and the gleaming new Mark II's and hit the slopes and let the ski air with its exhilarating clarity flush the glooms and stenches of jungles and army posts out of his head.

He sensed he was a marked man after the first job interview. He was apprehensive on the second and the turndown came without surprise. Thereafter he went from mountain to mountain, playing out the complete dialogue, all the way to the final, repeated, "I'm sorry, Mr. Griggs." Anticipating each rejection, he would become so antagonistic the operators found him oppressive, almost frightening.

After he was completely certain no operator would have the likes of him with his record and reputation working their precious mountain, he decided to spend a little time hunting. Get out his rifle, his other love, and get off a round or two at a deer. After watching the animal drop with a single, clean, perfect shot he suddenly made up his mind about what he was going to do. He immediately began planning details.

He had been a ski fanatic even as a child, a scrawny kid, often cutting school, always skulking around one or another of the mountains near his home in Vermont, listening to instructors teach rich kids, sneaking onto the lifts or stealing lift passes off jackets in the main lodge and skiing the slopes from sunup to dusk on a progression of stolen skis. He dropped out of high school in his junior year, bought an old heap, and drove from mountain to mountain, all over New England, satisfying himself that he was master of every slope. Having become a brilliant skier, he managed to get into a ski patrol the following year and within two more years was the youngest No. 1 ever in the patrol at Stratton, one of his favorite mountains with its profusion of runs. Then he was drafted.

When he began planning his payoff to the operators for their kindness and consideration, he remembered the Old Imperial run at Connally Mountain, a tough isolated slope with an antiquated lift, bucket-like seats strung out some 75 feet apart, slow-moving, the patrol member in the shed at the top stopping the lift and helping each skier out of the bucket. The run was steep in places, and long, a challenging and satisfying run for even the best skiers, which explained its popularity despite the time-consuming ride to the top.

And he also remembered the bend in cable direction as the run approached the summit so that only two chairs at a time were in view from the shed. He had only to get a rifle with a removable stock, ride to the top of Old Imperial with the dismantled weapon strapped under his coat, shoot the attendant in the back, and take over the mountain. After making a good solid kill he'd simply leave the lift stopped, ski down, get into his car, and drive away. He'd be gone before the patrol could get up to the summit on the "cat" to check out the problem . . .

He watched the next chair turn the corner and move into view with another target, a guy in a fancy sweater and stocking cap. No heavy jacket. Probably a good skier. This would be the last one. Pop him off and call it quits. He'd gotten enough to leave his mark, to make that day on Connally long remembered. No use taking unnecessary chances.

He sighted in on a couple of stripes in the sweater's design, a hair left of center. Perfect. Follow the target for a second or two, maintain concentration, squeeze. But a split second before he fired, the skier reached down to touch his boot. He'd missed completely!

The skier looked up abruptly, stared at the shed and at patches of woods to the right and to the left. Then he flipped up the safety bar on the chair and leaped quickly out of the seat, not even bothering to take his poles, dropping the ten or fifteen feet to the snow and falling over.

How had he missed? He had to get off another shot! Drop him quick before he got to his feet and skied around the bend and out of sight. He lined up on the skier as the skier struggled upright to start downhill. The same two stripes, from the back instead of the front. He squeezed but the gun clicked

197

harmlessly. Damn! Why hadn't he reloaded? Why hadn't he kept count? How could he have been so stupid?

The skier, starting a little slowly without poles, moved downward, gaining speed, and finally swept to the right, around the crook in the slope and out of view.

No need to panic. Just get rid of the gun and ski down. No clues. Nothing. He didn't know from nothing. That's all. No, he didn't see or hear anything. No fingerprints, even if they found the gun. He'd handled it with glove-liners and had rubbed it carefully to make sure. No panic, no panic.

He ran a few yards along the path to the summit, a spot just beyond the little hollow. The bodies were becoming speckled with snow. He stuffed the rifle into a drift near the base of a tree and smoothed over the spot where the gun went in. A few minutes of fresh snow and there'd be no trace. Nothing to worry about.

He hurried back to the shed, set down his skis, and stepped into them. Grabbing his poles and gloves, he moved back along the path. The lift was motionless, the nearest chair containing a crumpled body wearing skis, the second chair empty except for poles. He pushed off, skiing down the slope with style and grace.

The long ride down gave him time to think, to anticipate questions and plan his responses. No, he hadn't seen anything unusual going on. Accidents? No. Anybody with a gun? You kidding me? No.

And no, he didn't know of any reason why nobody'd come down the slope in the last little while. No, he didn't know why the lift wasn't moving—it was running fine when he got up there and he'd taken a bad fall on the way down and had stopped and rested a few minutes to get himself back together.

He began to feel strangely chilled and realized that despite the air temperature and the wind of skiing and the snow in his face, his body was steamy with sweat.

He glanced up at skiers stranded in the unmoving chairs and hoped they'd still be hanging there, freezing their noses off, when he drove away. He looked down and ahead. A good slope. One of the best. Let the people in the chairs watch a pro take it down.

As he reached the lower stretches of the run and the main lodge came into view, he saw the "cat" just starting up the slope, carrying two members of the patrol, each wearing his bright blue jacket and blue hat. They had a long ride to the top. He was moving a lot faster. He had plenty of time. More than enough. He'd had much closer calls than this in Nam.

He continued down toward the area around the main lodge where all the lifts took on their loads and headed up the mountain. Lots of skiers. They'd remember this day at Connally. They might even lose some of their interest in skiing. He had only to get through the crowd unnoticed, over to the parking lot, then get the hell out of here.

As he drew nearer he was able to separate the crowd into individuals. He picked out the skier in the fancy sweater, the one he'd missed with his last shot. The guy was standing in a group, right where the slope leveled out, watching him approach. Nothing to worry about. They couldn't possibly know anything yet.

Several in the group wore the mountain's bright blue jackets. He recognized the honcho who ran the mountain, a big over-age college Joe. He thought about the interview with him several months back and wondered if the creep would remember him. Then he spotted the fat guy who ran the ski school. And one or two more from the patrol. And a cop, the trooper, the big one with the mustache who'd been directing traffic, wearing his shiny, navy-blue jacket with the big badge and the fur collar, and the hat with the fur-lined earmuffs tied up and sticking out like wings. When it became obvious the group was waiting for him, he began plowing and slowed as he reached them.

"Excuse me," the honcho said, "but did you notice what's wrong at the top? The operator has stopped the lift and we don't know why."

No look of recognition. The creep didn't remember him. Still, his heart was pounding. This was it. The last hurdle. The parking lot was less than a hundred yards away. "Uh, everything looked okay to me when I was up top. I noticed the lift stopped, too. Why is that?"

"We thought you might be able to tell *us*. You just came down."

"No, as a matter of fact I left the top some time ago. Had a fall about halfway down. Stopped and rested a while. Sprained my ankle a little." He felt dizzy from his churning pulse and wondered if they could tell.

"You seem all right, now."

"Yeah, it's a lot better."

"This man says someone took a shot at him up there. Did you hear anything that sounded like a shot?"

"Shot? You kidding? What kinda shot? Hell, don't say that. I'll be scared to go back up. No, I didn't hear any shot."

"Did you see anyone with anything that might have been a gun of any kind?" the cop asked. "Anything at all?"

He hesitated, to appear to be trying to remember. "No. Not a thing."

"Well, we've sent up two members of the patrol," the manager said. "We should know something in a few minutes."

"Probably nothing serious." He started to ski slowly out of the group and toward the parking lot.

"Hey," one of the ski patrol said. "What's that all over the shoulder of your jacket? Blood?"

He stopped and froze. His mouth fell open and he looked at all of them, his eyes going from face to face. The chick! He dropped his poles and clutched at his right shoulder with his left hand, still looking from face to face. As he did, his right arm dropped against his side and he felt the box of shells, still about half full, in his jacket pocket. He'd forgotten to bury them with the gun.

"Well? What about it?" The cop studied his face, then reached out and tugged at his shoulder to look at the stain.

He didn't answer.

"I think you'd better wait here with us till the patrol gets to the top," the cop said.

"Uh, I can't. I gotta get going. I really got to go." He thought about trying to run but he was on skis and he'd dropped his poles. And he was surrounded by blue jackets.

"So early?" the cop said. "You've got an eight-dollar lift ticket there and it's not even time to break for lunch yet. You'd just better wait here with us till we hear from the patrol."

The manager squinted at him and said, "You look very familiar. Have we met before?"

But he hadn't even heard the question. He'd just remembered something funny. The blood on his jacket wasn't fresh. He had worn the jacket hunting and had messed it up lifting the doe he'd shot. A silly grin spread across his face and he began to snigger and then laugh uncontrollably.

This may sound corny, maybe, but this story, or at least fragments of it, did come to me in a dream. I did have a close and favorite friend in college named Bert, and he did in fact have an older brother named Harry in Hollywood who he claimed was a producer. In the dream, Bert and I were on a train heading West to visit his brother.

Nadigo

David Klemmer stood at the corner of two streets, shaken with disbelief at how he had come to be there alone. The town was small and flat. He could see the edges of town in all four directions, the faded little houses thinning out into desert. The horizons rippled with heat, exceptional heat for late afternoon in late December. Beyond miles of desert loomed tall bluffs. He was somewhere in Arizona.

The town was old and ugly. Two filling stations, a few parked or slowly moving cars, electric wires, and the black highway with the white line kept the town from being a perfect setting for a western. The buildings and even the sidewalks were mostly wooden, except for aprons to the service stations.

The idea had been preposterous from the beginning. He should never have left New York. Three days before, in the rooms they shared on West 123rd Street, he should have shrugged off Bert's invitation. But Bert's glowing word pictures were more than he had been able to resist.

"The glitter and green of California call," Bert had said. "We leave Wednesday for the Coast."

"Sure, Bert, what I need is a trip to California for the holidays."

But Bert had been serious. And he had the railroad credit card his very rich brother in California had sent. The winter of 1950 was tightening its grip on New York; and California, some far-off land he had never seen, was a tempting contrast to the nearby rumble of trains and the freezing rain outside. Work or no work. Dave had gone past the point of simply weakening. He continued to voice negative noises but in his own mind he had accepted the invitation and was planning to go.

★ ★ ★ ★ ★

The train ride had been all Bert had promised—a kaleidoscope of panoramic landscapes. Yet Dave struggled to keep himself tuned in, absorbed in thoughts of his work, suffering guilt for being away from it. Something in his thesis lab work just wasn't right. "Dave's a chemist," he heard Bert say to a quietly dignified elderly couple across the breakfast table on the third day. "He hates his work so much, that's all he ever thinks about. Me. I'm an English major," Bert continued. "We're going to California for the Christmas break. My brother's got an eleven-sided swimming pool." The couple opposite them studied them quietly, listening but seldom speaking. Outside the window, a brilliant, diamond-clear western day was opening up and sweeping by.

Around mid-afternoon, Bert became sick and began complaining of excruciating stomach cramps. "We've got to get off this train," he said.

"This train's non-stop the rest of the way, Bert. You'll feel better in a little while. We'll be getting into L.A. soon."

"I've got to get off this train."

"This train doesn't stop around here. We're in the middle of nowhere."

"All trains stop." Still holding his stomach, Bert got up and lurched forward.

"Bert, where're you going? Wait. Maybe there's a doctor on the train." Other passengers began to look up at them.

"I'm going to stop the train," Bert answered.

"You can't stop this train," Dave said, starting after him.

"I can stop any train!" He reached the front of the car and reached up for the emergency brake pull with the DO NOT TOUCH Sign.

"No. Bert, no!" Everyone in the car was standing.

Bert grabbed and yanked. Then he dropped into an empty seat and doubled over, holding his stomach.

A conductor burst into the rear of the car and came running up the aisle. "Who the hell pulled the rope?" Passengers began gathering.

"I did," Bert shouted. "Stop the train. I've got to get off." He was rolling from side to side.

"We're in the middle of the desert," the conductor said.

"He's sick. He needs a doctor," Dave said. "Maybe there's a doctor on the train."

The conductor disappeared and the train continued at a slightly slowed pace. Bert began to moan and continued rolling back and forth on the seat. Passengers gathered around them offering suggestions and sympathy. Bert practically cursed them back to their seats.

The conductor returned. "There's a small town in about five miles. You sure you want off?"

"Tell 'em to stop," Bert shouted. "We want off."

"What town is it?" Dave asked.

"We're still in Arizona. I think. That's the best I can tell you." The conductor started down the aisle again.

"Just get us off this goddamn train! You hear?" Bert shouted. Dave looked around quickly at Bert.

In a few minutes the train began slowing down to stop, the clean, rhythmic click of wheels starting to grind and grate.

* * * * *

They stepped from the train into choking heat on a side street in a tiny desert town. There was no railroad station. They were wearing winter clothes. Bert was still doubled over, holding his stomach, moaning. Dave carried their two suitcases. He glanced around and led Bert toward a slightly built-up area alongside a black highway with white lines. "C'mon, Bert, that looks like a main drag. We'll find a doctor."

They walked along the side street, in front of an auto repair shop and several small grubby houses and buildings, until they came to the highway, obviously the main street of the town. Dave looked around for some indication of the name of the town, some business named after it, a lumber-yard, a post office, anything. The buildings were one and two story, mostly wood frame. Fred's Cafe. Sidewalks were wooden all along one side of the road and covered, like in a western. Davis' Feed Store. General supplies. Across the street a dress shop, Mae's, with a garish, black-glass storefront. A drugstore. Hickman's. About two blocks down, two filling stations on opposite corners of an intersection. Standing alone, surrounded by cars, a small brick A&P.

They walked up on the covered sidewalk and approached a young man, perhaps their age, a handsome boy with steel-blue eyes, wavy hair, and neat shirt and slacks. "Could you tell us where we can find a doctor?" Dave asked.

The boy was leaning against a post with a match in his mouth. He straightened up and removed the match. "You two just get off the train? First time I ever saw it stop."

"My friend got sick on the train. Could you tell us where there's a doctor?"

206

"Sure, we got one. Old Doc Finger. He's a good doctor. He'll take care of him."

"Where's he at?"

He pointed down the covered walk. "About six doors down. There's his shingle hanging. Go up the steps."

"Thanks. Incidentally, what town is this?"

"You'd better get your friend on over to Doc Finger's. He looks like he's feeling pretty bad." The handsome boy turned and walked away.

Dave and Bert walked up the steps to a little foyer. A door to the left of the foyer led into a dingy, crowded waiting room. They went in, found two empty chairs, and sat down. Bert was pitched forward in too much pain to remain quiet. Dave did what he could to calm him, finally slumping back to match stares with the other patients, all older men. There was no receptionist, no nurse, no sign of the doctor or of any activity. As Dave stared at the other men sitting quietly, his mind blurred for a moment and he imagined the other men derelicts, rather like sunken boats in low water, one missing an arm, another a leg, an eye or an ear or a nose, even an entire face. One man had a four-inch hole in his chest through which the chair-back was visible. For an instant he thought he heard a train. He shook his head to clear it, and his thoughts wandered back to his thesis work. He cringed.

"If you hate chemistry so much, why don't you get out of it?" Bert often said.

"I've gone too far to turn back. Besides, what else could I do?"

He felt a need and nudged Bert. "Looks like it's going to be a few minutes. I'm gonna go look for a head. Be back." He turned to the man sitting to the other side of him. "Excuse me. Can you tell me where the nearest men's room is?"

The man thought a minute. "Don't know. Probably the

back of the bar and grill across the street."

Dave reached the street and looked for a bar and grill. Probably Fred's Cafe. He crossed and went in. The empty cafe was hot and the air heavy with beer and fried food. The heat was beginning to reach him. The waiting room had been hot. He walked straight to the back of the room and found a door marked MEN. The air in the tiny cubicle was almost unbearable. There was no basin in which to wash his hands.

He headed out, saying thanks to a man in a white paper cap and filthy white apron behind the cash register.

"Come back," the man answered.

As he reached the street, he thought about the crowd in the waiting room and wandered into the drugstore, over to the magazine rack. He stood for a few minutes thumbing through magazines, became absorbed in an article, and squatted to read it. He read another and, realizing some time had passed, dropped the magazine and walked back to the doctor's office. As he headed up the narrow wooden staircase, he found a padlocked steel folding lattice across the foyer. It was like the steel grillwork in front of New York pawnshops. Beyond it, the door to the doctor's office was closed, the glass window dark. He went up to the lattice and shook it.

Back on the street, wondering where Bert could possibly be, he spotted the boy who had directed them to the doctor. He hailed the boy and trotted over to him. "You haven't seen my friend, have you? You know, the one I got off the train with."

The handsome boy grinned at him. "Why? Should I have?" The boy's eyes were so clear blue it was like staring through two holes in his head at the sky beyond.

"I left him in the doctor's office and went out for a few minutes. The place was full of patients. When I got back, the place was locked up with that steel fence."

"Doc Finger's quick. Good hands."

"But where could they have gone? My friend was sick. Is there a hospital?"

"Nearest thing like a hospital is ninety miles. Your friend's probably well now and around someplace looking for you. Doc Finger's pretty good."

"Incidentally, why does he have that steel fence?"

"He keeps a little strong medicine up there. Kids broke in a couple of times."

"Where could I find Doc Finger now?"

"Maybe home if he didn't go hunting."

"Thanks. Incidentally, what's the name of this town?"

"You'd better quit worrying about a little thing like that and find your buddy, seems to me," he said with his persistent unwarm grin. Then he walked off.

Dave looked up and down the highway. There wasn't much activity, and he didn't see Bert anywhere. He could see to the horizon and would spot Bert if he were standing in a crowd five miles away. He went back into the drugstore and asked the old pharmacist if he could use the phone to call Dr. Finger.

"His office is just across the street."

"I just came from there. Place is all locked up." Dave reviewed his story for the old man.

"Sure, help yourself to the phone. Just pick it up and ask Annamarie, that's the operator, for Doc's house."

After several rings, a sullen woman's voice answered.

"I'm looking for Dr. Finger. Are you Mrs. Finger?"

"Yeah. I'm his wife, 'n he ain't here. Call him at his office." She answered as if she couldn't possibly imagine any other approach, as if no one had ever called for him at home before.

Dave repeated his story for her. "Has he called you or said anything about my friend or about taking him to the hospital or anything like that?"

"I ain't heard from him since this morning. Said he might go huntin' when he got through this afternoon."

"Thanks just the same." Dave hung up, looked helplessly at the old druggist and went back out into the street. Sunset was approaching and the town was getting uglier as the light changed. The realization began to slowly descend on him that he was dependent on Bert and the card, that he was in the middle of a nowhere of strangers, with remarkably little money. He clutched at his pants pocket to make sure at least his wallet was still there. He walked back to the intersection of the highway and the street where they bad gotten off the train. Surveying the town, he realized he could walk in and out of every public place in the town in thirty minutes. He had to find Bert.

He stepped into Davis' Feed Store and the sweet heavy smell of sacks of grain hit him. There were farm tools, a rack of rifles, counters stacked with men's work clothing, and two small-screen televisions. He smiled at the proprietor and left.

Black's Men's Shop, one of the few non-wooden buildings. He asked the proprietor if a . . . a stranger—and he described Bert—had been in.

The man laughed sarcastically. No. Nobody fitting that description. Dave flushed with intense dislike for the man and walked out. He surveyed a brightly lit well-stocked appliance store through the large glass window. There was only one person in the store. He stepped inside the dress shop, Mae's, and looked around. A fat proprietress with wild artificially blue-white hair and heavy make-up approached him. He quickly walked out.

He spotted the red white and blue of a revolving barber

pole. An arrow pointed up a flight of stairs: *Sweets Brothers Tonsorial Parlor*. He walked up the steps and through swinging doors into the sweetish stench of barbers' tonics and preparations. Five barber chairs were full and some ten or twelve young men sat in chairs ringing the room. They talked, waiting. This room, with the thick layer of matted hair covering the floor, was clearly one of the town's popular gathering spots. Dave noticed a striking similarity among three of the barbers. The Sweets Brothers. As he looked at them, their similarity, except for height, became more and more remarkable. They were one short, one medium and one tall; but their identical heads were covered with thin blond, almost nonexistent hair, and their faces were pinkish and boyish and bright-lipped, and they had matching incredibly sweet smiling countenances as they chatted with their particular customers of the moment and with each other.

Dave turned and walked quickly out of the shop. As he ran down the steps toward fresh air, he thought he heard the fading sound of a distant train.

When he reached the street, he ran into the handsome blue-eyed boy. "I just thought I heard a train."

The boy shook his head no. "Only passes through once a day and you were on it. You must be hearing things. You look like you just saw a ghost."

"That barber shop up there."

"The Sweets boys?" The boy grinned. "Yeah, they're some matched set. Find your friend yet?"

"Does it look like it?"

"Try the A&P. Maybe he wanted to pick up a few things."

Dave studied the boy for a moment. "Tell me something. What do you do for a living? You work at something? Go to school? Or do you just stand around and help tourists?"

The boy continued grinning. "I ride the range on my

211

trusty steed." He pointed at a '49 Ford parked on the street.

"Is that all?"

"Why? Isn't that enough? You like what you do any better?"

"You don't hang your whole life on doing something you don't want any part of," Bert had once said.

Dave walked away from him and crossed back to the drugstore. "Like to use your phone again," he mumbled at the old pharmacist. He picked up the phone. "Annamarie?" he said, like a native.

"She went home."

"Well, could I have Dr. Finger's house?"

The sullen woman's voice answered after several rings.

"Uh, hello, is Dr. Finger there yet? Or has he called you in the last little while? You may recall I called a little earlier about—"

"I remember ya, and I ain't heard from him."

"Do you know when to expect him?"

"Not if he went huntin'."

"Okay, thanks. Maybe I could call back later."

"I go to bed about nine-thirty."

"Does he have office hours tomorrow morning?"

" 'Course he does. Tomorrow ain't Sunday."

"Okay, thanks." Dave hung up. "I'd like to call the hospital," he said to the old pharmacist.

"Have to charge you fifty cents. That's long distance. Just ask the girl for the hospital."

A voice mouthed, "Something-Hospital," after one ring.

"I'd like to know if you have checked in a new patient there in the past couple of hours. A patient of Dr. Finger's."

"What's the patient's name?"

Dave told her and spelled Bert's last name.

"I'm sorry. Dr. Finger has no patients here at this time."

"Would you just check the name to be sure?" Dave spelled it again.

"There's no one here by that name. Sorry."

Dave paid the pharmacist and walked out into the street. Bert had to be somewhere. He decided to continue his search of every public place in the town. He walked into the beer-and-grease air of Fred's Cafe and looked around. He even walked to the rear of the room and glanced through the open door to the men's room. Again he thought he heard a distant train. He walked back out into the air. It was dusk. Mae's and Black's and Davis' were all closed. Ritter's Grocery, The People's Savings Bank, and Early Brothers Real Estate and General Insurance were closed. The Sweets Brothers' barber pole was still and dark. Red's Whiskey Store was open, but Red sat alone behind the counter, picking his teeth. Dave came to the sheriff's office—the Police, of course—but it, too, was closed.

Dave crossed an intersection to the red-brick A&P. He stepped inside and for a moment felt surrounded by normalcy. It was like all A&P's, bustling with housewives, boys in white aprons, aisle after aisle of brightly displayed groceries. For a moment in the more familiar surroundings he felt more secure and a little hungry. He paced the area just behind the check-out, looking up and down each aisle. He went down the last aisle and into the open area in front of the meat display. Bert wasn't in there but then, why should he be? Why possibly? But where was he? His momentary sense of security faded. Dr. Finger was apparently his only lead and where was Dr. Finger?

He went back out into the street. The town's two filling stations were at the next corner, one closed. He went into the other, which wasn't busy.

"You haven't by any chance seen a stranger in a gray jacket

and gray pants, maybe with two suitcases."

"Friend of yours?" the attendant asked.

"Yeah. Can't see why he would have come out this way, but I'm looking everywhere. We got off the train when he got sick and—"

The attendant jumped up and dashed out to pump gas for a car that had just pulled in. Then another rolled in. "Haven't seen him," the attendant shouted, looking back at Dave.

Dave walked out to the street and looked toward the edge of town. The highway was flanked on each side by houses. Several hundred yards out stood a small horizontal white sign on a white post. A town name sign, maybe. Dave started walking toward it and then broke into a trot. The sign was farther away than it had appeared. He finally reached it. In the rapidly dimming light, he read, NADIGO, ARIZONA, Pop. 1230.

He turned and walked back toward town. The filling station attendant had two cars. The A&P was closed. He suddenly felt very frightened. It was nearly dark. He had less than seven dollars. He went into Fred's Cafe and found the handsome boy sitting alone in a booth, a bottle of beer and a glass in front of him. "Nadigo," Dave said, walking over to him.

"Sure. Why not?" the boy answered.

"Where's the town's sheriff? I notice you have an office for one."

"He went to Phoenix today." The boy grinned.

"Well, isn't there any other police protection in the town? A deputy or something?"

"Springer went with him. He wouldn't think of missing a trip to Phoenix."

"Suppose something happened around here."

"Nothing much ever happens here. The sheriff'd take care of it when he got back."

"Nothing happens? My friend sure as hell disappeared."

"He probably just left. Got well and left." The boy grinned.

"He wouldn't leave without me."

"Might have. Certainly could have if he'd wanted to."

"How? You said there's no train stop."

"Could've taken a bus. Bus comes through twice a day, once around suppertime. Could've also hitched a ride."

"I haven't seen any bus."

"They come through. They don't usually stop unless you call Mason City. I guess you could flag them down, though."

"Is there a Western Union in this town?"

"Doc Hickman's."

"What about a post office?"

"Doc Hickman's, too."

Dave remembered seeing a barred window in the back of the drugstore which, as he thought about it, was marked for mail. He was hungry, but as he stood in the restaurant the foul smell discouraged any thought of buying food there. Then, too, he had very little money and wondered how long it would have to last. He glanced at the cash register and the candy display. He decided to have a candy bar, a big double coconut Mounds, and he began salivating at the prospect. He walked over, bought one, went out into the air, and opened it. It was stale, very stale, thick, dry, chewy. But he ate it.

He went back to the drugstore. "I don't suppose my friend's been in here," he said. The old druggist shook his head. "Just thought I'd ask. Gimme a Hershey bar," he said, taking one, "and let me use your phone again." The candy was fresher than the first one had been. He called Dr. Finger's house.

"No, I ain't heard from him yet."

"Well, when he gets in, would you ask him to call Hickman's?"

"I close at ten," the old man said.

"I suppose," the woman said, "if I'm still up."

Dave called the hospital again and had another fruitless fifty-cent exchange with the woman on the desk there. He put the phone down. It was a few minutes after eight. He tried to reconstruct the day's events, to make some sense out of the situation. It was inconceivable that Bert could have left without him. But where was he? Perhaps he was seriously ill, too sick for the hospital ninety miles away. Perhaps Doc Finger had to take him somewhere better, farther away. He was sorry he hadn't stayed in New York. But what would Bert have done without him on the train? It was good he had come along. But then, why had he left Bert alone for so long while he read a couple of crummy magazine articles? Bert had needed him and he hadn't been around. Or *could* Bert have left?

But the fact remained he was in Nadigo, Arizona, wherever the hell that was, and he didn't know where Bert was, and he might have to get out of there on his own. He needed help, or at least money. He picked up the phone again. "Operator, I want to place a collect call to Mr. or Mrs. Herman Klemmer in Macon, Georgia. My name is David Klemmer."

He listened to his sleeping mother being aroused by the phone call. She wasn't used to getting calls that late. There was a three-hour time difference. She seldom had long distance calls of any kind. Dave never called home. There were too many other more essential expenses in life. A long distance collect call from Arizona? From David? "David? Is that you, son?"

"Hello, Ma."

"Will you accept the charges?" asked an operator somewhere along the line.

"David? Is that you?" she shouted. Long distances are always shouted. "Are you all right? Where are you?"

The line went dead. The operator must have been getting Mrs. Klemmer's assurance that she would accept the charges. She had so little experience handling these matters, especially on being roused out of sleep.

The line opened again. "Hello? Hello? David, is that you? Are you all right?" she shouted.

"Hello, Ma, now listen, I'm fine but I need your help."

"David, where are you? The operator said Arizona?"

"Ma, please listen a minute and I'll try and explain. I'm fine. If you'll let me talk a minute, I know it sounds crazy, but I can explain. You know my roommate? You know, that I've written you about? Bert? Well, he's got a rich brother in Hollywood and we were going out to visit him during vacation and—"

"Hollywood? David, you don't have money to go to Hollywood."

"Ma, let me finish. It wouldn't have cost much of anything. Bert's brother has all kinds of connections. The problem is that Bert has both railroad passes and he got sick on the train, so we got off in this little town so Bert could see a doctor and now Bert's disappeared and I may need money—"

"Disappeared? What do you mean disappeared? Where is he? David, is everything . . . Are you all right?"

"Ma, if I knew where he was, I'd go to him. I left him with the doctor for a minute and when I got back he was gone."

"Where? Ask the doctor."

"Ma, the doctor's gone, too. He went hunting, or something. I didn't want to call and alarm you, but I need your help. You've got to wire me some money, right now, just in case I'm lost from Bert."

"David, are you sure . . . Is someone there with you . . . forcing you?"

"Ma, I promise you, everything is O.K. I know this whole thing sounds crazy, but it's just like I told you. I'm going to keep looking for Bert. But just in case I can't find him, go down to Western Union and wire me some money. Just send it to me, care of Western Union, Nadigo, Arizona. I'm in the Western Union office."

"David, it's late. Your father and I are in bed. We were asleep."

"Ma, I need your help. I'm all alone in this little town. I'm stranded. You've got to send me some money."

"How much money do you need?"

He thought a minute. "You'd better send me two hundred dollars. I may need enough to get back to New York and I don't know what the fare is. And I have to look for Bert."

"We don't have that much at home. We'll go to the bank tomorrow—"

"Get it from Uncle Max. He's always got that much. The son of a bitch is loaded. Wake him up if you have to and get it from him. Just send it to me care of Western Union in Nadigo, Arizona. That's N-A-D-I-G-O. I'll be waiting right here in the Western Union office. Now, Ma. They close this office at ten, and it's eight-thirty here. Did you get the town? N-A-D-I-G-O."

She sighed. "I've got it all. We'll manage. David? David?"

He put the phone down gently, as if the least disruption might make something go wrong. He looked at Doc Hickman, who had been watching him from behind the cash register. The old man smiled with quiet concern but said nothing. He only smiled and observed. He was the image of all the old Docs in all the drugstores Dave had ever seen.

"Nothing to do now but wait," Dave said.

The old man continued smiling.

Dave walked back over to the magazine display and squatted down on a low shelf of magazines to occupy himself while waiting. He watched the old pharmacist move into the back of the store and busy himself. He glanced at the clock. He thought about his mother calling her brother, Max, waking him with a story about her son, David. The college boy, Max would say, the scientist, like some kind of crazy person, stranded in some little town without money. Where? In Arizona? He could see his parents getting dressed, driving out into the night to Max's, pleading to make the story sound plausible for Max and the money, and then driving to Western Union. He tried to submerge himself in a magazine but the words ran together and he turned page after page, staring blankly at pictures, frequently glancing up at the clock and in the direction of the old pharmacist, expecting him every minute to come walking forward with his perpetual smile and a handful of money.

As the clock edged past nine-thirty, Dave took the phone and placed the long distance collect call home. There was no answer. Perhaps the weather was bad there. Perhaps they had had car trouble, maybe even an accident. Ordinarily, Dave always went to great lengths to avoid being a burden. He thought for a moment about Bert's whereabouts and his face grew hot with fear of something so incredibly unknown. He thought about his thesis work and another flush of heat swept through him. He wandered back to the magazines and squatted back down.

He watched the clock and waited for some sign of activity from Doc Hickman. There had been no customers in the store for some time. His parents had had time, plenty of time. He had stressed time. Don't telegrams travel with the speed of electricity in a wire? As the clock approached ten of ten, he went back to the phone and placed the collect call again. His mother answered and quickly accepted charges. She was more experienced now. "David? Where are you?"

"Ma, you know where I am. Where's the money?"

"The man at Western Union says there's no such place. He had a book and he said it had every Western Union office everywhere and he said there's no such place as Nadigo, Arizona."

"But Ma, that's crazy. I'm standing here. He must have made a mistake. Did you spell it right?"

"I wrote it down. N-A-D-I-G-O, Arizona. I even tried calling you there at Western Union but the telephone operator said the same thing. She said there's no such place. David, are you sure you're all right?"

"Look Ma, I'm talking to you from here . . . What did the operator say when she asked you to accept my call?"

She paused a moment. "She asked if I would accept a call from you from Nadigo, Arizona."

"Ma, now listen. It's too late to do anything tonight, but first thing in the morning . . ." Dave glanced toward the back of the store. The old man was turning off lights. ". . . first thing tomorrow, go back to Western Union and don't take no for an answer. It's N as in nowhere, N-A-D-I-G-O, Nadigo, Arizona. You've got to do it, Ma."

"Where are you going to sleep tonight? Will you be all right?"

"I'll be fine. Just send me the money in the morning, O.K.? I've got to go now, Ma."

Dave hung up and walked out onto the planked walk with the pharmacist. The old man locked the door. "Guess I'll see you in the morning," Dave said. The old man nodded, smiled, and disappeared around the corner, leaving Dave very much alone. Dave looked up and down the totally deserted street. There was no automobile traffic. The buildings were all dark. A few widely spaced street lights produced splotches of dirty illumination. Where would he wait till morning? He was suddenly overcome by a wave of extreme terror. He wanted to cry out for Bert, for any friendly face. He turned around and around, staring helplessly in all directions at the desolation that contained him. The blue-eyed boy with the cold smile who always appeared when he had a question—where was he now? The little black Ford was gone. Fred's Cafe was dark. "Oh, my God," he muttered to himself, beginning to feel the nausea of overpowering fear.

He glanced at Doc Finger's dangling shingle. He could barely make out the stairwell leading up to his office. Doc Finger had seen Bert. He was the last link with Bert. Dave crossed the road and walked to Doc Finger's. He would wait there for him, at his door, taking no chances on missing him the next morning. He climbed the stairs in the dim light that leaked in from the street. The landing was hot and dark, almost pitch black.

Dave took off his jacket and slumped down into the corner where the steel fence met the wall. Below him, the doorway onto the wooden sidewalk glowed in the darkness like the square mouth of a cave or a mine.

He began to think about his work, about what he'd done last and what he'd do next. He could almost smell the sweet chemical air of his lab. This was a sensation he liked, wasn't it? He did look forward to a lifetime of solvents searing the inside of his nose and cracking the skin on his fingers, didn't he? What choice did he have? The face of the blue-eyed boy with the cold grin suddenly appeared in his thoughts. "I ride the range on my trusty steed. Do you like what you do any better?"

Bert drifted back into his mind as he sat in the darkness

221

staring at the door below. A wave of guilt swept over him and he tried to retreat further into his little corner of floor, wall, and steel fence. He closed his eyes, and Gorman moved into his mind. Professor Gorman and the indecipherable molecular models on the lecture bench. "Do something else, Dave. Chemistry's obviously not for you." "But Bert, I'm already in graduate school. It's too late." "It's not too late, Dave. Don't you understand? It's not too late."

The boy with the blue eyes crossed his mind. Then Nadigo's main street. Yes, Nadigo. It was warm in Nadigo. It was cold in New York. Cold and damp. Nadigo was warm and dry. He thought about his parents going to Uncle Max— No! Not back to Uncle Max for more money! Let Max keep his lousy money.

The doorway below was the slate gray of dawn. He had been asleep. He raised his cramped body and stretched and walked slowly down the steps. The street was still deserted. He sat down on the wooden steps at the edge of the street to watch the town wake up. The early morning air was crystalline. The monumental bluffs seemed a short drive away.

He waited and watched. The day gradually warmed and brightened. A man in work clothes, the first person of the new day, walked by and nodded. A car moved slowly by. Mr. Davis opened his feed store. More cars passed. The lights were on in Fred's Cafe across the street and the tiny thread of bacon scent that reached Dave was sweet, as sweet as he had ever smelled. Old Doc Hickman smiled and waved as though he had seen Dave there every day. The town was fully alive and the sun warm. The A&P and the filling stations had traffic.

The little black Ford pulled up in front of Dave and the boy with sky blue eyes smiled at him. "Find your friend?" His smile was suddenly warmer, more sincere.

"I don't need to find him any more."

"What about you? You planning to go back?"

"What for? I like it here."

"A little later, why don't we go out for a ride? Ride the range. Pretty country around here. I'll show you sights you can't see back East."

"I'd like that. I'd really like that."

"Meet you in half an hour up at Sweets," the blue-eyed boy said. "I need a haircut. Wait for me up there." The boy pulled the Ford away from the wooden sidewalk and moved down the street.

Dave glanced toward the stairway to Sweets. The barber pole was turning. He sat in the sun for a few more minutes and then walked up to the barber shop. All five barber chairs were occupied and most of the ring of waiting chairs were full. Dave went over to an empty one and sat down.

While he was waiting, a young man came in, somewhat in a hurry, an intense dark-haired young man wearing winter clothes. His facial expression was harried, unnerved. He looked around as though looking for someone. He walked over to the closest of the Sweets brothers. "Did a friend of mine come in here? Guy named Dave Klemmer? He was about so tall and was—"

"Look around," Sweets interrupted. "See if he's here."

The young man slowly scanned the faces of everyone in the shop.

Dave smiled as the stranger's scanning eyes touched him and moved on. Dave continued to smile for a moment or two as he watched the young man complete his scan and hurry back down the steps to continue his search.

We occasionally see a homeless person around, usually at some intersection on the Boston Post Road, or some ramp off of I-95, with a roughly hand-lettered sign that says, "Homeless Hungry Please Help," or maybe, "Will Work for Food." One day I saw two, a man and a woman, at the actual spot I described in the story, and I fantasized for a moment about what would happen if I took them to lunch at the Burger King. This story came so fast, it practically wrote itself.

Homeless, Hungry, Please Help

He'd seen a lot of them around, but this was the first time he'd seen them as a couple, a man and a woman. Usually, it was one or the other, standing on the street divider at the light by the Sears Shopping Center. The person would be holding a sign written in large letters with a heavy marker or crayon on a battered piece of corrugated carton:

HOMELESS
HUNGRY
PLEASE HELP

Sometimes the signs read: WILL WORK FOR FOOD.

As cars pulled alongside them, waiting for the traffic light to change, some drivers would lower a window and hand them a coin, or often a bill. Although Sam was annoyed by panhandlers in general, if he got stuck right in front of one, and made the mistake of making eye contact, he sometimes found himself reaching into his pocket and holding a bill out the window.

225

But this time there were two of them, a white couple, man and woman. They were on the street divider in the middle of the Post Road, at the light in front of the Milford Post Shopping Center, and in the bright midday November sun, they appeared younger, cleaner, and better dressed than the usual pathetic, ragtag variety. He guessed they were in their mid-thirties, easily a good twenty or more years younger than he himself was.

The man was sitting on the concrete divider, his legs crossed in front of him, holding the typical hand-lettered sign. He had a thick but close-cropped beard and mustache to match his head of wiry dark hair, and deep-set, very intense eyes. The woman stood behind him and was not unattractive, with short brownish hair and a slim figure. They were dressed alike, almost stylishly, in jeans, plaid shirts, and denim jackets. A large plastic bag, presumably holding their few belongings, was on the divider next to them.

As Sam waited for the light, studying the two of them, they looked in his direction and made strong eye contact, and the little needle of guilt pricked him. He was an obvious "have," behind the wheel of his large Mercedes, and they were "have-nots." He was in the wrong lane to hand them something out the window, but he definitely felt intrigued by their so completely atypical appearance. Then a crazy whim hit him.

He knew it was a dumb idea and a bad mistake as soon as he lowered the window, but he was curious about them, and since he was thinking about having a bite of lunch somewhere anyway, he muttered "What the hell?" to himself, and went ahead with it, something he wouldn't have done if his wife, Martha, had been with him. She was generally sympathetic to the homeless but didn't want any direct contact with them. He waved and yelled, with a friendly smile, "Whatta ya say? Wanta have lunch?"

The man jumped to his feet.

Sam pointed at the Burger King on the corner across from the shopping center and yelled, "Meet me over there."

He drove into the Burger King parking lot and got out of his car as he watched them hurry toward him. "I was just thinking about having lunch," he said when they reached him, "so I decided that inviting you to join me was something I could do to help out." And then he picked up the faint trace of an odor. Not strong. But detectable. Unbathed bodies. Homeless, like their sign says. But at that point, it was too late to do anything about it.

"You're a good man," the man said, looking him over, without smiling, and then looking at Sam's shiny Mercedes. "Maybe we can give you a hand with something to try and help you out in return. We're always ready to do a little work for a meal."

"Thanks for offering, but that's not necessary. Don't give it a thought. Glad to do it. Let's go in." Then he said, "Well, since we're going to have lunch together, my name's Sam. What're yours?"

"Hello, Sam. Name's Vince. And she's Loreen."

"Hello, Vince, Loreen."

Sam realized immediately that he didn't like or trust this man. There was an intensity, an air of threat about him. As for her, he couldn't tell much about her. Other than the fact that she wasn't bad-looking. She did justice to her jeans. But he already regretted what he'd started. It was a really stupid thing to do. But he'd get through the half hour and next time be wiser for it.

Once inside, Sam motioned at the lighted menu signs and said, "Help yourself. Whatever you'd like, it's yours. The sandwiches are good and the fries are the best around."

"Sounds like you come here often, Sam," Vince said, smirking.

"Well, once in a while, anyway. I kinda like it when I'm in a real big hurry."

Sam watched the two of them study the menu and then order. Each of them ordered two Double Whoppers, a large fries, a large Coke, and a slice of pie. Two Double Whoppers? That's a full pound of beef! And pie? That should hold them till their next meal, whenever and wherever they got it. He ordered himself a chicken sandwich and a Diet Coke, and they went to a booth and sat down. He watched them begin eating. Yes, they were definitely hungry.

"Sam Champion!"

Sam looked up, startled, and tried not to show his dismay. His friend, Harley Spence. "How's it going, Harley?"

"Sam, what the hell're you doing eating here?"

Hesitantly, "I come here once in a while when I'm in a hurry. What about you, Harley? What're *you* doing here?"

"Same thing. Want to introduce me to your friends?"

"Vince and Loreen . . . My friend, Harley."

"Why do you two look familiar?" Harley asked . . . Then he glanced at the big plastic bag and back at the two of them, and a flush of recognition crossed his face. He glanced in the direction of the street, and then back at Sam with a broad smile. "Sam, you're too much. You know that? . . . I'll leave you to your *friends*. See you at the club." He walked away and got in line to order.

"Your last name's Champion?" Vince asked.

"Name only. I was never champion of anything."

"I know I've seen that name on something, somewhere, but I don't quite remember . . ." Loreen said. "Wait. Champion Lumber?"

". . . Yes . . ."

She smiled and rolled her eyes in appreciation. "I remember seeing that big sign facing the Turnpike."

"I'm not around there much, anymore. I'm more or less retired, now."

"You live somewhere around here?" Vince asked.

"Around. Not close by."

"You married? Live alone? What?"

"My wife's in Florida at the moment. We have a place down there, and I'll be going down sometime soon." He was becoming a little annoyed by their questions. "But, wait a minute. What about yourselves? You two just don't look like homeless types. What's the story, here?"

"We both got laid off and finally had to give up our place."

"Where?"

"In Boston. We were both working in a shoe factory."

"And you couldn't find *anything* up around there?"

"Nothing." Vince said it with a little heat.

"So, what now?"

"We're gonna head South if we don't find something pretty soon," Loreen said.

"You have people down there? Family?"

"We don't have anybody anywhere," Vince said.

"No friends in Boston, or up that way?"

"Nobody in a position to help us out."

"How'd you get here?"

"We hitched," Vince said. Then, "Sam, I'll bet you could find something for us, couldn't ya? At your lumberyard? Or your place? How about your place? We're good workers. Between the two of us, we can do just about anything. And do it well."

"Afraid I can't help you. I have nothing to do anymore with running the lumberyard. And there's nothing around the house."

229

"Nothing at all around your place? Come on now, Sam. There's gotta be something around there that could use some doing."

He was feeling pressure that he didn't need. "Look. There's nothing. Okay?" He said it with an air of finality, trying to get a message across to them, to put closure on the discussion. "It's been my pleasure to take you to lunch. I'm glad to do it. But once we walk out the door, we're never going to see each other again. I hope that's understood." He looked at Vince, who was scowling.

"Well, you were awfully nice to buy us lunch," Loreen said, and she smiled at him.

"As I said, glad to do it." She wasn't bad-looking at all when she smiled, but he had the feeling there was something bogus behind that smile. He'd had enough of them both. It was time to get the hell away from them, and let the whole dumb, regrettable business become history. He got to his feet. "Look. I'm finished eating, and I've got stuff to do, so I'm taking off, but you two can stay here as long as you want. Rest, use the bathrooms, even have free refills of your Cokes if you want. See that sign? Free refills? And the best of luck to you both."

"Thanks again, Sam," Loreen said.

Sam drove his Mercedes downtown to his broker's and sat a while, discussing his portfolio, and then stayed a while longer, watching the tape. This was how he spent his days, now that he'd retired from the business. Some men went to the track. Others went fishing. Still others played golf. He liked watching the Market, while his sons ran the lumber-yard—and had been doing it very nicely for some years. He'd sent them to college so they'd be able to do exactly that.

After having enough of watching the Market, he drove home, stopped at the mailbox, and headed up the long, circular drive, past stately trees and lush plantings, to the imposing stone home completely hidden from the road. He pulled up to the doors of the three-car garage . . .

And then he saw them.

Loreen was sitting on the steps of the door leading into the house through the laundry room, and Vince was raking leaves. Sam's first reaction was to turn around, drive back down to the road, and call the cops on his car phone, but Loreen smiled and waved and stood up and came walking toward him, and Vince was industriously working, trying to make a dent in the deep blanket of leaves that covered the vast rolling lawn. Not that he needed Vince's help. His landscape service would come with a crew and clear the leaves, using blowers and other equipment, just like they did every other year.

Without putting the car in the garage, he cut the engine.

"Hi, Sam," Loreen said, walking toward him with a pleasant smile. Vince walked over, carrying the rake.

"What the hell are you guys doing here?"

"We came to see if we could do a little something to show our appreciation for the nice lunch," Vince said.

"How'd you get here?"

"We walked."

"Walked? That's got to be over five or six miles."

"It wasn't so far," Loreen said. "We're used to walking."

He tried to picture them walking the roads in his upscale town, carrying their big plastic bag. Definitely not a typical everyday sight. "How'd you know where to find me?"

"You're in the phone book," Vince said. "All we had to do was ask around for directions. Nice spread you got here, Sam."

"Thanks."

"Bet it's real nice inside."

Sam controlled a rising sense of anger and frustration. He could thank his friend Harley for having blurted out his last name . . . What the hell business did they have coming to his home? But somehow, he felt safer playing it nice and laid back rather than getting nasty with them. He was alone with them and nobody knew they were there. He began to envision all sorts of lurid headlines. "Look. I already told you that you didn't have to feel obligated for the lunch. What's going on here with you two?"

"Sam, do you think . . ." She hesitated. "Sam, do you think we could come in and get cleaned up? We won't be any trouble."

Jesus! Now what? "What do you have in mind?"

"Could we . . . come in and take showers?"

"We'd really appreciate that, Sam," Vince added.

He repressed a strong wave of impatience. He really didn't want them in the house, but he could understand their need . . . "There's a room above the garage with a bathroom that's got a shower. And there's towels and soap. Just bring your towels down to the laundry room when you finish."

"You're a good man, Sam," Vince said, looking like he'd just won something. "Let Loreen go up there first, and I'll keep working on these leaves."

"You don't have to. I have a service coming to do that."

"Save your money, Sam. Let me handle it."

"It's a big yard. You won't get very far doing it like that. And besides, you're about to run out of daylight."

"I can handle it."

Sam shrugged. "Well, if you insist on doing it, however far you get, you'll need a tarp to carry the leaves off into the woods down behind. I've got a tarp in the garage." Sam reached in his car door and operated the garage door remote. One of the doors rose. Another car, a Chrysler convertible, was parked inside. Sam pointed. "See that tarp? Right over there beyond my wife's car."

He watched Vince walk in, around the convertible, and over to where an array of tools and miscellany were stored, gazing around him, carefully taking in the other car and all the garage's other contents. Vince picked up the tarp and headed back to the yard.

"How do I get up to that room?" Loreen asked.

Sam pointed. "Through that door and up the stairs." He watched her as she walked to the door and started up the steps. Yes, she did fill out those jeans rather nicely . . . But who in hell *were* these two people? Then he got into his Mercedes and drove it into the garage.

Inside the house, he went into the den and sat down at his desk to go through the mail. Most of it went directly into the wastebasket, but there were some dividend checks, which he endorsed and set aside to take to his broker's. And that done, he got into an easier chair and began reading the *Newsweek* that had also arrived. He heard a door open and approaching footsteps and was not surprised when she walked into the room, looking and smelling clean, scrubbed, and refreshed.

She gazed around as she entered, very impressed. "I just wanted to thank you again, Sam, for everything."

"It's okay." Something about her demeanor was patronizing, and he didn't like it. What was coming next? "Where's Vince?" he asked. "We need to talk about taking you two back to town."

"That's what I wanted to talk to you about. It's too dark outside for Vince to keep on the leaves, so he's cleaning up now, and . . . Sam, that room we're using up there has a double bed in it. And since it's dark, and there's not much we can do and no place we can go after dark, do you think we could stay there, tonight? I'll strip the bed in the morning and wash the sheets and make it back up, and do a little cleaning up around the house for you, and while I'm doing that, Vince can continue working on the leaves, and—"

"Hey, Loreen, hold it. All I wanted to do was buy you two lunch, and now you're moving in on me. What gives here?"

"Sam, you can't imagine how much we appreciate just being able to get cleaned up . . . and do you know how long it's been since we've slept in a nice bed? Even one night? And that room's just sitting there, not being used for anything. Sam, don't you think . . . ?"

How in hell had he managed to let them into his house? But they were there. She was being very very nice, but he didn't like or trust Vince even a little. He thought about calling the police. He knew the chief of police in the town, knew him well, in fact, but the chief wouldn't still be in his office, and if he called the number and asked for any kind of help, a car would show up with some young cop he didn't know. What would he say to him?

And if he didn't call, what was he going to do? Drive them back to the Post Road and leave them standing there in the dark?

If he let them stay, this not only let them into his house but also led to the next piece of business. Another meal, and then breakfast. Except for breakfast, he ate most of his meals out when Martha was in Florida. He ate at the club, or at one of a couple of restaurants that he liked but Martha didn't much care for. When Martha was home, they had a lady, Roberta, who came regularly and both cooked and cleaned. With Martha already in Florida, Roberta came once a week to clean, on Fridays. And Friday was four days away.

What to do for a meal? He wasn't going out to pick up something and leave them alone in his house . . . Pizza. He'd ordered it a time or two before, when his grandsons were visiting . . . "Okay, Loreen, you guys can use the room tonight, and I'll take you back over to town in the morning. I'll order some pizza for dinner."

"We'll never forget you for all your kindness to us."

"It's okay. Glad to help." He didn't like all the phony, bogus bullshit. All he wanted was to get through the next twelve hours and get them the hell out of there.

"I'll go tell Vince."

He ordered a couple of pizzas and then went to the kitchen and put three place settings on the table in the dining alcove: paper plates, knives and forks, a pile of paper napkins, and tall glasses, which he filled with ice. He set an unopened two-liter bottle of Coke on the table.

The pizzas arrived and they sat down around the table.

"Beautiful place you got here, Sam," Vince said.

"Thanks."

"Uh, don't you have any beer?" Vince asked.

"What's wrong with Coke?"

"Coke's okay, but I sure would like a beer or two with pizza."

"Well, sorry, you'll have to settle for Coke. We're fresh out of beer."

"No you're not. I saw some, there, in the fridge."

"When were you looking in the fridge?"

"A little while ago. I was looking for some cold water."

Were things getting a bit out of hand? Hopefully not. Besides, he liked beer with pizza himself. He looked at Loreen and forced a smile. "What kind of drunk is he? A sweet drunk, a rowdy drunk, or a nasty drunk?" He tried to say it with a light touch, just kidding around, but he was fishing for a clue. He did not like the idea of giving this man any alcohol.

"A sweet drunk," she said, almost too quickly. "In fact, he

never gets drunk . . . And, tell you the truth, we both kinda like beer with pizza."

Sam went to the fridge and got three cans of Heineken.

"The good stuff," Vince said with a nod. He got up and dumped the ice from his glass into the sink, and then did the same with the other two glasses. He sat back down and clearly enjoyed pouring the fancy imported beer into his glass. He took several swallows, groaned with pleasure, and wiped his mouth on his sleeve.

Sam watched as his dinner guests wolfed the pizzas and guzzled the beer. Vince got up without a word and took two more beers out of the fridge for himself and Loreen. This made Sam not just pissed but a little concerned. Vince seemed to be getting progressively more brusque as he drank, but nothing dramatic or overt. Nothing that spelled real danger. Sam watched Vince finally get up and help himself to the last of the six-pack in the fridge.

"You guys want some ice cream for dessert?" Sam asked. Maybe this would soak up some of the alcohol.

"Sure," Vince responded.

"Loreen, there's a half gallon of chocolate in the freezer, and you'll find bowls right up there, and spoons in that drawer." He pointed to each as he spoke.

Loreen served it in big portions, leaving the carton on the table, and it became a source of amusement to Sam to see how much food these two could consume. He'd had a total of two slices from the two large pizzas and both pies were finished. As he watched them attack the ice cream, he wondered if any of that would survive.

When they'd gotten their fill, Loreen returned the remnant of the ice cream to the freezer, cleared the table, putting everything in the sink, and then began washing the dishes. Sam showed her how to put things in the dishwasher, once they were scraped and rinsed clean.

"What are you gonna do, now?" Vince asked Sam.

Curious question. "Not much," Sam answered. "Watch a little TV for a while, and then, go to bed. See you in the morning."

"Hey, Sam, hold up. Mind if we watch with you?"

What could he say? No, you can't watch television with me? Just go to your room and stare at the walls, and be glad you've got a place to put your head down tonight? . . . What the hell? Another eight or ten hours and he'd be rid of them . . . "Well, long as you like watching football. I watch football on Monday nights."

"That's fine. Me and Loreen love football."

They followed Sam, not missing a thing along the way as they gazed around them, until they came into his TV room, where Sam had several pieces of plush, relaxing furniture facing a giant-screen TV. Sam took his usual leather recliner, and Vince was fascinated by the deep, upholstered armchair he took that swiveled.

Loreen sat stretched out on a sofa. Yes, she wasn't a bad-looking woman. Nice lean flanks. And suddenly the presence of her full breasts inside that loose shirt became apparent. Martha's figure had surrendered to the invasion of cellulite years back. Eons, it seemed. Her limited interest in sex had disappeared, as well. And she occasionally commented on what she called "his fascination with bosoms and buns."

"Sam, where's the nearest bathroom?" Vince asked.

"What's wrong with the one you've been using?"

"I figured there was one closer."

Sam looked at him. *You couldn't use the one I'd already provided you? Too far to walk? Maybe sixty, seventy feet? Just make yourself at home, my esteemed guest . . .* Another few hours . . . "Through that door and to the right. You'll see it there, on your left. A little powder room." He wanted to try and be reasonably pleasant and sociable for the few more hours they'd be on his hands, but be wasn't finding it easy. He didn't like Vince.

The sound of Vince's exiting beer found its way back to where they were sitting. Vince hadn't bothered to close the door. The crude bastard! Jesus, couldn't he have just closed the door? Loreen tried to give the impression that she didn't hear it.

"Is there another bathroom I could use?" Loreen asked.

She couldn't wait until Vince got back and use the same one he used? Of course not. She wanted to see more of the house. "Uh, Loreen, through the door, there, and turn left. All of those bedrooms have their own baths."

She left and Sam followed her path by listening to her footsteps. She paused at every room and looked into it, then went . . . up the steps to the master bedroom? She was helping herself to an unescorted tour of the whole place. He thought briefly about Martha's jewelry but remembered that Martha always locked it up in the wall safe before leaving for Palm Beach.

They watched whatever ABC offered without much interest or conversation until time for the game, which featured America's Team, the Cowboys, against a lesser opponent, and as the intro for the game came on, Vince asked Sam if there was any more beer.

"We've had enough beer, Vince."

"A cold one goes awfully good with a football game, Sam. If you've got some more around."

Sam looked at Loreen and she smiled and nodded her assurance that it would be okay. Besides, he really liked a beer with the game himself, and Vince seemed to be behaving, so . . . A few more hours. Just a few more. Maybe it'd keep Vince sleeping better. "I think there's more in a fridge in the basement, Vince. I'll go take a look."

"Keep your seat, Sam. I'll go. Just tell me where." He was on his feet.

"The door to the basement steps is in the kitchen and the fridge is right at the bottom of the steps. You'll see it."

Vince left and returned with another six of Heineken. "You keep yourself well stocked, don't you, Sam? That thing was full." He handed one to Sam, one to Loreen, and popped the top on one for himself. He took several long swallows and then groaned his pleasured groan. They settled back to watch the game.

By the middle of the third quarter, the game had become a one-sided bore, and Sam suggested they give it up. He wanted to go to bed. They reluctantly accepted this. Sam had had one of the beers, Loreen, one, and Vince, three. Vince took the remaining one with him. Sam went up the steps to the master bedroom . . . Just a few more hours . . .

★ ★ ★ ★ ★

Sam's light sleep was disturbed by a deflection of the mattress, as if someone had just sat down on the edge of the bed, behind him. He froze in the total darkness, his heartbeat accelerating. He'd locked the bedroom door, but the lock was only a privacy lock, easy to open from the other side with a small screwdriver, or even a bobby pin. Martha'd wanted the lock to keep the grandchildren out when she napped.

Was he about to feel a blade at his throat? Whoever was there was between him and the bedside night table under which he'd hung a holster that held a fancy little handgun. Should he try to quickly shove whoever was there and go for the gun?

"Sam?" A tentative whisper.

It was Loreen.

239

He took a deep breath and rolled over on his back. He raised himself on his elbows. "What the hell are you doing in here?"

"I just came to pay you a little visit. You know, to show my appreciation for how nice you've been to us." Her voice was different. It was quiet and throaty, not the patronizingly saccharine small talk he'd been hearing all day.

"Are you out of your head? Get the hell out of my bedroom."

"Come on, Sam. Don't try and tell me you don't like the idea of my being here. I've seen the way you've been looking at me all day. Besides, I like you, Sam. You're a nice man." She put her hands on his chest and began running them over him, his chest, shoulders, arms. "Hey, Sam, are these pajamas silk? They are, aren't they?"

He flung her hands away. "Will you get outta here?"

She put her hands back on him. "Real silk. God, what class!" She put her hands back on him and moved them down toward his belly.

He grabbed her hands again and threw them aside. "Will you get the hell out of here? What about your husband? What if he wakes up and finds you not there? I think you'd better go back to him."

She put her hands back on Sam once again and began massaging sensuously. "To begin with, he's not my husband. And second, he doesn't own me. And third, he ain't gonna wake up. He's dead to the world. All that beer he had? . . . Sam, when was the last time you had yourself a great time in the sack? I'm talking a really great time. Come on. Be honest. I've seen the picture of your wife, downstairs."

"Martha's a lovely lady."

"I'm sure she is, Sam. And she's really hot, too. Right?"

He couldn't think of a snappy reply to that. "Listen, I ap-

240

preciate your wanting to be so nice to me, but you get the hell out of here and back where you belong. Go on."

"Like you really want me to. Right?"

"Right. You've got no business in here."

She slid her hands inside his pajamas and leaned over and nibbled his earlobe. "Come on, Sam," she whispered. "I can see you don't mean it. And don't worry. I even brought a condom so you wouldn't have to worry about anything. And you wouldn't have, anyway, because I know how to take care of myself. Now, relax, Sam, and have a night to remember. What've you got to lose? Vince is out of it, and your wife's not here . . . God. Silk. Pure silk . . . Here, lemme help you out of those . . . Easy . . . Let's don't rip the buttons off." Her breath in his ear affected him despite himself as she began fumbling with the drawstring on his bottoms.

"Uh-oh, Sam, I think it got knotted."

"Don't worry about it." He yanked them off without untying it. "What are you wearing?" he asked.

"Nothing but a T-shirt, and I'm gonna be out of that in about two seconds."

He held his breath and felt his pulse accelerate as he listened to the wispy sound of the cotton T-shirt being peeled off her body in the darkness.

"Come on, Sam. Move over a little . . . That's it, sugar." Her feet were a bit chilly, but the rest of her . . .

★ ★ ★ ★ ★

He smelled coffee when he came downstairs. He walked into the kitchen and they were there. He looked at Vince to see what he could read in his face, but couldn't tell anything for sure.

Loreen, all sweetness and light again, said, "I found some eggs and some cheese, so I'm making eggs and cheese. Sound good?"

241

He seldom ate eggs. It was usually orange juice and instant oatmeal, and maybe a cup of instant coffee. "Don't make me much of that." He got himself a glass of juice. She'd set the table and he saw toast sticking out of the toaster.

They sat down and he managed a few bites of the eggs but wasn't impressed with her cooking. And that was a major understatement. He had some of the toast and coffee . . . Just a little while longer . . . "Okay, now that we've had breakfast, where in town do you two want me to drop you this morning? Back over there where I found you?"

"That's not what we had in mind, Sam," Vince said quietly.

"What's that supposed to mean?"

"I think we'll be staying here a while."

"You'll what?"

"I think we'll be staying here."

"You don't have that option, Vince. Hear what I'm saying? Now, look. I've provided you two with three meals, a night's lodging, drinks, and entertainment, and that's it. Let's get you back out there where you can be on your way. I told you yesterday after lunch that I never expected to see you again. And you showed up here. What the hell's going on here, Vince?"

"Sam, you're gonna *like* what we have in mind. We're gonna stay here and help you out. Make your life easier. We'll work around the place, inside and out, and between us, handle most anything. Cooking, housekeeping, outside work. You're gonna be pleased as punch."

"Forget it, Vince. C'mon, get your stuff together and I'll be pleased as punch to take you back to town, wherever you like, and that's it." He was firm but kept his voice quiet; he didn't want a dangerous situation to develop, and he was becoming a little unnerved.

"Sam, why don't I talk it over with Martha?"

What? "What are you talking about?"

"I already had a little chat with her this morning. But I didn't tell her about anything much. Like some of your *late night* activities. Or where I was calling from. At least not yet."

Sam felt sick. Like he'd taken a boot in the solar plexus. "You called Martha? Where'd you get the number?"

"Off your little bulletin board here in the kitchen. And just so I wouldn't lose it, I wrote it in permanent ink across my belly. But don't worry about it, Sam. I'm sure we'll work something out, and maybe I won't have to call her again."

He looked at Loreen and she was smiling. A winner's smile . . . So that was the way it was. This would take some thought, but no precipitous action, at least for the moment. He got up and walked out of the room, his fists clenched.

★ ★ ★ ★ ★

He couldn't leave the house. Not even to shop for groceries. He didn't want to leave them alone in it. And he certainly wouldn't give either of them a car and money to go off shopping. He'd just order everything from "Tiffany's," the small supermarket known by that nickname for very good quality stuff and even better prices. Tiffany's delivered.

Since he was less than impressed with Loreen's culinary skills, he ordered simple foods, deli for lunches, and steaks and chops, which he'd grill, and potatoes, which even she could bake. And desserts. Pies and ice cream. And beer by the case.

He spent time watching the Market on cable and talking to his broker by phone, reading the *Times*, and sitting around, watching other stuff on television. The days dragged. He was a prisoner in his own house. He didn't want to get the cops involved, even though he knew the chief. Most everything that happened in town requiring police involvement found its way into the town's weekly, and often into the *New Haven Register*. He didn't want that . . . And there was always the fact that Palm Beach could be reached by phone.

The beautiful weather held and Vince would go out and disappear, always taking a few beers with him. Loreen lolled around, doing little, often disappearing into some room where there was a TV. She seemed to love running the laundry. Apparently, washing towels made her feel like she was taking care of the house . . . He had to think about what to do with them . . . And, do it soon!

"Sam, here's your mail."

"Vince, just do your stuff and let me get the mail. Okay?"

"I thought I'd do you a favor and save you the walk down to the mailbox."

"Don't do me that favor. I happen to *like* the walk down to the mailbox."

He didn't want Vince to be seen at the road. And what if Vince knew how to recognize the window envelopes that contained checks. "Wanta do me a favor, Vince? Just get the leaves done."

"I've got that under control. It'll get done."

"It's got to." He wanted to call his landscape service and have them come and do it, but what would he have left to keep Vince occupied?

★ ★ ★ ★ ★

"Vince, I've got another job for you. Know how to split logs into firewood with a wedge and maul?"

"Sure, I can do that. Like I told you, I can do anything."

"There's a big oak down near the edge of the lawn in back. It's been cut into logs, but they need splitting. Think you can handle that? You'll find the wedge and maul in the garage."

"I'll take care of it."

"You're still a long way from finishing the leaves."

"It'll all get done. Don't worry about it."

Always that cocky assurance, and the man didn't do squat.

* * * * *

"Sam, me and Loreen're gonna move from that little room over the garage into one of the bedrooms here in the house."

"Is that so?"

"Yeah. That bed's too small for the two of us. We got used to a king-size when we had our own place. And this one's also not too comfortable. And besides, sleeping over the garage makes us feel like outsiders. You don't want that, do you? One of the bedrooms off the hall, here, has got a king-size bed, and a TV. And a *nice* bathroom. And nobody else is using it. So we're moving, today."

"Is that so?" He had to think of something! He had to get them out of his house!

"Don't make yourself too comfortable," he said in a quiet voice, after Vince had left him.

* * * * *

"What *are* these, Sam?" Loreen asked.

"They're veal chops. Rib veal chops."

"They must be two inches thick. I never saw any kinda chops anything like this. And you really cooked 'em good."

"And you did a nice job baking the potatoes, Loreen."

Vince got up from the table and got himself another Heineken.

"How're you coming with the work outside, Vince? The leaves aren't up, yet. What gives?"

"Everything's coming along nicely."

"And the log splitting?"

"Don't bust a gut, Sam. I'm dividing my time between that and the leaves. It'll all get done in due time."

He hadn't done much of anything with the leaves. What did he do out there besides drink beer? Sam clenched a fist so tightly beneath the table that his hand ached. He had to get rid of them!

★ ★ ★ ★ ★

"Sam, I've been thinking. We've been here a few days now, and working very hard, and I feel like we should be paid for all the stuff we're doing. A person needs a little money in their jeans or they don't feel like a person. You know that. Right?"

Now they want to be paid for accepting free room and board. What next? "That's interesting, Vince. Tell me what you have in mind."

"I was thinking two hundred a week apiece, for now. That'd be about right. Maybe later on, when we get a better handle on what needs to be done around here, I might want to negotiate a little better deal for us. How's that sound?"

Like rape. He had to get them out of there! He took out his wallet and removed four one-hundred-dollar bills. He handed two to each of them. "That'll hold you for a week."

"And, Sam," Vince said, stuffing the two bills into his shirt pocket, "when do you plan to head south to be with Martha?"

"Don't know, just yet. Why?" What was he up to, now?

"Because I decided that what we're gonna do is stay here while you're gone and take care of the place for you over the winter. That way you won't have to worry about a thing. I'm sure you'll like that, and I know Martha'd agree. And we can even run the other car every once in a while. You know, it's not good to leave a car standing around without ever running it. 'Specially in the winter. You can just mail us our money."

Now they planned to spend the winter playing house in his house with a fancy new convertible to drive around and four hundred a week to spend on food and drink. They'd probably even move into the master bedroom. "I don't think that'll be necessary, Vince. We've been leaving the house in the winter

246

for years with no problems."

"I think you need to take advantage of my offer, Sam. Maybe I'll call Martha and discuss it with her."

"I don't want you calling my wife, again, Vince. Ever. Okay?"

"Well, then you better think seriously about my offer, Sam."

He had been thinking seriously about the situation. And he had to come up with something. Soon! "I'm going to do that, Vince. I'm going to think about it."

They hadn't called Martha and identified themselves. At least, not yet. He called her at night, every couple of days, and she never mentioned them. But he believed they'd called the number to check it out, and were holding the threat over his head. He didn't want them carrying out that threat.

★ ★ ★ ★ ★

He lay in bed, wide-eyed, unable to sleep, staring into the darkness, his face hot, radiating the heat of total frustration over what to do about getting rid of his boarders . . . his house staff.

His thoughts skittered back to the time he'd spent in Vietnam, and he recalled the first time he was positive he'd been solely responsible for a kill. It had been a strange sensation. The next time it happened, and each time after that, it became a little less strange. He came home from there with a profoundly changed sense of appreciation for weapons and what they could do.

After returning home, he married Martha and got into the family business, the lumberyard, and took up hunting for recreation. Killing a deer got to be practically kid stuff. Bringing down that moose—now that had been excitement! And he thoroughly enjoyed stopping off in Tennessee, on his annual drive to Florida, to shoot ducks with old army friends. What great fun! Just aim and squeeze and watch 'em flutter to the ground . . .

He sat up in bed, turned on the TV, and flipped from channel to channel for a couple of hours, watching one thing and another, until his brain finally cooled down a little. Then he put his head back down and managed to get some sleep.

★ ★ ★ ★ ★

He *had* to make a run into town. His broker had some important papers for him to sign, right away, in front of a notary. He had his usual juice, toast, and coffee, and left the two of them packing away messy-looking bacon and eggs. He drove toward New Haven, and some ten minutes along the way, realized that in his haste, he'd forgotten some dividend checks and other papers he'd meant to take with him. He headed back home. He wasn't worried about the checks; he felt sure that if Vince got into them, he had the brains to see that they were already endorsed for deposit at his broker's.

When he reached the house, Loreen wasn't anywhere downstairs. She was usually doing laundry or wandering around, looking like she wanted to think the place was hers. "Playing house." He went into the hall and heard their voices. They were upstairs in the master bedroom, laughing and talking loudly because no one else was there.

He walked quietly up the carpeted steps and into the master bedroom, taking them totally by surprise. Vince was stretched out across Martha's favorite satin bedspread, his filthy shoes on the bed, the beer in his hand also resting on the bed. Loreen was going through drawers.

"Sam!" Loreen gasped. She looked at Vince, who quickly sat up and dropped his feet over the side of the bed.

"Looking for anything in particular?"

"Oh God, Sam, I'm so embarrassed, but you know I'd

248

never bother anything. Just looking. Everything's so beautiful."

"Let me make you two an offer. I'll give you a thousand dollars apiece to leave here and never come back." He watched Loreen look at Vince to see how he was going to respond.

"Thanks, Sam, for the offer," Vince began, over the shock of Sam's sudden appearance, "but I think we'll stay here. I really like the idea of being able to stay around and take care of things for you and Martha over the winter."

"Let me sweeten the offer. I'll make it two thousand apiece."

"I think we'll still settle for the two hundred a week and the chance to be of help to you, Sam."

"Here's my final offer. Three thousand apiece. You think about that one. That's a lot of money between the two of you."

"That is a good offer, Sam, but I still say we'd rather stay here, being of service, for just our little money every week." Then, Vince winked at him.

"You're missing out on a very good deal, Vince. I hope you know that."

Vince shrugged and didn't bother to comment or remove the half smile from his face.

"Well, I've still got to make the quick trip into New Haven. See you later. And incidentally, Loreen, if you find something up here you really want, check with me later and maybe I'll let you keep it." Sam smiled, watching this line take them by surprise.

Sam left for town. It was time to do something before *they* did something. Get them before they got him. He was ready to go to Florida, and it was duck-hunting season in Tennessee. And he wasn't about to leave them in his house all winter, and pay them money to stay there and enjoy themselves.

★ ★ ★ ★ ★

Sam was hungry when he returned from town. He went into the kitchen and fixed himself a good sandwich, something he'd found that Loreen couldn't do. As he thought about it, neither of them could do much of anything, and neither seemed to have a trace of a work ethic. He'd worked his own ass off during his years running the lumberyard.

He wasn't surprised they'd been fired from some factory in Boston. Assuming their story was true. If they worked for him he'd fire them in a minute . . . They'd been good, though, at setting up a little scam for taking him. They'd done that beautifully. Whoever heard of panhandlers turning down six thousand dollars?

After eating the sandwich with a beer, he decided to take a walk around the property and see what Vince was doing. He went outside, into the brilliant sunlight. October and November, so far, had been perfect, the fall colors spectacular. He often wondered why Martha rushed to Florida so early. She was missing the best part of the year. And he missed her.

The leaves needed doing. Vince had hardly started. If they weren't up by the first snowfall, the lawn would be wrecked. He walked down toward the back of the grounds and, as he approached the oak logs to be split, got a good look at just what Vince's work ethic was. Vince was sleeping in the sun, his head resting on one of the logs, his arms folded on his chest. The maul was beside him, its handle also resting on the log. Three empty beer cans lay nearby.

Suddenly Sam's pulse began to pick up speed. The time had come. A complete plan popped into his head. This was it!

He looked in all directions. He could not be seen from anywhere. Not even from the house. And no one knew the two of them were there. This was it! He walked right up to Vince and Vince didn't so much as blink. He reached down and picked up the maul, not trying to do it quietly, and still Vince didn't stir. He felt the heft of the maul. It was heavy, but he could still handle it. His heart was pounding. *This was it!* Could he do it?

He walked around behind Vince and set his feet. He was in the batter's box . . . Or on the first tee . . . He brought the maul all the way back and then, with all his strength, swung it down, feeling bone give way under the mass of dark curly hair on Vince's head. The experience was a sensation suggestive of hitting a pumpkin. Vince's limbs jerked violently with the blow and then shuddered a few times before falling still. His eyes and mouth came open . . .

A good clean kill. No real mess. A little blood in Vince's mouth. Now that he was started, he wanted to move quickly. And think clearly. Not overlook anything. He reached into Vince's shirt pocket and took back his two hundred dollars. Vince wouldn't be needing it. He pulled out his own shirttail and polished the maul, head and handle, and the wedge. He picked up the beer cans. He had a large bag of those to take to the supermarkets and feed to the recycling crushers.

And now for Loreen. His .22 target pistol came to mind. After all the TV he'd watched and the detective novels he'd read about nice clean gang killings, it sounded like just the ticket. He went into the garage, left the wedge and maul, and pulled the three beer cans out of his pockets, dropping them into the big garbage bag of returns.

He moved down the back steps into the basement recreation room where his hunting arsenal was stored. He got the gun out, dropped the clip, inserted a few rounds, and shoved the clip back into place. He noticed a small first aid kit among the hunting stuff and picked out the largest Band-Aid he could find. He dropped this into his pocket.

Loreen was in the laundry, pulling a load of towels out of the dryer, and as he walked toward her, his right hand behind his back, she looked at him curiously, as if she couldn't quite make any sense of the expression on his face.

"Sam?"

He walked right up to her, and with his hand shaking, abruptly jammed the gun under her chin, aimed upward, and fired two quick shots. She crumpled to the floor. He looked her over. Good job. The bullets had not come out. He fumbled in his pocket for the Band-Aid, managed to get it unwrapped and stripped, and stretched it over the entry hole. He wanted no blood anywhere. He worked his hand into her tight jeans pocket and found *her* two hundreds.

He went into the garage, got a couple of heavy sections of the *Times* out of the recycle basket, and lined the trunk of his Mercedes. Then, back to Loreen.

The phone!

He walked uneasily into the kitchen to answer it. "Hello?" He could see Loreen from where he was standing.

"Sam, how's my friend, that benefactor of the downtrodden?"

It was Harley Spence. Sam took a couple of deep breaths. "I'm fine, Harley. What can I do for ya?"

"You sound out of breath. I catch you at a bad time?"

He took another deep breath. "No, I'm fine. What's up?"

"Haven't seen you around much, lately. What'cha been up to?"

"My usual. Watching the Market. Getting ready to head south."

"What'd you do with those street people after you fed them?"

"I sent them on their way."

"You're too much, Sam. You know that? Listen, we haven't seen you in a while, and I know you're alone, with Martha in Palm Beach, so I called to invite you to have dinner with Letitia and me at the club, tonight. Whatta ya say?"

That would fit quite nicely into things. And he could use a good meal, for a change. "I'd be delighted, Harley. What time?"

"Drinks at seven?"

"See you then."

He returned to Loreen, dragged her into the garage, hoisted her torso over the rim of the trunk of the Mercedes, then her legs, and closed the trunk. He backed the car out of the garage and headed across the grounds toward the woods behind, thankful the place was as big as it was. How would he explain to someone passing why he was driving his Mercedes around the yard? He reached Vince and struggled with Vince's limp body. He now had just about a full trunk of dead blackmailing panhandlers. He pulled a scrap of newspaper from under them, wadded it up, and stuffed it in Vince's mouth. No bloodstains in the trunk, please.

He drove back to the garage, went into the house, and sat down to make a list. He had a bunch of stuff to get done in one afternoon if he was to be on his way south that night: pack a few things, stop by the post office and leave his change-of-address card, take all the beer cans to a supermarket and crush them, call the landscape service to get them on the leaves, clean all perishables out of the fridge, run the dishwasher, cut off the water to the outside faucets, put the thermostats on the winter settings, go over the house for all of *their* stuff and throw it into a Salvation Army Dumpster somewhere, wash the linens they'd been using and make the room back up, notify the alarm company and the town's police that he'd be leaving so they'd know to keep an eye on things for him, and what else? . . . Call his friends in Tennessee and check on the duck hunting . . .

★ ★ ★ ★ ★

He declined valet parking when he got to his country club. He didn't think he'd leave his keys with them. But he gave the boys a couple of bucks tip anyway, since he knew them all so well.

The evening just hit the spot. A few good Scotches with hors d'oeuvres, followed by a perfect steak dinner and a fine red wine. His first good meal in a while. He could hardly believe how relaxed he was, considering the contents of his trunk, and Harley's jabbering to Letitia about how he'd taken a couple of homeless types to lunch.

He left the club after ten, drove to the Wilbur Cross Parkway, headed south to I-287 westbound, and onto the Tappan Zee Bridge. Bridge traffic was light at that hour, as he'd expected, and when he reached the middle of the structured section, he slowed down almost to a stop, lowered a window, and heaved the target pistol, into the middle of the great wide Hudson, just past the truss superstructure. Let them find it there.

After the bridge, he drove until he came to the exit for the Palisades Parkway, southbound. He was headed for a perfect spot he remembered, one of the parkway's secluded, off-the-road, high-bluff overlooks, facing the river. It was nearly midnight when he made the U-turn and pulled into the unlit area.

And almost before he could decide which way to position the car, a Highway Patrol car roared up to him, seemingly from out of nowhere.

The trooper got out of his car and came walking over. He shined a flashlight into the car and into Sam's face.

Sam lowered his window.

"What are you doing in here at this hour?" the cop asked.

"These are for daytime use."

"Uh, officer, I was driving down the parkway and getting a little sleepy and decided I needed to take a snooze before I fell asleep at the wheel. I was afraid to stop on the road, out there."

The trooper looked around the back seat with his flashlight. "Is that a weapon in back, there, in that leather case?"

"Yes, it is, officer. A shotgun. I'm on my way down to Tennessee to go duck hunting with friends."

"May I see your license and registration? And step out of the car, please."

Sam got the registration out of the glove compartment and climbed out of the car. He was beginning to get a little shaky.

The trooper examined them. "Champion. Champion. Sounds familiar . . . That wouldn't be that big lumberyard by any chance? I used to live up that way."

"My sons run it now."

The trooper's tone changed. "Small world. I used to buy a lot of stuff there. Mr. Champion, I wouldn't recommend staying here very long at this hour."

Sam managed a smile. "Matter of fact, I think I'm awake enough now that I can make it onto the Jersey Turnpike and rest at one of the rest stops there."

"Good idea, Mr. Champion." Then, with a chuckle, "You wouldn't have anything in your trunk you wouldn't want me to know about. Right?"

Sam felt faint. "Just more luggage and stuff."

"Have a good time duck hunting, Mr. Champion." He walked back to his car and roared out of the area, onto the parkway.

Sam was trembling when he got back into his car. *Did he dare still unload there? . . . Did he? . . . He didn't know of any- place else!*

He started the car and maneuvered around until it was parallel to the large rocks near the edge of the cliff. He cut the engine. And then his pulse really began to flood. He just sat for a few minutes. What if someone else showed up? . . . Not at that hour. And the trooper had left. He wouldn't come right back. Sam pulled the trunk release.

Shaking like a leaf, he managed to get Loreen's body over the rim of the trunk, onto the ground. He dragged it to the edge of the cliff and pushed it over, into free fall in the darkness. Judging from the sound, it dropped a long way before hitting anything. Hopefully, it would disappear into the brush and not be noticed; too bad the leaves were disappearing from the trees. He went back for Vince and, struggling harder because he was heavier, sent him after Loreen.

He drove out of the area and to the New Jersey Turnpike. He pulled off at the first rest stop and cleaned the newspapers out of the trunk, throwing them into a trash receptacle. Then he went inside and had coffee. He'd get the car cleaned and vacuumed when he got to Florida.

He returned to the turnpike and drove for a while longer. Spotting a motel sign, he got off and took a room for the night.

★ ★ ★ ★ ★

The duck-hunting season proved to be one of the best ever. From there it was on to Palm Beach and their condominium at the Biltmore, where Martha immediately dragged him kicking and screaming into her usual social whirl. She seemed to know everyone there, just as she did in their circle back in Connecticut.

Vince and Loreen had almost completely disappeared from his thoughts when, a few days before Christmas, a local plainclothes cop came to call, escorting a detective from New Jersey.

256

"Mr. Champion, we're investigating a couple of homicides involving two people who were found . . ."

Sam found it hard to listen. He absolutely didn't want to hear it. He hoped it didn't show on his face. That or the fact that he was trembling.

". . . and the reason we wanted to talk to you is that the male of the two had an envelope in his pocket containing a rather large check made out to you. A dividend check, I understand. We contacted your chief of police, who helped us find you down here."

Think! Keep your wits about you! "You know," Sam said, "the two you describe sound like a couple of homeless I befriended and bought lunch for at a Burger King"—*Harley saw me there*—"back one day in Milford. Afterward, they showed up at the house, looking for work, and he must have taken the check out of my mailbox. I'd been wondering about whether I wasn't supposed to be receiving that check, now that you mention it.

"Since it was late that day, I fed them pizza"—*Domino's may have a record of the order for two large pizzas*—"and let them stay overnight in our servants' quarters, and sent them on their way the next day. And now, I find out, I did all this after he'd taken a check out of my mailbox. What do you think of that?"

The New Jersey detectives seemed impressed that Sam had been so kind to a couple of homeless, but he caught a glimpse of Martha raising an eyebrow and shaking her head when she heard this. She apparently couldn't believe her husband had done anything like that. The detective asked more questions, but not in a manner suggesting he might consider Sam a suspect, and the two cops finally left.

Sam felt a little ill. Vince and Loreen weren't out of his life just yet. *If the case came to the attention of that highway trooper and it probably would, he could place Sam on that overlook late at night!* Were there any other details he'd forgotten? He'd found no blood or other traces of any kind in the trunk after getting to Florida. What about the excessive quantities of food and beer he'd ordered from Tiffany's over the days preceding the scene on the overlook? Not typical of any past shopping pattern. And his total absence from the club, and his broker's, over that same stretch of days . . . *And, oh, God! Had Vince really written the Palm Beach phone number on his belly? And was it still legible when they found him?* . . . Maybe Vince had been bluffing. Wouldn't the cops have mentioned that? Had they missed it? . . . Or were the cops playing cat and mouse? . . . He wasn't going to be sleeping too well for a while . . .

If he became a suspect, and all of this stuff came out, and possibly more stuff he hadn't yet thought of, could he beat the rap? Maybe. With a very good lawyer. Or team of lawyers. Everything was circumstantial and coincidental. Yes, maybe he'd beat it. But not without a great deal of notoriety and expense, neither of which was among his favorite things . . .

And all because he'd taken a couple of homeless people to lunch.

*Marilyn and I were once on a vacation at a, I guess you could
call it "resort," and when we asked about tennis, they sent us to a
completely deserted and secluded court a mile or so down the road
from the entrance to the resort. We began playing and from what
seemed like out of nowhere, a young girl, maybe twelve years old,
materialized and wanted to shag balls for us. We let her, but it,
somehow, made me a little nervous . . . But I came home with an
interesting idea for a story.*

Six-Four, Four-Three, Deuce,
A Ghost Story of Sorts

By mid-afternoon the excitement gradually quieted down.
Although the accident was still the major topic of conversation
around the lodge, the guests began returning to their recreational activities. It had been a spectacular accident. The car literally dropped from the sky. It came hurtling over the bluffs,
down some fifteen hundred feet, and landed just in front of a
horseback party from the lodge.

Yes, it had been quite a day, something of more than routine interest for the guests to tell about when they returned
home. State troopers and other investigators had been
coming and going all day, studying the accident. An official
photographer took scores of pictures. The bodies were recovered from the wreckage and taken into the nearest town to a
funeral home. Since it wasn't possible to get a hearse or even
a truck to the site of the wreckage, the bodies were wrapped
and brought into the lodge slung over horses.

The manager of the lodge had been in a state of near shock
all day as he moved among the guests, muttering in stunned

disbelief that he didn't see how it could have happened, that there was a sign, a large sign. One of the guests circulated the story that investigators considered it strange there were no tennis balls in the wrecked car. Had the accident occurred on arriving or on leaving the court? Had the victims forgotten to bring balls or had they played and discarded the balls? There were no witnesses whatsoever. The victims were a young couple from Connecticut, the parents of three children; their name—Grenelle.

★ ★ ★ ★ ★

Lynn and Larry Grenelle had put a great deal of time into planning their two-week vacation. This year for the first time they were going away without their kids. Lynn, a zealous planner, acquired reams of travel information from state tourist bureaus, AAA, and the like. She interrogated friends and acquaintances and as she combined this information with her myriad folders and brochures, the ideal vacation gradually began to crystallize. It would be the Lakes Region of New Hampshire in early August. And it would be a place that offered tennis and everything else they wanted on the premises, because once they arrived, they didn't want to start their car for two weeks.

Having narrowed their choice, they went over a stack of brochures and, by a process of elimination, selected Land's End Lodge.

Preparations went well. Their request for reservations was acknowledged with a cordiality that was almost flamboyant. "I didn't know anyone could want me that much for any-thing," Larry commented. And, they found a pleasant old Irishwoman to stay with the children.

"I take it you approve of her," Lynn said as they were fi-nally leaving on Saturday morning.

"I think she's great."

"If only you had the same enthusiasm for children that you have for the people who take them off your hands."

They arrived at Land's End Lodge in time for a dinner which fulfilled its promise. After dinner, they unpacked the car and returned to the recreation hall for the evening's entertainment, dancing. They milled around, exchanging pleasantries with the other guests.

"I think we're going to have a wonderful two weeks, Larry," Lynn said.

"A little on the dude ranch side," Larry commented, "but not bad. Did you see the getup on that woman over there?"

"I wonder how the kids are. Why don't we call?"

"For gosh sakes, relax. They're all right. I think I'd like to completely forget about the kids for a while. Incidentally, did you see the tennis courts anywhere as we drove in?"

"No."

"Neither did I. Well, we'll find them in the morning."

★ ★ ★ ★ ★

After breakfast, they walked around the grounds in their tennis whites, looking for the courts. Finding horseshoes, Ping-Pong, paddle-ball, shuffleboard, an area of swings, slides, and climbing mazes, all crowded with children, the waterfront, the pool, the stables, and a gymnasium, but no tennis courts, they strode into the manager's office.

"You drive back out to the main road, to the left about a mile and a half and take another left on a gravel drive between two concrete columns. A hundred yards past a small bridge, you'll see the court."

"I thought your folder said, 'Tennis on the premises.'"
Lynn was in a state of controlled rage at having been taken.

"It's on the premises. We own the property. It was once the town's camp for wayward girls. The townspeople hated having it around here. Many years back, when money got tight, the owners of this lodge convinced the town fathers to stop supporting the camp. Then they bought the property from the town to get the tennis court and more room for horse trails. There's nothing left over there now but the court." Then the manager added with a smirk. "No one felt the least bit bad except the girls themselves. They got pretty nasty about it. But that was years ago."

"We chose this place because we thought we could come here and not have to get in our car for two weeks," Lynn said.

"Your battery might run down," the manager said with unexpected glibness. Then remembering the credo inherent to his position, he added, "It's really a very nice court. I'm sure you'll find it satisfactory."

"Is there only one court?" Larry asked. "Do we need to reserve it or anything?"

The manager smiled. "To tell you the truth, we have very few guests with an interest in tennis. You'll have the court pretty much at your disposal while you're here."

"And you say it's a nice court?" He was beginning to see greater possibilities for satisfying his tennis appetite.

"It's an all-weather court in perfect condition. And you'll be able to enjoy it in complete privacy."

"I'm convinced," Larry said, starting to leave.

"Don't get lonesome over there," the manager said. "There's not much around except the court. And, oh yes, be careful parking your car. The road . . ." He paused and smiled at the word "road." "The road ends at the court and the land drops off rather suddenly to the bluffs. Please be careful."

★ ★ ★ ★ ★

They came to the concrete posts and turned off, finding themselves engulfed by the stillness of a windless morning among tall trees, very tall trees, that filtered the sunlight, producing a million shades of translucent green and only occasionally allowing the sun to glint through. They drove along the double-rut, one-lane road, awed by the sudden green quiet that surrounded them.

As they neared the bridge they came upon a large number of children playing in the creek bed to the right. "Why there must be thirty of them!" Lynn said. "And I believe they're all girls!" They all appeared to be between the ages of nine and twelve, or perhaps thirteen. None was particularly attractive and several were fat and large. Although they were highly animated and noisy, they were not laughing as they went about whatever they were doing. Three of the larger girls were holding a massive stone between them, as if ready to drop it. Most of the others chattered and hopped about, pointing at something in the shallow water. A few simply stood with immobile faces and watched. They all stopped and stared impassively at the car rolling very slowly over the wooden bridge.

"Larry, where do you suppose those kids come from?" Lynn asked. "They couldn't be from the lodge. And they couldn't live around here. There's nothing for miles but the lodge. And what on earth are they doing?"

"What a bunch of monstrous-looking girls," Larry answered, as if certain all children other than his own were, in fact, monsters. "Maybe the girls' camp is still operating," he added with a chuckle. "Maybe that greasy character in the office at the lodge is putting something over on us."

"There's nothing around. Just trees. And there's no bus, no bikes, no counselors, nothing. I wonder how they got here. And from where?"

"You're asking me?"

The court came into view and as they approached it, they surveyed it intently. It was fenced only at the ends but the surface and net were adequate, they agreed, at least as far as all-weather courts go. They continued rolling forward slowly, studying the court, when Lynn suddenly threw up her hands and screamed.

Larry slammed on the brakes. Then he dropped his face on his forearms leaning on the steering wheel. He had stopped only a few feet from the point where he would have lost control of the car on the sloping ground leading to the bluffs. Because he had been so engrossed in studying the court, he had not seen the warning sign on a tree: DANGER! DO NOT GO BEYOND THIS POINT. SUDDEN DROP-OFF. He stayed motionless for several minutes, almost choking on his heartbeat. The motor continued its whisper-like idle as he remained still, his leg aligned in death-like rigidness with the brake pedal. Lynn sat with her face buried against the back of the seat, visibly shaking.

As Larry's composure began to return, he cautiously put the car in reverse and backed up to a level spot that was even with the middle of the tennis court. He cut the engine and set the emergency brake. He stepped out of the car and rubbed his face with his hands as a shudder traveled down his body. Lynn finally raised her head and climbed out of the car, following Larry as he walked with short, careful steps towards the edge to peer down and reconsider what might have been.

"Our slick friend wasn't fooling about being careful when we park," he said.

"I wish you'd look," Lynn said, holding onto Larry's arm. "It must be, what, about two hundred feet?"

"Nearer two thousand," he answered, easing them back from the edge. "Don't knock any balls over the back fence."

They returned to the car and got their rackets and balls. Not certain they still wanted to play, they walked onto the court.

"I understand why the manager said we'd have the court

to ourselves," Lynn said. "Really, there's something about this place . . ."

" 'Land's End'?" Larry said, smiling at her.

"At least that." She trembled slightly. "Well, let's play tennis . . . I suppose. We're here."

They begin volleying and soon settled down to pleasant tennis. They had almost finished one set when a child, a girl, apparently one of the group they had seen under the bridge, came wandering up. She was smallish, wiry, sandy-haired, and around nine years old.

"Hello," Lynn said with a warm smile.

The child responded with a cool, unsmiling nod that discouraged Lynn from following her usual tendency to make friends with children. Instead, Lynn continued to smile blandly as she returned her attention to the game.

A few minutes later another child walked up to the court and stood next to the first one. She was quite similar in size and coloring but she had long pigtails instead of short hair and bangs. They stood in expressionless silence and watched the tennis game.

At one point Larry almost fell while chasing a shot that was out of reach. He stumbled clumsily but managed to regain his footing. The two little girls laughed.

Larry reddened. "What's so funny?" he asked, glaring at them. "Nothing," said the one with pigtails, her smile evaporating.

"You almost fell. That was funny," said the other, still smiling.

"I don't see anything funny about it," Larry snapped.

The two girls started laughing again.

Larry managed a little restraint and returned to the game. He was serving, and in his controlled fury, double-faulted, both serves being quite high, moving on a line into the screen behind Lynn. He let up on his next serve and struck Lynn's return a glancing blow off the handle of his racket. It flew past the two little girls standing by the end of the net, going past the car and into the tall grass beyond. "What do you say one of you kids gets the ball for me?" Larry asked.

"I don't think so," the short-haired child answered, ignoring the tone of authority in his voice.

"Suppose I say please?"

"I think we'd rather just stand right here."

"If you can stand right there, you can get the ball."

"I think we'd rather just watch."

"Now look." Larry was beginning to redden. "You kids do as you're told."

"Larry, please," Lynn said. She walked off the court and over to the ball. The two girls watched intently, watching first her and then checking Larry, turning their heads back and forth. Lynn returned to the middle of the net where was Larry waiting. They stood with their backs to the two girls.

"Have you ever seen a pair like these?" Larry asked.

"Larry, there's something about these children that absolutely frightens me."

"They're just a couple of really snotty kids," Larry answered. "C'mon. Let's play tennis."

"Hey, mister."

Lynn and Larry turned around.

"We want to play tennis."

"We don't plan to stay much longer," Lynn answered. "You can play in a few minutes, after we leave . . . We came a long way to be here on vacation and play tennis."

"We want to play now," said the child with pigtails.

"We don't have any rackets or balls," said the other child. "We want to use yours."

Larry snickered. "I wouldn't even let *her* use my racket,"

he said, pointing at Lynn.

"We can play good, as good as you," said the child with pigtails.

"I'm sure you can," Larry answered, "but not with my racket and not on my time."

The two girls looked at each other. Then they turned and started towards the bridge in a hurried manner, running, then walking briskly, then running again.

"Larry, let's go," Lynn said, after the two young girls had turned out of the clearing, into the road and out of sight. The aura of stillness and greenness that surrounded them was like a vast, enclosing dome to Lynn. It was a setting which might ordinarily have inspired her to marvel at its natural beauty, but she suddenly felt oppressed. The highway was less than a half-mile away, a bustling resort less than two miles, and yet she felt isolated, almost lost. "Larry, let's go," she repeated. "We can play tomorrow."

"Let's finish this set."

"Let's finish it tomorrow."

"For God's sake, let's finish it now. Those two little brats are gone." He walked towards the back court.

Hesitantly, Lynn returned to playing position. They began playing but their game had degenerated into a listless affair. More shots were missed than hit and the game had become an endless task of walking around, picking up tennis balls.

They both looked up at the sound of chattering voices. The group of children from under the bridge had turned the corner in the road, entered the clearing, and was approaching the court. They stood and watched as the girls came nearer, their chattering growing louder.

The girls walked up to the court, assembled around the end of the net and become quiet. They stared at the speechless Lynn and Larry, vague smiles playing on their faces. "Well," said a shapeless giant of a young girl, perhaps, twelve or thirteen years old. "Go ahead and play." A tinkle of laughter rose from the group. "Don't let us stop you," the large child added, and a wave of shrill, chattering laughter raced all through the bizarre gallery.

Larry continued to stare at the children. They appeared nondescript, unattractive, arrogant. Finally, he wiped his mouth on the shoulder of his shirt and asked, "Whose serve is it?"

"Don't you think we ought to leave?" Lynn asked.

"It's your serve," Larry said, lobbing the balls to her.

Lynn hit an easy serve, one which barely cleared the net. Her serves were usually much harder but in her indifference towards continuing the game, she had tried only to get the ball over. Larry, playing back in a position to return her usual serve, charged at the ball. He missed, and in charging turned his ankle, fell, and skidded on his knee. He rolled over, clutched his knee and yelled several times from the intense pain.

Laughter poured from the group of girls.

Lynn came around the net. "Larry, these children are unreal. Please let's go."

"We're finishing," Larry shouted, almost in a rage. This remark brought a wave of cheering and applause from the gallery.

Lynn turned to the girls. "Why don't you kids run and play somewhere else? We're almost finished and in a few minutes we'll be leaving and you can have the whole area to yourselves."

"We think we'll stay right here," said one.

"We like to watch," said another.

"Hit a hard one to old bloody-knee." Laughter.

"See if you can knock him down again." Laughter.

Lynn turned and looked plaintively at Larry. He walked in a very deliberate manner to the other side or the court and into position to receive the next serve. Lynn returned quietly to the back of her court and served again. Once again her serve was easy, and Larry, better positioned, charged the ball and slammed it. It went on a line past Lynn into the screen behind the court. He made a motion as if to strike the court with his racket but restrained himself.

"Look at Mr. Red-knee go!" The gallery was alive with laughter. "He almost knocked a home run! He almost knocked down the fence!"

Larry walked over towards the girls. He spoke quietly, in a state of restrained temper. "You kids get out of here until we finish." He was answered by another wave of laughter, laughter that resembled the sound of breaking glass. He reddened. "Either get out of here or be quiet!" The shiver of laughter continued to circulate through the group. He turned and walked back into position, feeling somewhat less sure of himself. "Go ahead and serve."

Lynn couldn't believe his obstinacy; she had become terrified of the gallery. She glanced nervously at them and then served again.

It was another slow serve and Larry, in good position, swung easily, hoping to start a decent volley. The ball hit the handle of his racket and bounded over into the middle of the girls. One of them picked it up and tossed it to another. The gallery began spreading into the open area between the car and the court, the girls tossing the ball back and forth among themselves.

"Give me that ball!" Larry shouted as the pitch of their laughter and the fervor of their game increased. "Give me that ball!" He started walking towards them. As he approached the one with the ball, she turned and hurled the ball towards the bluffs. It bounced two, three times and then disappeared. "What on earth . . . What's the matter with you? What did you do that for?" he shouted. "You go get it."

"It's over the cliff and far away," said one of the girls and all the others laughed.

Another child ran onto the court and grabbed a ball lying by the net. She threw it out to the group and the girls began tossing it around Larry, who lunged helplessly at the ball with his racket. Then, without warning, one of the girls caught the ball and threw it towards the bluffs.

"Do you know what you need?" he said to the girl who had thrown it. "Do you know what you need?" he said, walking towards her. As he approached her the girls quickly regrouped in front of Larry. "What are you kids up to? What do you want?" He began backing up towards the court. His instinctive, paternalistic interest in doling out punishment dissolved into fear—simple, old-fashioned fear. "What are you kids up to?" he reiterated as the quiet, menacing group moved towards him. "You kids need a good spanking every one of you. Hear me? Hear me?" He continued moving backwards, away from the advancing cordon of grim, silent girls.

He tripped on the edge of the hard surfacing, fumbled his racket, and fell on his back. The girls swarmed over him. An ugly, hefty child of twelve or thirteen threw herself across his chest. A roly-poly, freckle-faced blob with short, stringy black hair and a sickish smile landed on his stomach, knocking his breath out. Others fell in pairs on his arms and legs. One wiry little child ran around behind him and locked her fingers in his hair to hold his head down.

Lynn, spellbound and horror-struck by the unpredictable events, recovered her senses enough to scream. She ran towards Larry but part of the gallery around him split off and intercepted her. She stopped, began backing up and babbling, "Now, you children don't know what you're doing . . . You've got to stop. Don't worry about the tennis balls . . . You children are nice children . . . Nice children don't bother people . . . We'll buy you all some ice cream . . ."

Three of the girls around Larry moved off the edge of the court and came hobbling back, carrying among them an extremely large stone. They returned to where Larry was being held and suspended the stone over his face. Lynn screamed and gasped "No!" as the stone fell. Her knees went weak as she heard the dull, wet thump. The blow did not quite knock him unconscious. He twisted his head back and forth, blood showing here and there on his face; he was screaming incoherently. The stone-bearers lifted again, this time higher, and dropped it, this time on the side of his head. His body movements stopped and he was silent.

Lynn screamed again and tried to move towards him but the group in front of her stiffened. The little pig-tailed child darted around behind her and squatted. The others pushed her and swarmed over her, holding her down as they had done Larry. The stone-bearers came hobbling over, joined together by their common load, taking short, mincing steps so that they resembled a six-legged spider. Lynn screamed as the stone materialized over her face. It fell one time and she was quiet.

All of the gallery stood up and looked around for a quick moment. Then the stone-bearers returned the stone to where they'd found it. The others began dragging the two limp forms by the arms towards the car. With feverish efficiency the children put the two bodies into their natural positions in the car and fastened the seat belts. Another child tossed the tennis rackets onto the seat. Still another took the tennis ball can and the single remaining ball and threw them over the bluff. A large child released the emergency brake and gave the gearshift a knowledgeable shove. The children pushed. They were quiet, serious. The car began to gain speed. It gradually pulled away and moved suddenly out of their sight as it nosed forward, bounced, left the ground, began somersaulting end-over-end into space. They walked to the edge and looked over. The wreckage was out of sight, obscured by greenery. They turned and began walking, then running, back towards the bridge, leaving the court once again deserted and silent, and freckled with sunlight on a warm, windless summer morning.

This is another story that grew out of a dream right when I needed one. I did work in Oak Ridge many years ago, did have an interesting friend named Wally, did go spelunking with him once, and did take target practice in a deserted quarry with him and his guns. The rest of the story is pure fiction but he was definitely an interesting character. I wonder whatever happened to him?

A Night in The Manchester Store

It all started one night as we were driving home from La Guardia. Wally said to me, "Whaddaya say we go to The Manchester Store on our way."

Out of the clear blue sky? I said, "Wally, are you serious? Now? What the hell for?"

"I want to check on something."

"Check on what?"

"Something. I might even buy it, tonight."

Or steal it, maybe? "Wally, it's almost nine now. And we're a good fifteen minutes away from there. Don't they close at nine?"

"Nine-thirty."

"Well, that still doesn't leave us much time. Can't it wait? Because I'd really like to get home. We've been away for three days. Is this something important?"

"Yes, it is, or I wouldn't have brought it up. And you'll be glad we stopped. You're going to have a great time. Count on it."

I'll have a great time watching him shop? Or I'll just have a

273

great time? What the hell did that mean?

What was he up to? Was this going to be another one of his crazy-ass things? . . . It'd been a lot of years since the last one. A long time. Was there going to be some element of risk involved, this time? . . . I decided not to bother responding to his comment about the "great time." Just sweat it out and hope for the best. So we'd be a few minutes later getting home. And he was the boss.

And since *he* didn't say anything further about it, we just lapsed into a period of quiet as he continued driving. He loved to drive, usually very fast. He thrived on doing reckless things, taking chances of all kinds, challenging fate, it always seemed to me, and I don't recall his ever failing, or getting caught, at anything he'd decided to do. He simply never got caught . . .

Wally Hunter and I go back a long way. We'd worked together at the national lab in Oak Ridge. He was a brilliant engineer, and he did his expected work, more or less, but he was also a cynic, always spouting sardonic humor about everything around us, knowing, as I guess I also did, that the project to which we were assigned was never going to produce anything. An aircraft engine powered by a nuclear reactor was not a realistic objective and was never going to fly.

And so we joked and laughed a lot about it. And we attended the regularly scheduled progress meetings, listened to all of the optimistic feasibility reports, carried out our assigned tests and experiments, compiled our data, and wrote up our results. It was, as they say, a living.

But that was only part of what made life with Wally Hunter in Oak Ridge so fascinating. I never thought of him as a close friend. He really wasn't that likable. And he wasn't someone I ever saw or even expected to see socially. I never met his wife. I thought of him instead as a very intriguing fellow worker, a sort of "what will this nut come up with next?" kind of guy.

And what made my association with him so unforgettable was that he occasionally sucked me into some wacko thing to do, either on or off the job, but mostly off. A Saturday morning adventure for two engineers with weekends free. I was always a little nervous about what he'd get me into, but somehow I was drawn to him, and I seldom resisted the opportunity to spend time joining him in one of the far from routine things he came up with, despite some element of risk or danger that was always involved.

Like the cave. He was, among a myriad of other things, a spelunker, someone who loved to explore caves, and he'd found one that contained this unique chamber he said I just had to see, so one Saturday morning we drove to it, parked the car, and with his waterproof flashlight, which he'd probably stolen somewhere, we plunged ahead, into the depths of the cave.

We came to a passage he'd known about, of course, but never mentioned, where we had to crawl through an opening no larger than our bodies, and which had water, very cold water, running through it. But it was summer, and our clothes would dry, so what was the problem? He went first and snaked right through the hole. Then it was my turn.

I started through and got stuck! I couldn't move in either direction! Although he was at first amused by this, I was in a state of panic, and despite having my belly in cold water, I began to sweat profusely. I *absolutely couldn't* move! Stuck in a hole in a cave? Who needed this? What kind of crazy business was this for a nice Jewish boy? Better I should have been in the synagogue, attending services with my wife! . . . Not that we went that often, frankly. But at that terrifying moment, wedged tightly in that hole in solid rock, blocking the passage of the freezing water, which was beginning to deepen under my chest and approach my face, my brain was also alive with poisonous snakes, water moccasins with dripping fangs, and all sorts of other fearful creatures, and with visions of being stuck there who knew how long, wondering if I'd ever get out alive.

After he'd enjoyed his moment of amusement at my panicked state, he finally began reaching under me, cleaning out the small stones and gravel, and then he grabbed me by the hands, told me to exhale, and pulled me through the opening, leaving my poor chest and belly, and a couple of spots on my back, rubbed raw.

He led me to the subterranean chamber he'd brought me to see, and I guess it was everything he'd promised it would be, but all I could think about at the time was the return trip through that hole to get back to the outside world. And to this day, I still shudder at the thought of having been stuck there.

And then there was the abandoned quarry, just a stone's throw off one of the main roads inside the government-restricted area. On another Saturday morning we went there with his .22 rifle and his .22 target pistol and all the bottles and cans we could scrounge up, and we set up our collection of targets on a rock, down in the quarry, and climbed up to the rim, sat there, and had a little target practice.

It was great fun but it was also very illegal. We were fooling around with firearms inside the government-restricted area and definitely had no business being there. We could have easily found ourselves trying to deal with the rotten local gendarmes, redneck deputy-sheriff types who were allowed access to the roads. Or maybe government security types connected to the plants. But of course we didn't . . .

. . . And I still wonder where some of those shots might have gone as they ricocheted off that rock. What goes up must come down at virtually the same velocity it went up, it seems to me. Gravity is gravity. What if . . . ? But that was years ago.

And Wally was a master thief. He simply loved to steal. He was constantly taking things home from the lab. Tools, expensive instruments, electronic stuff, whatever . . . At times he could hardly lift his briefcase when he left work and walked through guard stations to the parking lot. And of course he never got caught. The same was true when he visited the various stores in town, satisfying his love for thievery. He never got caught. I was with him one afternoon in a small downtown department store, and when he began lifting things, I didn't quite know what to say or do. All I wanted was to get the hell out of there.

And being as smart as he was, he spent most of his time at the lab, on company time, writing for several technical magazines, articles totally unrelated to his job at the laboratory, and he was getting paid good money for them. And he was never questioned, even when he got our company secretary to type them. Because he never got caught at anything.

He left the job in Oak Ridge several years before I did, and I never expected to see him again. Finally, years later, when my wife and I decided we'd spent enough of our life in that unique community, we, too, decided it was time to leave. I went to an employment clearinghouse at a convention, got several offers, and took one which brought us to Connecticut. Senior engineer at Metals and Materials Technology, Inc.

On my first day on the new job, the personnel director said to me, "I understand you already know the section chief you'll report to."

"I do?"

And in walked Wally Hunter. "Welcome to 'Met 'n Mat Tech,' " he said with a wide grin. And he was wearing a suit and tie. All those years in Oak Ridge he'd worn nothing but

jeans or suntans and sport shirts, while most of the other professionals around him, including me, "dressed for business"
and wore jackets and neckties to work.

He led me to his spacious office, and after we'd gabbed a
few minutes about whether things had changed much in Oak
Ridge since he'd left, he advised me that he'd been able to get
me a separate office, and with a window, no less. "I refused to
let them toss you into the bullpen where most of the fresh
meat gets thrown," he said.

Then he added, "And the salary offer they made you? The
one that you accepted? I insisted on having it increased a hundred a month. They don't do that too often, around here,
once they've gotten an acceptance, but I told them you had
special skills that our section needed badly, and I didn't want
to take any chances on losing you." Listening to all of that, I
was rapidly getting over the shock of running into him again
and discovering that he was my new boss. I was even beginning to feel a little pleased about it.

The first year of working with him went by fast. He was
still the same old Wally Hunter in most respects, entertaining
to be around for his total cynicism, but a little more scary
than I remembered. He'd become much more intense in his
attitudes toward the world around us, and the fact that it
owed us a living. His cynicism could at times become almost
incendiary.

Since we were no longer both living in the same small
Southern town where there wasn't much to do, the "Saturday
morning adventures" were ancient history. All of that small-
town stuff was behind us. We were out of the sticks and into
upscale areas in the civilized world, living in widely separated
Connecticut towns within commuting distance of the plant.

But, occasionally, when on the road together, we'd do
things I considered a little strange. One night in Chicago he

insisted we go to a notorious gay bar and have a couple of drinks so we could observe how "that other ten percent" lives. In offhand comments about his own sexuality once, he'd suggested that he was into "limited," or "mild," sado-masochism, from the sado side, of course. I'd still never met his wife.

At the end of my first year at Met 'n Mat Tech, he called me into his office one day for my "annual review," and rather sternly asked me, as an opening remark, how much salary increase I felt I deserved. I was hesitant. "Whatever you can get me, Wally. Seven, eight percent, hopefully something over five. I'd feel very good about ten."

He broke into a broad grin and said, "I got you fifteen."

And that was the end of our so-called annual review, a type of corporate activity he considered to be total bullshit. One of his favorite forms of larceny was getting me, and I suppose others in our small section, as much money from the corporation as he could manage. He signed my expense accounts, and when we traveled together, he'd often say, "You lie and I'll swear to it." It was these attitudes toward company funds which probably explain the strong sense of loyalty we all had to him . . .

When we arrived in front of The Manchester Store, he didn't pull into the store's private lot, but parked instead on the street, around the corner from the store's main entrance. I asked him why.

"I like this better," he said in a familiar tone of voice he used once in a while when he didn't want to be questioned further about something. We got along well, but on the occasions he used this tone, I'd learned to just cool it.

Before getting out of the car, he opened his briefcase and took out his cell phone, dropping it into his jacket pocket.

"Just curious, Wally, what do you need with that?"

"Why not take it with us? The company pays for it. If I decide I want to make a call, I'll have it handy. I don't want to have to use a public phone or go through the store's switchboard."

Knowing Wally, that somehow had a little bit of a scary sound to it. What call would we want to make some fifteen minutes before the store was closing? Why were we even going in there when all the clerks would be anxious to leave? But what the hell? This was Wally.

The Manchester Store was unique. It was large and complete, with huge, tasteful spreads of just about everything a department store could offer. In addition to extensive, major-name-brand departments for clothing and footwear, and of course, perfumes and cosmetics, it also specialized in furniture, appliances, fine jewelry, toys, and sporting goods of every description, including a widely respected department of everything needed for hunting and fishing, and finally, a rather nice restaurant.

But it wasn't its size and completeness that made The Manchester Store unusual. It was its style and character. The Manchester Store was an old, long-established family business, and the Manchester family was dedicated to preserving the store's venerability, maintaining the special charm and ambiance of earlier years. Only recently had its management made such radical changes as installing escalators, while still maintaining those ornate old elevators with the filigreed silverish doors. The store had even finally started accepting credit cards other than those issued exclusively for use in the store. The Manchester Store, an ageless example of period architecture among other things, stood alone in all respects, including location. It was a very popular alternative to the fancy New York chain department stores and the gigantic malls where they were usually found.

We walked around the first floor for a minute or two, among other customers still milling around, and then went to the fancy jewelry department, where Wally shopped for an expensive string of cultured pearls, presumably for his wife. A very proper elderly lady waited on us, unlocking the glass case and taking out the one he pointed at, and it became quite clear that he knew more about pearls than she. But this didn't surprise me. He knew more about most things than most people.

As he discussed them with her, I glanced at my watch and saw the store was to be closing in a matter of minutes. The saleslady was growing impatient. He asked her about gift cases and she hurriedly pulled one out of a drawer and showed it to him.

Finally, he told her he'd think about it and led me away. "Let's go up to the fifth floor, to furniture," he said.

"Wally, the store's closing in a couple of minutes."

"Come on."

"For what?"

"Because I want to go up there. And I'm driving. Come on. We'll have a ball."

A ball, now? What the hell kind of a ball? It was no use. It had been a long time, but once again, I sensed that I was being sucked into one of Wally's things. And this time I had no idea what the hell it was. But this one clearly smelled of trouble, serious trouble, and I was beginning to feel more than a little damp around the collar.

We took the escalator to the top floor, strode toward the furniture and bedding area, and as we arrived there, the ear-splitting bell rang for some twenty to thirty seconds, announcing that the store was officially closed. We looked around and there wasn't a salesperson in sight.

"Wally, they're closed. We've got to get the hell out of

here, now, or we're going to get in trouble."

"Relax, for Christ's sake. Follow me. There's a men's room right over here, and I've got to go bad."

"Can't we just leave? Can't you wait until you get home?"

"No way. Come on!"

I followed him. We went into the men's room and I stood there while he calmly pulled a paperback from his jacket pocket, went into a stall, hung up his jacket, dropped his pants, and sat down. The paperback was a spy novel he'd been reading on the plane. He consumed paperback spy stuff. But was this the time to be doing it? I looked at my watch. Minutes were ticking away and I was sweating heavily. What the hell was this? The reading hour?

When he finally came out, he asked, "Don't you have to piss or anything?"

I wasn't sure I wasn't too nervous to perform any bodily functions, and I was getting worse by the minute. But I figured it was probably a good idea, because I had no idea what was going to happen next, so I fronted up to a urinal and, with considerable concentration, managed to get it done. "Wally, you want to tell me what the hell's going on, here?"

"I thought we'd spend the night here in the store. Do a little easy unhurried shopping."

Had I heard him right? "Wally, did I hear you right?"

"Relax, man. I've done it before. We'll have a ball."

He was serious! I felt a little dizzy. This topped anything from the Oak Ridge days by a couple of quantum leaps. "Wally, we've got to get the hell out of here! Now! Before they shut the place down and turn on their security setup! If we don't, we're going to be in a lot of trouble."

"Will you relax? I told you, I've done this before."

And he was relaxed. Completely. I couldn't believe it. "Well, look," I said, "I want to get on home. I told my wife I'd be home around ten, ten-thirty, and that's what I want to do. I don't want her worrying."

He pulled the cell phone from his jacket pocket and handed it to me. "Here. Give her a call. Tell her we missed our flight and she'll see you tomorrow."

"What if I just leave now and I'll go look for a cab home? You can stay if you want. I can get my suitcase from you to-morrow."

★ ★ ★ ★ ★

He looked at his watch. "You're too late, pal. The front door's already shut. Nobody's down there. And if you start looking around for somebody to let you out, you're going to run into some rather tedious problems . . . Why don't you relax? We'll have a great time here, tonight. I told you before. This is not my first time doing this."

"What do you do?" I asked, partly as a joke. "Sleep in the furniture department?"

"Of course," he answered with his usual cynical grin, "and then be the first person in the coffee shop for a great bacon-and-eggs breakfast in the morning." Then he handed me his phone. "Call your wife and tell her you'll see her to-morrow."

"I don't believe you. I don't think you've ever done this before. You can't walk around this store at night. They must have some kind of fancy electronic security system, motion detectors, closed-circuit TV, some damn thing, that'll pick us up and start ringing bells and have police coming in here like gangbusters. What I do think is, you've gotten me in a lot of trouble, and I have to tell you, Wally, I'm sweating bullets. How in hell are we going to get out of here?"

"Will you take it easy? First of all, they don't have any fancy electronic stuff here. In The Manchester Store? Never. It wouldn't be in keeping with the store's image. What they do have is a night watchman who walks the store once an hour, on the hour, and sticks his key in one of those old time clocks on every floor, and then returns to his little office in the basement, where he does have closed-circuit TV monitors covering all the outside doors to the building."

Then Wally looked at his watch. "Keep an eye on that middle aisle of the floor. He'll go walking down it in about five minutes to go to the time clock on the back wall, back there in appliances. We'll stay down, out of sight, but I'll bet he doesn't even look in this direction."

"Well, when he shows up, I hope you don't mind, but I'm going to tell him I accidentally got caught in here after the doors closed, and ask him to let me out. And I'll look for a taxi to take me home."

"A taxi ride from around here to where you live, even if you could get one, which I doubt, could cost you a couple hundred bucks. Have you got that kind of cash with you, hot-shot? I doubt it. And taxis don't take credit cards. And even if you do have cash, you can't put that on your expense account. Whether I sign it or not, it won't fly."

"I don't care. Wally, I'm a nervous wreck. What I want to do is leave."

"Well, you can't. If you do, he'll call the cops to come and investigate, and the cops'll write it up. And you don't want that. Do you hear what I'm saying? Why can't you just relax and have some fun doing a little shopping? It's great not having a bunch of stupid clerks trying to wait on you."

My shirt was getting damper by the minute and clinging to my body. "Wally, I'm scared out of my head being in here like this, now."

"Jesus, I thought you'd love it." He looked at his watch. "It's just about time for the night watchman to come traipsing through. Let's sit here on this sofa and keep our heads down and we can watch for him. You can call home after he's gone."

I did as I was told. I had no idea what else I could do. And I was shaking. What if the guard decided to come walking over to the furniture department to browse? He could. He could be in the market for a sofa. Maybe even the one on which we were slumped, watching for him. "Tell me, gentleman," he could say, when he came strolling over, "how does this sofa sit? Nice? Comfortable? And try to keep your dirty shoes off of it. I may want this particular one. And by the way, you're under arrest."

And just as Wally had said, we heard elevator doors open, followed by footsteps, and finally, there he was. The area had been darkened from what it had been during sales hours, but from our crouched position, peering over the back of the sofa, we could still see him clearly. Wally had picked us a spot where we could watch through a maze of lamps and stick furniture, and easily go unnoticed. The guard was a big man, middle-aged, burly, tough looking despite a potbelly.

He walked slowly along the middle aisle of the floor, glancing in all directions. He moved out of our view as he reached the back of the floor, in appliances, and, in the quiet, we heard the small mechanical sound of his key being inserted into the time clock. He then walked back toward the elevators, and we kept our heads down until we heard the elevator door open and close.

"That's a different watchman from the one I saw the last time I was here," Wally said.

"It is?"

"This one's a *big 'un*. The last time I was here, the guy was so old and puny he looked like a good strong fart would knock him down."

"Wally, you're not making me feel any better."

"Oh, for Christ's sake, relax. We're not going to be seeing him up close. We'll be seeing him just like we did, then. From a distance. Every hour on the hour. And in between his hourly visits, we'll do a little shopping."

"He thinks he's alone in this store, Wally. What makes you so damn sure he won't do something different?"

"Because that's his job. He's gotta hit every one of those clocks at a specific time, and he spends the rest of his time sitting on his ass in that office in the basement. They provide him with a television to keep himself occupied."

"How do you know that?"

"I've been down there. I talked to the other guy down there one night, just before closing. I started picking his brain and he was more than happy to spill his guts. He told me everything about his job. They provide him with a TV to watch while he's keeping an eye on all those closed-circuit screens monitoring the outside doors."

I was impressed, as usual, with Wally's research. Almost as much as with his nerve. He was a crazy man. But he never got caught at anything. Never.

"Here," he said, "take the phone and call your wife."

I couldn't think of an immediate alternative. I told her the flight had been canceled because of mechanical problems, and I'd be home the following day. Then I returned the phone to him. "I guess you can call your wife now."

"She'll see me when she sees me." He stuffed the small phone into his jacket pocket. Then he said, "Let's go do a little shopping. We've got a good forty-five minutes before he gets off his ass again."

"How about if I wait here for you?"

"Are you kidding? Come on, I'm going to help you with your Hanukkah shopping. Make a real hero out of you. Let's go."

I reluctantly got to my feet and went with him. I guess it was out of a long-established habit of letting him talk me into doing things that I was absolutely sure I'd regret doing. This was crazy. This was no cave exploring or deserted-quarry target practice. This was big doings. Felony-sized . . . So what else was new?

We walked to the escalator, which was silent and unmoving, turned off for the night. Then it was cautiously down the steps, tiptoeing just far enough to be able to survey the next floor before continuing down into it. I followed behind him, gradually becoming a little more relaxed. I had to marvel at the fact that he really seemed to know what he was doing. He'd never gotten caught at anything. Despite his almost deranged driving habits, he'd never to my knowledge even gotten so much as a ticket.

We approached the first floor, and after surveying it longer than any of the others, we moved toward the fine jewelry area. Despite the subdued lighting, visibility was still adequate. Wally stepped behind the counter where he'd seen the fancy pearls, and it was at this moment that I knew for sure he'd been planning this. He reached into a pocket and pulled out thin, plastic-film gloves! As he slipped his hands into them, he whispered, "You keep your hands in your pockets."

I understood perfectly. He and I had come to Oak Ridge during a time when all new employees were fingerprinted on being hired, and those prints were still on file somewhere. I was more than glad to do that. I had no desire to touch anything. I wanted no part of the whole business. But I did have a question: how was he going to get into those jewelry showcases? They were all locked.

And as quickly as I wondered about the question, I got my answer. He poked his hand into his pocket and came out with a bunch of those little metal things that locksmiths use to open locks.

"I'll bet you were wondering how I'd get into this show-case without breaking any glass," he said with his cynical smile.

"As it matter of fact, yes, I was."

"You think I want to smash the place up? That wouldn't be any fun. I'm not here to rob the store. The challenge is just to do a little shopping without their help. And if they do notice that something's missing, which I doubt will even happen, they'll maybe ask a few questions and then write it off to employee pilferage and get the loss reimbursed by insurance."

"And those lock picks? Where'd you get those?"

"I've got a buddy who's a key-and-lock guy, and he's been checking me out on this particular skill. These little locks on the jewelry showcases? Shit! These are kid stuff."

Another of my firmest beliefs shattered. Locksmiths sell absolute security. It's their stock-in-trade. So it goes. "And The Manchester Store is your favorite store," I said. "Right?"

"A fine old store. Everything is of highest quality." And with a flourish, a smile, a wave of his hands, and a softly whispered musical "ta-da," he opened the display cabinet.

He reached inside and from an extensive array of pearl necklaces, he carefully lifted out a necklace, a double strand of large cultured pearls priced at thirty-five hundred dollars. It was not the same one he'd looked at before. That had been a single strand, and much cheaper. He avoided disrupting the arrangement of necklaces in the black velvet tray, pushing the others together just enough to eliminate the gap left by the missing one.

He next opened the drawer in a side cabinet, the drawer opened by the saleslady earlier, and took out one of the black gift cases. He laid the necklace into it and smiled. Then he began opening other drawers until he found a small box made to contain the gift case. He put the case into this box and slid it into his jacket pocket. Then he looked at me. "Which one would you like?"

"What?"

"Pick out one. Come on. We haven't got all night."

"Uh, no. Really. No thanks."

"Come on, pal. Don't be a schmuck. We're standing here. Pick something."

"No. Really, Wally. Forget it. It's not necessary. Actually, to tell you the truth, my wife's not much into jewelry." And what a whopper of a lie that was. But I'd made up my mind.

"Shit! For Chrissakes, will you pick out something? This is last call."

"Nothing for me, Wally, but thanks." I backed away a few feet from the showcase. He was hot, but somehow, I just couldn't make myself be a party to it.

"Schmuck!" Wally snapped. "What the hell's the matter with you? That's why I brought you here." He relocked the showcase. "Come on, then. Let's get back upstairs."

We made our way back up the escalator steps to the fifth floor, and furniture. I still couldn't believe what was happening. Did he really think I was going to be able to sleep through the night up there? But it was still early.

We just sat and stared at our watches until eleven o'clock approached, and then we began to anticipate the next pass by the guard. And he appeared, as expected, just as Wally had assured me he would. He walked the length of the floor, this time, hardly looking around, until he entered the appliances area, where he disappeared. He looked even larger this time than I'd remembered from his first pass. We heard the sound of his key in the time clock and then he reappeared as he made his way back to the elevators.

After we heard the elevator door open and close, Wally said, "How about that? Everything right on schedule." There was still a trace of annoyance in his voice, but he was cooling down.

I asked, "And he just sits down there in an office and watches the tube for an hour, and then repeats his rounds?"

"If he doesn't key those clocks on schedule, *he's* in a lot of trouble. Maybe one of these days, during store hours, I'll take you down there and show you around. There's a lot of stuff going on down there." Wally smiled. "If he's there, we'll get him to give us a tour."

"And are we supposed to just go to sleep now, and wait for morning?"

"First, I've got one more little item to shop for, as soon as he's had time to get back to his office, and after that we can think about getting a little rest. Matter of fact, I could use some sleep. It's been a long day. We got up early in Chicago this morning, did a day's work, drove to O'Hare, and flew home. And we were up late last night, running around . . ." Then he looked at me and grinned one of his familiar teasing grins. "How about you, hotshot? Think you'll be able to get to sleep after all this excitement here tonight?"

He'd read my mind. I felt a little weak at the knees every time I remembered just where the hell we were . . . But I had to hand it to him. He was right at home. How many times *had* he done this, before?

Then he said, with his playful smile, fully aware of my state of unrest, "Okay, let's go. One more little purchase and then we can turn in." He chuckled. "I'm a pretty good customer here, you know? My wife loves this store. She spends a fortune here. She'll love getting this gift, knowing it came from The Manchester Store. She doesn't much like all the

New York stores they have around, up this way."

"What floor this time?" I asked.

"The fourth."

"What department?"

"Sporting goods."

"Oh? Whaddaya need?"

He glanced briefly in my direction and gave me one of his special, wait-and-see smiles. "Be surprised."

As soon as we entered the sporting-goods area, he walked directly to a large, glass-topped showcase filled with handguns.

"A gun, Wally?"

"I've been thinking that I need a good handgun for protection at home."

"Don't you already have handguns? I remember that day in Oak Ridge when we went out shooting, you had a handgun. I remember shooting it."

"That was a twenty-two target pistol. They're strictly for recreation. You'd have to hit a man right in the eye to stop him with that. If it was on the line, I wouldn't want my life depending on the protection I'd get from that." Before touching anything, he once again slipped on his plastic-film gloves and then brought out his lock picks. It took him a matter of seconds to open the cabinet.

He looked through the glass top of the cabinet at the array of guns inside and the first thing he lifted out was an ornately engraved, oversized revolver with a very long barrel, probably the kind of thing only a collector would think of buying. He broke it open to see that there were no cartridges in it, then snapped it shut again, aimed it at the middle of my chest, and clicked it a couple of times. "How do you like this cannon?" he said. "Shit, I'd be Wyatt Earp with this thing. Hit a guy in the chest with a slug from this baby and you could send him right through a window." He put it back and continued studying the selection.

While I was nervous just being there, I was fascinated with what he was doing. I didn't own a gun of any kind. Not even a rifle. He wanted to be prepared to win a shootout involving heavy artillery right in his own home. I couldn't imagine such a thing. But watching him was like watching a movie. "Well?" I said. "See the one you want?"

"You bet your ass." He picked up a heavy-looking handgun that appeared to be like one of the new guns cops carry these days. He played with it for a moment, getting the feel of it, aiming it, examining it . . . He pressed something on it, allowing the clip to drop out of the handle, into his hand. "Nice," he breathed. "Very nice." He was a baby with a new toy. He snapped the clip back into place. Then, without warning, he abruptly tossed it at me. "Here, hold this in your hand and see how you like it."

I clumsily managed to catch it and then took it and played around with it for a moment as he had done. It was kind of a kick. But I couldn't possibly imagine owning something like it. "This is a pretty high-caliber weapon, isn't it, Wally?" What did I know about such things?

"Yes, it is."

"Wouldn't it have a lot of recoil when you shoot it?"

He nodded. "Quite a bit. It'd tear a big-ass hole right through you, too."

"I'll bet it would." I handed it back to him. And then the thought occurred to me that my fingerprints were on it. But if that was the one he kept?

He surveyed a glass-doored cabinet behind the counter that was filled with boxes of cartridges and finally located the match for his new toy. He pulled on the knob and this cabinet was also locked. But that posed no problem. He took out his little picks and had it open in seconds.

He lifted out a box of the shells, dropped the gun's clip, and began loading it.

"You're loading it now?"

"What good's a gun if it's not loaded?"

What? . . . But I decided not to ask any further questions. No point in sounding any more naive to him than I already did. What the hell? He wasn't planning to shoot me. At least I didn't think so.

"You want to pick something out for yourself?" he asked. "How about it? While we're standing here with the showcase open. I'll help you pick out something if you want."

"No thanks, but thanks for offering."

"How about just a twenty-two target pistol? You had a great time that day at the quarry back at the Ridge. You did pretty good with it, as I remember."

"I'd shot twenty-twos years ago, Wally, when I was just a kid at camp."

"This is last call, pal."

"I don't want anything, Wally. But as I said, thanks anyway."

"Listen, nobody should be without some kind of protection in their home in today's world."

I didn't respond.

He was amused at my skittishness. I could see it in his eyes. But this was nothing new in our relationship, which had existed over a lot of years, and after the scene an hour earlier in jewelry, I guess he decided it wasn't worth the trouble of knocking himself out trying to do me a favor.

He moved the guns around in the showcase until it no longer looked as if one was missing, and relocked it. Then he locked the cabinet behind the counter. And *then*, he stuck the gun into his belt, just like he was one of the "wiseguys," and stuffed the box of shells into a jacket pocket. "What say we go turn in?"

★ ★ ★ ★ ★

I was dead asleep when I felt the hand shaking my shoulder. I hadn't expected to be able to sleep, but after we dropped ourselves onto beds in the furniture department, I disappeared into a world of dreamless slumber with remarkable swiftness. It *had* been a long day. Driving from our hotel to our customer's offices in Chicago, making our pitch, taking them to lunch, with drinks, getting to O'Hare, flying to La Guardia, driving to Connecticut, and then, a late evening of "shopping" at The Manchester Store. A full day.

And as I began to wake up, I felt I had slept long and well. I felt rested, but still a little groggy. It was apparently time to get up and get moving. Wally had set the alarm on his fancy-schmancy watch, which he'd probably stolen somewhere, so we could get up at the exact right moment to swing into action, Wally-style. But why was he shaking me so damn hard?

"What in the name of holy hell are you guys doing in here?"

That voice! I looked up at . . . It wasn't Wally! . . . He looked like he was nine feet tall, standing over me! It was the night watchman! With his huge shoulders and arms, and his slight paunch, he looked like he weighed three hundred pounds. He had a handlebar mustache and a bulbous nose, and graying, light hair. He gripped my upper arm in his ham hand and he was still shaking me, shaking my entire body, in fact, like I weighed nothing.

I got up on one elbow and looked around. Wally was lying there, apparently still asleep. I sat up, rubbed my eyes, and asked, "What time is it?"

"It's six in the morning," the man answered, "and I want to know what in hell you two are doing here."

As I hesitated, trying to think of something intelligible to say, Wally stirred, rolled over, and sat up, dropping his legs over the side of his bed, and I wondered what he was going to do at this point. Would the man see the gun in his belt? I muttered, "Uh, what happened was . . ."

"What happened was . . . ?" the watchman snapped, mocking me. He was hot and I could see that he was a man who could rightly be called one big, tough, mean, son of a bitch! I glanced at Wally again, and he had buttoned his jacket. The gun was hidden. "Uh, what happened was . . . what happened was . . . uh . . . we were in the men's room, up here on this floor, when the bell sounded, and by the time we got down to the main floor, all the doors were locked, and nobody was around, and we couldn't get out."

"That must have been one hell of a leak you took, because the bell rings at nine-thirty and the main door doesn't get locked and left until at least nine-fifty, nine fifty-five."

"Well, that's what happened." I tried to look as straight at him as I could. "I have this intestinal problem, which—"

"I don't need the bullshit! I don't know what you two are doing here now, but it ain't kosher, and it'll have to be written up. We'll have to get the police in here on this."

"Oh, come on," I pleaded, "it was nothing. Really. I promise you." Then I looked at Wally, and he had the gun out, leveled at the watchman. I suddenly felt dizzy.

Seeing my expression, the watchman turned to Wally, and shock registered on his face. "Where'd you get the gun?"

"Downstairs in your gun department."

"Is it loaded?"

"Of course it's loaded. What good is a gun if it's not loaded?"

The watchman knew he was in trouble. He held out his hand. "Look," he said, "if you'll just give me the gun, I'll let you guys leave outta here, no questions asked, no police, no nothing. We got a deal?"

"Sorry," Wally answered flatly.

"All right, then," the watchman said, "keep the gun. Just put it away. And I'll let you two out, and you can go on about your business, no questions asked, no police, no nothing. We got a deal now?"

"I don't think so."

"Why not?"

"Because we have no way of knowing what you'll do after we walk out the door."

"I'll do whatever you tell me to do."

"But after we leave, how will I know that?"

"Look. You tell me whatever it is you want me to do. I'll go along with whatever you say. Okay?"

"You can say that, but I'll have no control over it."

I was listening to Wally's mind working, his very sharp, analytical mind. And if I'd felt stricken when I first saw that he'd drawn the gun, I was suddenly feeling lightheaded.

The watchman saw it coming, too. "Then what do you want me to do?" he asked.

"Nothing," Wally answered.

I looked at Wally's hand and saw his grip tightening. *"No, Wally! Please God, No!"*

"Sorry," Wally said, to the man, almost in a whisper. "Nothing personal." He fired twice, point-blank, into the man's chest. The shots were deafening and echoed around the huge display floor. The man's body jerked from the impact of the slugs, one of which exited from his back, splashing out a little blood and stuff with it as it shattered the base of a table lamp across the area. The man crumpled to the floor, ending up in a contorted heap, his eyes still open and glazed.

"Wally?" I gasped, looking back and forth between him

and the dead man on the floor.

"It was the only way we were going to walk out of here, completely clean," he answered quietly. "Think about it."

His analytical mind.

Wally squatted next to the watchman's body and disconnected the man's loaded key ring from his belt loop. "One of these'll open one of the doors to the street. It's early. There won't be any traffic outside. We'll go to the diner near the plant and spend a couple of hours having some breakfast and then go into the office. If anybody asks, just say we caught the five A.M. out of O'Hare. That works out about right."

Shortly after leaving the vicinity of the store, we drove onto a bridge over a river. There was no traffic at that moment. Wally slowed down, lowered his window, and tossed, first, the man's keys, and then the gun, and box of shells, into the water.

★ ★ ★ ★ ★

I don't know how I got through that day at the office. I could still hear those two shots ringing in my ears. I felt sure everyone could see in my face that I was beyond just a little disturbed about something, but, bless them, nobody inquired. I avoided spending time with Wally the rest of the day.

I took off a little early and drove home in my own car, which I'd left in the company's parking garage. And of course, I heard all about it on a local radio station as I drove. The watchman had a wife and four children.

I was sure I'd find two men in suits, two of our small town's detective squad, waiting for me when I arrived home, to lead me away in handcuffs. But when I got home, they weren't there. And they didn't come the next day or the day after that, or the day after that. And the thing I wondered was, if they finally did come, would they believe my story? Would anybody ever?

But the two men haven't come looking for me . . . And it's been quite a while . . .

Additional copyright information:

"Hello! My Name Is Irving Wasserman" was first published in the Adams Round Table Collection, *A Body Is Found*, published by Wynwood Press, New York, 1990. It appeared again in *The Year's Best Mystery and Suspense Stories—1991*, Walker, New York, 1991.

"The Ransom of Retta Chiefman" was first published in the Mystery Writers of America anthology, *Women's Wiles*, Harcourt Brace Jovanovich, New York, 1979.

"I'm Sorry, Mister Turini" was first published in *Alfred Hitchcock's Mystery Magazine*, February 1975.

"The Everlasting Jug" was first published in *Alfred Hitchcock's Mystery Magazine*, January 1973. It was Mr. Cohen's first published mystery short story, written as an exercise in a creative writing workshop.

"The Case of Grand Cru," a pastiche on a story by Poe, was first published in *The Strand Magazine*, Issue III, 1999.

"Just Another New York Christmas Story" was first published in the Adams Round Table Collection, *Murder in Manhattan III: Missing in Manhattan*, Longmeadow Press, Stamford, 1992.

"Those Who Appreciate Money Hate to Touch the Principal" was first published in *Alfred Hitchcock's Mystery Magazine*, April 1975, and was reprinted in the Mystery Writers of America anthology, *Every Crime in the Book*, G. P. Putnam's, 1975. In 1983 the story was the winner of the Veuve/Clicquot Times Award in the annual competition held by the British Crimewriters Association, and was reprinted in *The London Times* on May 13, 1983.

"Neville" was first published in *Alfred Hitchcock's Mystery Magazine* in March 1992.

"The Battered Mailbox" was one of the winning stories selected by the jury in the competition held at the Third Crime

Writers' International Congress, Stockholm, June, 1981. The winning stories were first published in *Crime Wave*, William Collins & Sons, London, 1981. The story was reprinted in the collection, *Choice of Evils*, Davis Publications, New York, 1983.

"How Much Justice Can You Afford?" was first published in the Adams Round Table collection, *Justice in Manhattan*, Longmeadow Press, 1994.

"I'm Sorry, Mister Griggs" was first published in *Ellery Queen's Mystery Magazine*, June 1974, under the title, "That Day on Connally." It was first reprinted in *Best Detective Stories of The Year—1975*, Dutton, New York, 1975, and has since been printed in several other collections, both in the U.S. and abroad.

"Nadigo" was first published in *The Mystery Monthly* in September 1975. It was reprinted in the Mystery Writers of America anthology, *When Last Seen*, Harper and Row, New York, 1977.

"Homeless, Hungry, Please Help" was first published in the Adams Round Table anthology, *Murder on the Run*, published by Berkley, New York, 1998, and has since appeared in publications in Germany and France.

"Six-Four, Four-Three, Deuce, a Ghost Story of Sorts" was first published in *The Mystery Monthly*, July 1976, under the title, "A Game of Tennis."

"A Night in The Manchester Store" was first published in the Adams Round Table Anthology, *Murder Among Friends*, Berkley, New York, 2000 and has since been reprinted in *The World's Finest Mystery and Crime Stories*, 2001, Tekno Books.